D0492626

The Balmoral Incident

By Alanna Knight

THE ROSE McQUINN SERIES
The Inspector's Daughter
Dangerous Pursuits
An Orkney Murder
Ghost Walk
Destroying Angel
Quest for a Killer
Deadly Legacy
The Balmoral Incident

THE INSPECTOR FARO SERIES
Murder in Paradise
The Seal King Murders
Murders Most Foul

THE TAM EILDOR SERIES
The Gowrie Conspiracy
The Stuart Sapphire

The Balmoral Incident

ALANNA KNIGHT

Allison & Busby Limited
12 Fitzroy Mews
London W1T 6DW
www.allisonandbusby.com

First published in Great Britain by Allison & Busby in 2014.

First Edition

ISBN 978-0-7490-1721-7

Typeset in 11.25/16 pt Sabon by
Allison & Busby Ltd.

Paper used in this publication is from sustainably managed sources.
All of the wood used is procured from legal sources and is fully traceable.
The producing mill uses schemes such as ISO 14001
to monitor environmental impact.

Printed and bound by
CPI Group (UK) Ltd, Croydon, CR0 4YY

For Sandra and Donnie,
with love

CHAPTER ONE

'Danger comes in many disguises.' So said my stepbrother
Vince wearily considering the Beast snorting and casting
clouds of steam onto the roadside as it awaited liquid
refreshment.

But to begin at the beginning.

We were to have a summer holiday at Balmoral
Castle, or rather in an estate cottage, for although Dr
Vince Beaumarcher Laurie was a physician to the royal
household, that privilege did not extend to members of
his family. HM King Edward, now in residence for the
deerstalking and the shooting season, did not care for
children, not even his own, from all accounts.

'Indeed, even the most innocent of situations can
turn quite threatening,' Vince continued back inside my
house as he considered my shelf of logbooks from the
year 1895. That was ten years ago when my career as a

lady investigator began soon after I arrived back home to Edinburgh, wrapped in grief and uncertainty, refusing to believe that since my husband Danny McQuinn had disappeared in Arizona I was probably a widow. I had not the least idea what the future held or that I was destined to follow, somewhat hesitantly, in the footsteps of my father, Chief Inspector Jeremy Faro, a legend in his own lifetime.

In my case, the role had been unwillingly forced upon me by an accidental meeting in an Edinburgh store with an old school friend, who tearfully whispered over afternoon tea that a servant girl had been murdered and her husband's odd behaviour aroused horrified thoughts that he might have been involved. She had no one to turn to. Would I help her? I had been so good at solving puzzles at school. And so I did and very successfully trapped the real criminal, not without considerable danger to my own person.

That was the first of my less dramatic cases as a self-styled 'Lady Investigator, Discretion Guaranteed'. Cases mostly of fraud, thieving servants, domestic incidents, clients all with good reasons for not wishing such problems to be put before the Edinburgh City Police and dismissed on lack of evidence. And what if the incident involved a close relative or those blackmailing letters bore the grim shadow of a former indiscretion?

My clients were mostly female. Except in the direst circumstances men were suspicious and publicly scorned the powers of a female detective, apart from an occasional gentleman of some importance in the city in a state of desperation. Threatened by indiscreet letters to an ex-mistress, in terror not only of publicity but of bringing about the end of a now happy marriage.

And then there were murders.

'Yes, my dear,' Vince had continued, turning his attention away from the logbooks with their accounts of homicides which I have already chronicled through the years. 'You undoubtedly have had a charmed life.' He laughed, tipping the contents of a hip flask containing some exotic liqueur into his innocent cup of Earl Grey tea: 'Dangers can lurk in the least expected places.'

This less than profound statement I was to learn referred not to humans but in this instance to the latest addition to his accoutrements as physician to the royal household. The motor car was the very latest passion for wealthier members of society and ranked a trifle higher on the social scale than the bicycle which, ten years ago, I had adopted as the most suitable means of covering the two miles between my home in Solomon's Tower on the lower slopes of Arthur's Seat, and the city of Edinburgh.

Learning to ride simply by falling off and getting on again, one could only stop and jump off when the treadle was at its lowest point, the brake an uncertain plunger upon the front wheel. Consequently I was often carried on beyond my destination, to the alarm of onlookers, shocked by this apparition of a female riding perched on such a precarious vehicle and in danger of exhibiting her lower limbs.

But the bicycle was the swiftest thing on the roads. The change from horse-drawn to mechanically propelled vehicle did not take place without a period of transition during the last decade, when solid rubber tyres and the pneumatic tyre made the bicycle an acceptable means of transport for ladies. This daring new fashion soon caught on: ladies bicycling became the smart thing in society, lords and ladies had their pictures in magazines, riding in the park, wearing straw boaters, while ladies took to knickerbockers under their frocks. Scandalous and shocking was the cry, but really rather grand.

But Vince was enchanted by this new Rolls. Nicknamed the 'Beast', since it snorted and roared, and not yet quite reliable enough to rival the royal train, it was locked in that other royal residence at Holyroodhouse for use by HM or other trusted members of the family, and also by Vince, since he was regarded with particular affection by the King who had been wayward Bertie, Prince of Wales for such a long time and, on occasions when travelling, had had to rely on Vince's discretion to ease him out of some rather indelicate situations.

Bertie loved a challenge and had transferred some of his devotion to horses onto the Beast. Out riding, however, he would pat his present favourite mount and remark: 'It is quite extraordinary: you have been replaced by a snorting steaming engine with a ferocious roar instead of the gentle biddable creature with four legs that you are.'

Back in Solomon's Tower, Vince was telling us that he had arranged this month in the country as a special late treat for my stepdaughter Meg's seventh birthday. Vince's wife Olivia had been persuaded to come from their London residence at St James for a short visit, bringing their youngest, Faith, with her. The two boys, more than a decade older than their sister, were firmly established with lives of their own. Jamie was now a young intern at St Thomas's Hospital and Justin, a law student in his final year at Oxford. Faith, that late and unexpected child, frail and delicate, so unlike her sturdy brothers, was subject to every prevailing cold wind that blew.

Summers in Scotland were known to be notoriously variable and Olivia had consistently refused to risk the anxiety of a bedridden Faith regardless of the fact that her father was an excellent physician. He did, however, manage to overcome her fears, needing less persuasion this time. Olivia's best friend from schooldays, Mabel Penby Worth, was also heading for a holiday in Ballater and they would be meeting for the first time in many years, their friendship sustained by an exchange of letters. Mabel, who had never married, was a career woman of sorts.

'I know little of her private life, only that she writes for magazines and occasionally for *The Times*,' Olivia had added in tones of awe. 'And she travels a lot, often across to the Continent, quite alone.' Suddenly the chance of spending a few weeks with this accomplished lady was irresistible.

Mabel was the reason for Vince's presence in Edinburgh. As always, he had worked at the plan, smoothing out all the possible difficulties so that it sounded much simpler than indeed it proved to be. He would drive the Beast and collect Mabel who had been taken by hired carriage off the London train at Newcastle railway station and carried to Peebles to visit an elderly relative.

Peebles was also near the home of my husband Jack's parents and a reasonable distance for the Beast to travel. Jack and I normally did the journey by train, however Vince produced a road map where the house was indicated and, certain that Mabel would enjoy this daring new experience, he would drive her back to Edinburgh where we would meet Olivia and Faith at Waverley Station, board the royal train to Ballater and thence the eleven miles to Balmoral.

Jack would only join us whenever his duties permitted. That was sad but inevitable. As Senior Detective Inspector Macmerry of the Edinburgh City Police, he was in the middle of a case.

'Will we be staying at the castle?' asked Meg. 'Won't that be terrific, Mam?' she laughed, whirling me round a wild dance of delight.

'Alas, no,' Vince shook his head.

Meg released me and demanded sternly, 'Why ever not?'

'We will be very near the castle, in a cottage of our own.'

I knew there was no question of staying in Balmoral while Vince wrestled with plausible explanations to a now disappointed Meg, explaining that the cottage was very handsome, complete with every luxury for a royal person wishing to relax away from the trials of state. Abergeldie had filled this role adequately for HM in his days as Prince of Wales, but was now too public; he had devious private reasons for wanting his privacy other than a retreat from domesticity. The wild prince who had been Bertie still existed under the sombre royal crown and the less said about that the better, according to Vince. All he would say was to repeat that HM disliked the presence of noisy shrill children, and that included his own.

Mabel had written to Olivia that she intended staying in a hotel in Ballater to which Vince responded that there was no need for that, as the so-called estate cottage would have ample room for us all.

Olivia had looked doubtful, clearly recalling a vision of estate cottages as somewhat primitive in matters of sleeping accommodation and sanitation.

'I told Livvy that we'd let Mabel decide about that when we see her,' Vince said, adding a cautious, 'after all, it is years since they met.'

Meg had turned her attention to other more important items. 'Thane will love it too, won't you?' she said giving the massive deerhound a hug.

Glances were exchanged. No one had thought about Thane and anxious looks were diverted in my direction.

Meg had taken it for granted but here was a quandary indeed. In pre-Meg days Jack and I had cheerfully left Thane to his own devices. Feeding him had never been a problem. He was, in truth, a wild animal, still a hunter and as such made his own arrangements. There was plenty of wildlife on Arthur's Seat to satisfy his appetite as well as keeping him exercised. There was no walking the dog required with Thane, he was too large and strong – the size of a pony, he made the hint of a dog lead absurd.

I looked at him sitting close to Meg. There had been a change in his habits since Meg's arrival four years ago. Suddenly he was Meg's dog and had spent less time out on the hill and more indoors, transformed into the role of a domestic pet. Seeing him lying contentedly before the kitchen fire or happily at Meg's side, I had some misgivings.

Was this change an indication that Thane was feeling the weight of his years? Worse was the thought that this might indicate that he was soon to leave us. A future that seemed desolate and sorrowful for me, since Thane had been an integral part of my life for ten years, since the day when he had rescued me from the drunken tinkers on the hill. I had no idea how old he was then, fully grown and quite immaculate in appearance, his coat was shiny and neat; the mystery of his presence on Arthur's Seat had never been satisfactorily explained. But in ten years he had not aged in the slightest and what Meg did not realise was that in the natural law of canines, they did not live as long as humans, and calculated by a factor of seven, Thane was now eighty-four years old. I looked for signs of age, a greying muzzle, a general slowing down. There was none.

Jack shared my anxiety, mostly on Meg's account I must admit, although he made light of my fears; but refusing to countenance that Thane had always been an enigma, he would say: 'She'll get over it. He's just a dog after all, Rose, he isn't immortal.'

'Try telling Meg that,' was my reply. 'I don't envy you.'

We knew nothing of Thane's origins, except that deer- and wolfhounds belonged in the pages of history. Deirdre had one with her in Glen Afric, King Arthur had one always at his side and in the present day, Sir Walter Scott was devoted to the breed with Maida at his side on his memorial statue in Princes Street.

I had also heard from a doctor owner a remarkable story that deerhounds were capable of renewing themselves.

According to his account, Thane would not visibly grow old. He would suddenly disappear. We would mourn his passing and looking out on Arthur's Seat realise that he had gone to rest in one of its many secret caves. Having resigned ourselves to never seeing him again, we would get on with our lives. Then one day, a joyous bark and he would be back with us again.

The same dog? Well, not perhaps exactly the same, although Jack would say of course he was Thane. But we would never know the truth. It was magic and there was some consolation that Meg believed in magic.

One afternoon she had arrived from the convent school down the road at St Leonard's, run by the Little Sisters of the Poor. Uncle Vince was on one of his rare visits and their delight was mutual.

'How was school?' Vince demanded after a final hug. 'Are you good at sums?'

Meg threw down her uniform hat. 'I do quite well, thank you, Uncle.' A sigh. 'But the nuns are much better at teaching us how to sew and do useful things like cooking.' She frowned, looking at Thane who had rushed to her side. Stroking his head, she said: 'There are so many things I want to know that they haven't got answers for, and they get very cross when I insist.'

'What sort of things?' Vince asked gently.

Meg sighed again. 'When I talk about magic, like you, Thane.' Pausing to kiss his head, she looked up at Vince.

'It's very odd, but he seems to know what I'm thinking, as if he can read my mind sometimes. Better than Mam and Pa here, or anyone else,' she added with an apologetic glance in my direction.

I knew that feeling well. Long before Meg came into our lives, Thane and I had shared this strange kind of telepathy.

'It's a kind of magic,' she said. 'How can they deny that when Jesus was magic? But when I try to tell the nuns that of course magic exists they just cross themselves and whisper that it is . . . is . . .' and struggling to find the word, 'blasphemy. They say I must be punished.' Bewildered, she shrugged and looked at us. 'But it isn't wicked; if you believe in God, then that is a sort of magic, isn't it?'

We were saved from being plunged into deeper waters of theology when Jack arrived.

As I made tea I only half-listened to the conversations, their laughter echoing round the ancient Tower. Jack and Vince, Meg sitting on her father's knee. How alike they were, physically, anyway, and clever too. Meg was the brightest pupil in her class at the convent. So bright, in fact, that the nuns had to keep on moving her up into the next class. At that rate she would soon be with the eleven-year-olds.

Sister Josephine was perturbed, almost apologetic. 'She is quite brilliant, advanced for her age, in every way,' she added with a frown at my little gasp of pleasure.

She shook her head. 'It isn't quite natural, Mrs Macmerry.' And the hand raised, about to cross herself but she remembered in time. 'It distresses the other little girls when she seems to see things and know everything.'

I explained that all little girls were like that, a kind of natural jealousy and she smiled, looked relieved. 'If you say so,' and we left it at that.

When I told Jack about my visit, that the Sister had wanted to see me, he looked up sharply.

'Nothing wrong, I hope?'

'Far from it – seems our little girl is quite brilliant, well ahead of her class.'

Jack had relaxed with a grin of delight, proud as any father could ever be, until I got to the bit about seeing things. He shook his head. 'Takes that from you, love, definitely not from my side of the family.'

We both laughed. Meg was not our child. She was Jack's and I was her stepmother.

'Wonder who she gets it from,' he said and we both looked at Thane who also knew things before they happened. Not altogether rare in animals, this extra dimension – the sixth sense which had long ago been lost by humans, or most of them.

I called it my intuition, this awareness, an awareness I had reason to bless. My father, Chief Inspector Jeremy Faro, had it and the credit, he claimed, lay in our Orcadian background and the rumour that we had selkie blood in the family. But there was no way Meg could have inherited it.

I remembered fondly this family scene, Vince, Jack and Meg with Thane close at hand. A perfectly natural little seven-year-old sitting happily on her father's knee, stroking Thane's head. If she was different from other girls of her age it was because she had no interest in toys or dolls, loved books and was happy for hours with a box of paints, and where her classmates had a pet dog, cat or rabbit, she had Thane.

'Children love small animals,' said Jack approvingly. But Thane was huge and no ordinary dog, despite what Jack wanted to believe.

He was fooling himself. Thane had powers beyond human explanation. He was a powerful force in Meg's life from that first meeting and it seemed that he was capable of infiltrating her mind. A scary thought, although he would never use that power except to protect and help her, but it made me uneasy for some reason.

Meg loved living in Solomon's Tower and there had been many changes since she first came into our lives as a scared three-year-old who had suffered many trials and cruelties before I tracked her down, this orphaned child of Jack's first, brief, unhappy marriage. At least some of the responsibility of Meg lay with me, for he had married her mother on the rebound since I had sent him packing. They were strangers, he knew nothing about her and was never quite sure if the child was his. When Margaret died shortly after Meg's birth, much to Jack's relief her childless, married sister Pam gladly took over the responsibility of his baby daughter and during those first three years of her life it was almost as if he tried to forget her existence. When I first set eyes on her, all my own misgivings melted away. I knew she was Jack's and at their first meeting their likeness was undeniable. As a little girl she was his image. The sandy, slightly curling hair, the large hazel eyes, the wide mouth. Indeed, as the years passed she grew even more like him but with a gradual refinement of features hinting that one day she would be a young woman whose good looks a father would be proud of – if it were possible that Jack could be any prouder than he was of her at this moment.

I would look at them sometimes and sigh. Life had been good. Here we were, a happy family the three of us, four if we included Thane, Meg with parents who loved her and loved each other. She did not know it, but this happy family was because of her own existence, since having lost my beloved first husband, Danny McQuinn, in tragic circumstances I had consistently refused to marry Jack Macmerry. Meg's presence had changed all that.

As I made tea, Vince had been telling Jack about the Balmoral visit. Jack came over and put his arm around me. 'I'm sorry, love, that I can't come too. It sounds such good fun. Pity about Thane.'

Meg was stroking Thane's head. She looked up, said very firmly: 'I'm not going with you. I'll stay here with Thane.'

What a sacrifice, I thought, to love him so much. As we seated ourselves round the kitchen table, Jack said sternly: 'You can't stay here alone.'

'Who is to take care of Thane if Mam and I are all away?'

In the normal way Jack would have done so. But as Jack was on a murder case with leads in Aberdeen and Glasgow, his movements from day to day were unpredictable.

And long before I met Jack Macmerry I was well acquainted with the situation that dominated a senior detective's domestic life, its inevitability had stalked my early years, the rare holidays my sister Emily and I looked forward to with Papa. The last-minute changes, the tears and disappointment, and after I married Danny McQuinn and lived in Arizona where he worked for Pinkerton's Detective Agency, I had learnt to respect that. If a policeman's life was not an easy one, neither was his wife's. I knew what I was taking on. As Robert Burns put it, 'the best laid plans o' mice and men' could well and often be asundered. I was fortunate, I could take refuge in my own career.

Meg regarded us pityingly. 'I won't be alone. Thane will look after me.'

Jack shook his head. He was at a loss to explain and I could see how he hated having to disappoint Meg who was no longer smiling, her happy mood lost, her small fists clenched, her lips quivering as she fought back tears. And before any of us could think up an answer she said: 'I am not going – anywhere – unless Thane comes too.'

Vince, well served in diplomatic dealings with royalty over the years, stepped in. He put his arms around her and contemplated Jack and me over her head. 'That is no problem, dear. Leave it to me. I'll arrange everything. There are plenty of dogs in the stables near your cottage. One more won't make any difference. We will take Thane with us, if your Mam and Pa approve, that is.'

How on earth would this work? I had qualms and Jack's frown was doubtful but I sighed with momentary relief, echoed by Meg, who flung her arms around Vince. 'Oh, thank you, Uncle Vince, thank you.' And to Thane who showed not the slightest interest in this conversation as if it did not concern him in the least, 'Isn't that lovely, Thane? You will love it and we will have a splendid time – all those lovely grounds for us to play in.'

I wasn't too sure about that, either, as I thought of the vast assortment of dogs and horses.

Jack obviously had the same misgivings. 'Hope you don't all end up in the Tower of London.'

CHAPTER TWO

And so the plan of departure took shape. I would drive down with Vince in the Beast to collect Mabel, who would stay overnight with us. The next morning we would join Olivia and Faith on the royal train in Edinburgh and continue the journey to Balmoral. As the motor car was not yet in general use, I suspected that we would be met on arrival at Ballater Railway Station by the old style carriage, the same as used by the King's mother Queen Victoria, but perhaps a safer and surer way for four adults, a small girl and a very large dog to travel the twisting roads to the Castle.

We were not to journey to Peebles alone with the Beast. On hearing Mabel's collection address, Jack had consulted his maps. Penby House was only four miles from his parents' farm at Eildon. And as it was his mother's birthday next week, a perfect opportunity to call in, drop off a present. Meg could deliver it in person, giving Andrew and Jess Macmerry a visit from this adored and (from their point of view) too-rarely seen only granddaughter.

'Meg put you up to this, Jack,' I said.

He laughed. 'Truth is, she's mad keen to have a ride in the Beast and she's made something at school, a tea cosy, specially for Grandma.'

Meg could have asked for the moon, neither Vince nor Jack could resist her. I considered staying behind but Vince insisted there would be room enough for Meg between us in the front, with Mabel and her luggage in the back seat. I could only pray that there wouldn't be rain to accompany us.

Vince merely smiled at that. 'Umbrellas will be provided.'

And so we set off. Meg with an almost tearful farewell to Thane. 'Why couldn't he come along too? He could run alongside,' she wailed.

'No,' said Vince firmly, 'that is out of the question. A motor car will cause enough consternation where we are going without a dog the size of a pony.'

And so we set off, Meg clapping her hands in delight, thrilled beyond words at this new adventure, with some misgivings on my part. However, I got used to the looks of amazement from passers-by as Vince occasionally applied the horn, a sound like the wrath of God, and the Beast only let us down twice on the journey, requiring his liquid refreshment. The frantic search for water from a ditch had been overcome by Vince carrying a large bottle of water with us.

* * *

Jack had sent a telegram from the Central Office and at Eildon the Macmerrys were waiting to receive us. They did everything but put flags out. What a reception. Andrew went into ecstasies over the Beast which Jess regarded with some apprehension concerning the safety of its occupants, in particular her precious wee granddaughter. Her relief was evident when we reached the farm in safety as if we had travelled not merely the miles from Edinburgh but across the high seas from China on an old-style clipper.

The cosy farmhouse with its peat fire, a feast set out on a snow-white tablecloth. Pies, scones, cakes, biscuits, everything that became a banquet was visible. I was relieved that the pies did not include veal, observing that the fatted calf, happily grazing outside, had not been sacrificed.

Kisses and cuddles were in abundance while across the table Jess studied Vince with reverence. Normally she never stopped talking but she hadn't a word to say, staring at Vince round-eyed. She almost curtseyed; overcome by his royal associations she didn't know what to call him, something between Your Highness and Sir. I certainly gained prestige for possessing such a famous stepbrother.

With so much food in evidence, and drink, drams provided by Andrew, with small sherries for the ladies, Vince was having a whale of a time and, even knowing his capacity and aware of the hip flask, I hoped he would be able to continue the drive for Mabel, whose existence had been temporarily forgotten as the reason for our visit. 'This lass you're down here to collect,' said Andrew, 'whereabouts is she staying?'

This interrupted the serving of more trifle to Vince. As Jess called him 'sir' Vince's eyebrows shot up and touching her hand gently, he said firmly: 'I presume you're teasing me, Jess Macmerry. I'm not "sir" to anyone but the stable boys.' He took her hand, kissed it and smiles were exchanged. To Andrew he said:

'Mabel Penby Worth is the lady's name, she's a school friend of my wife Olivia, visiting an elderly relative at Penby House—'

Across the table Andrew laid down his glass and said slowly, 'Penby House, did you say?'

'Yes indeed, I gather it's just a mile or two up the road from here.'

'Well, by all that's holy,' said Andrew thoughtfully. He looked quite shocked.

'Fancy that,' said Jess.

Vince laughed. 'What's wrong?'

Andrew shook his head, in the manner of one busily rearranging unpleasant thoughts. 'Well, it's just that – oh, I don't know, but there's always been a lot of gossip about the Penbys. Never very popular with the locals. Bad landowners. The old lady is the last of them, an invalid for years and not quite right in the head. Tried to commit suicide over an unhappy love affair, so the story went.'

'That was donkey's years ago,' Jess put in. 'And she's been a recluse ever since. Poor soul.'

I was eager to hear more of this local scandal which was cut short as Meg bounced back into the kitchen from feeding the hens. Clocks were consulted, it was time to leave. Meg clutched to her adoring grandmother's bosom,

26

with a tearful plea to stay, Jess eyeing the Beast warily and embarking on a catalogue of possible disasters, despite Vince's attempts at consolation.

'What will happen if you get stuck somewhere?' she demanded and with a protective arm around Meg. 'That monster and our precious wee darling?'

Vince chuckled. 'If you think our Beast is an odd-looking vehicle you should have seen its predecessor.'

Andrew nodded enthusiastically. 'Aye, saw one myself at a cattle market in Stirling, in the eighties. That was a sensation! Terrified the crowds. For all the world like a hansom cab rattling along the road – lacking a horse! Weird!'

'There the likeness didn't end,' Vince put it. 'Like the horse it frequently stopped and had to be encouraged to proceed. In this case by restorative drinks of water.'

'How did they manage that?'

'Usually with a teacup from the nearest ditch.' Vince shook his head. 'Sometimes this disagreed with its digestive system and made it cross, so it blew up and spattered the driver with orange spray out of the boiler.'

They both laughed as Vince went on. 'And at any steep hill it was not equal to the horse. It simply stopped dead, sat there breathing asthmatically while the luckless occupants had to get out and push.'

'In the middle of nowhere, man, that's a terrible thing to happen,' said Andrew while Jess continued to clutch Meg, unconvinced about this strange-looking machine's merits.

Vince smiled. 'Ah well, the age of chivalry still exists. It was a code of honour that a moving motorist should not pass by on the other side, leaving stranded a less fortunate fellow motorist.'

Andrew said: 'I remember fine reading about that. The fraternity of the road was to acquire a new meaning since the days of the highwayman and the Red Flag Act.' He nodded doubtfully, 'Aye, all well enough, but I still like to feel the solid warm flesh of a horse under me when I travel.'

Kisses were exchanged. We were on our way.

Warned that the house was remote and a little difficult without a made-up road, we were especially grateful for Andrew's instructions.

His cut-short history of Penby House's inhabitant had led me to expect a forbidding Gothic ruin but instead we approached a large characterless box-like mansion with many windows, perched on a small incline overlooking the Borders farmlands and a distant view of the Eildon Hills.

A short drive to the front door, in spite of an echoing bell, it remained ominously closed. Were we expected?

At last the door was opened by a pale young woman, presumably the maid. As we waited for her to announce us, the house smelt unpleasantly old, as if everything and everyone had gone to dust long ago. A vast cold reception area, an array of dark and somehow forbidding ancestral portraits lined the lofty staircase walls with uncarpeted treads guaranteed to echo every footstep.

Meg shivered. She was conscious of this air of desolation and held my hand tightly. 'What is this place, Mam?'

I didn't say so, but it had the cold unhappy air of an institution, and I guessed we were both reliving the warmth of that world we had left at the Macmerry's farm. Love and laughter were long vanished from this house, had they indeed ever existed within these grim walls.

Meg was staring up the stairs as we waited for the maid to summon Mabel.

A sound of footsteps and a tall figure, Mabel Penby Worth, appeared from what was possibly the drawing room. The young maid who had opened the door to us was now at her side, carrying her luggage. Lily by name and, surprisingly, her personal maid, who was to accompany her to Ballater.

As for Mabel's elderly relative, the reason for her visit, we were not to meet her.

'Aunt Penby does not receive visitors these days.' We were not really surprised for we had gathered from Andrew and Jess that she was a recluse. My imagination painted a Miss Havisham and I suspected that all three of us, Vince and I, and particularly Meg, were glad indeed to be leaving and deprived of the pleasure of that meeting.

Vince murmured that we were short of time but as we walked past an open door, I was conscious of another smell invading the emptiness.

Cigar smoke. Very prevalent and very expensive. Where was the man? Or did the old lady have eccentric habits too? We paused while Mabel had a final check on her items of luggage and I noticed on the hall table a few scattered photographs. One signed – of a younger King Edward, as Bertie, Prince of Wales and some other royals, indicated that Penby House had indeed seen better days.

Vince indicated the signed photograph. To Mabel he said: 'You have met His Majesty?'

'My mother lived here one summer when she was a girl.'

'Did she meet him?' asked Meg in tones of reverence.

'I have absolutely no idea,' and the cold reply said the subject was closed.

We boarded the Beast, which wiped the smile of delight from Mabel's rather sullen countenance when she realised she was to share the back seat with Lily and the luggage, since she was larger than Meg and I who occupied the front seat with Vince.

I turned, saw a shadow at a corner of the house, standing still, watching us. A working man, perhaps a gardener. Tall, lean, black hair and a long, rather pale face. He saw me looking in his direction and quickly withdrew. I felt almost embarrassed. Strange how any man who resembled Danny, even vaguely glimpsed, could still after all this time make my heart leap.

Later in our acquaintance when I asked Mabel did her aunt live alone in that vast mausoleum of a house, Mabel confirmed that she was a recluse and had no servants living in.

'Her physician looks in fairly regularly.' Had our visits coincided and was that the answer to the cigar smoke, quite unrelated to the man outside who was, to judge by his appearance, possibly the gardener?

I was puzzled why Mabel, one gathered by her conversation, much used to comfort and luxury, had taken the trouble to stop off en route to Edinburgh. As if aware of my unasked question, I was informed: 'One feels duty-bound, family obligations – that sort of thing – when one is in the area, coming north.' (Which of course, she was not. Peebles was quite a circuitous route from the direct train to Edinburgh.)

'We used to visit in the old days, and it would have seemed quite callous to ignore her now,' she went on, 'one's only remaining relative.' There was a slight pause and I said: 'So you know Penby quite well.'

She nodded, with a slight shudder. 'It was always a cold house, never seemed to get warm, even in high summer. I suppose border houses are like that.'

She would have been pleasantly surprised had she been with us at Eildon.

CHAPTER THREE

Mabel Penby Worth. I wasn't sure what I expected, perhaps a replica of gentle Olivia. Mabel was a surprise and I didn't know quite why then, except somehow she wasn't the image I had from Olivia's description. She looked like a fighter, not the kind of woman who would take defeat easily. In fact, the personification of the women's suffrage movement to which I was to gather she had dedicated her existence. A consoling thought, indeed.

I was impressed, we suffragettes could hardly lose with females of Mabel's calibre on our side. Quite tall, robust in frame, a strong, determined countenance under that bonnet and a strong handshake to go with it, as did the sensible, rather mannish travelling costume, a long tweed tailored jacket and skirt and a wide-brimmed velvet hat.

Her maid Lily was an addition we had not been

expecting, but Vince indicated that was an easy matter to sort out as he arranged them in the Beast, which did not altogether please Mabel who gave us a helpless look. As if to suggest there might be some other means of transporting Lily to Edinburgh. There was no alternative so Mabel sat as far away as was possible from one's personal maid on the back seat of a motor car.

We had not the slightest sympathy for her. As far as I was concerned she had missed the whole point of the suffrage movement that all women from all walks of life were equal, or should be. However, Mabel soon forgot her discomfiture and waxed lyrical about this means of transport, sentiments which soon became urgent whispers of doubts when we had to stop several times on the hilly return journey, to relieve the Beast's snorts and breathing problems with administrations from the water bottle.

Once in sight of Solomon's Tower, she again waxed eloquent at such antiquity. While Vince returned the Beast to Holyrood before taking a hired cab to Waverley Station, we were home and Mabel looked disappointed, not to say actually shocked, obviously having second thoughts about the Tower, which did not stretch to accommodation for acquaintances, especially a modern, unmarried lady's requirements, travelling with her maid whose voice we were soon to discover rarely rose above a whisper.

After a brief tour of the Tower, its reality of worn spiral stair treads, chilly stone walls with their tapestries in the somewhat shabby Great Hall failing to live up to her expectations of grandeur, Mabel seemed relieved to return to the warm kitchen and to sink into a worn but comfortable armchair.

'I feel as if I know you already,' she said, looking around our humble kitchen and I was not sure that this was a compliment. My few visitors were usually welcomed with a cup of tea and a scone. Mabel's changed expression indicated that she found it quite extraordinary to be taking tea in the kitchen, obviously expecting that we would be seated at either end of the enormous dining table in the Great Hall. A direct descendant of the round table used by medieval knights it had been installed centuries ago when the Tower first came into being, not far short of the Middle Ages. And there it had remained simply because having been built in, it would have been an impossibility to remove.

I looked at Mabel whose expression indicated that having been led to expect great things, she was being let down. Tea in the kitchen with her maid, indeed, who she stared at resentfully from time to time as if she should be serving tea rather than being seated at the table and consuming scones alongside her betters.

As the conversation tended to flag, Mabel glanced towards the bookshelf, with the long line of my logbooks for the past ten years.

'You have such an exciting life,' and pointing at a poster I had forgotten to remove of the Women's Suffragette Movement, of which I was the Edinburgh Branch chairman, she smiled.

'I am sure we are going to be great friends, Rose, for we have much in common. One of my main reasons for choosing to come north is for our meeting in Aberdeen.

Perhaps you already know about it. Dear Emmeline and Christabel are intending to be present, although that has not been advertised,' she added in a whisper. 'They are so well known, so they prefer to travel incognito—'

I had indeed heard of this great occasion, but dismissed it as an unlikely event for me to attend. Instead it now seemed well within my reach. For not only were the Pankhursts well known but achieving notoriety having smashed windows and gone to prison and suffered for the cause. My interest quickened. The mention of the Pankhursts and I was now listening intently: 'They have long been my heroines.'

'And mine,' she laughed. 'And I have the honour of being well acquainted with dear Emmeline over the years.'

My eyes widened. What a stroke of luck, one of my ambitions about to be fulfilled. To meet them at last . . .

'My dear,' Mabel was saying, 'you simply must come with me. You would be most welcome considering that you have such an interest and a prominent role in our movement.'

Vince, who had just returned from stabling the Beast and heard this part of the conversation, nodded approvingly. 'A jolly good idea, Rose, you can stay the night in Ballater or we will come and collect you both.'

It was then I had my first moments of disquiet. It was all too well planned, even to a meeting with the Pankhursts. Naturally suspicious through years of dealing with problems, I knew how readily things could go wrong. It sounded wonderful, too wonderful. All planned so meticulously, a visit long overdue from Olivia and Faith, seeing us all in a train heading for a holiday in, of all places, Balmoral Castle. Everything fitted in beautifully for everyone, even Thane.

I tried to shake it off, ignore one of my strange feelings, as Jack described them. A touch of ice in the heart, that something was about to go terribly wrong.

CHAPTER FOUR

Hiring cabs are somewhat reluctant, to say the least, about taking animals on board. The presence of even tiny dogs can upset the horses. One of Thane's proportions would be impossible, so it was decided that Vince, Mabel, the maid Lily and Meg would ride. I would take my bicycle and Thane would run alongside on our journey to Waverley Station, where the royal train carrying guests from England for the royal shooting party would be waiting.

I had already decided that my faithful bicycle would provide excellent transport between the Balmoral cottage and Ballater. It would also provide something equally important, namely independence, used as I was in Edinburgh to making my own way.

Jack and I waved the others off. I let them go ahead as I needed to attend to some last-minute details in the

Tower, including a store of non-perishable food for Jack who, totally engaged on a murder case, was apt to forget such minor details. He was looking a bit sad and wistful watching the cab disappear down the hill and I knew the main reason for that. He hated the prospect of being parted from Meg.

We looked at each other and he sighed, gave me a hug. This was the first time in four years since she had come back into his life that she had ever gone on holiday without both of us and I reminded him of his promise, that he would take leave and join us on Deeside.

'Who knows? I might well be in Aberdeen soon and Balmoral isn't all that far away.'

'That's great! When will you know for sure?'

Avoiding my eyes, he shrugged. 'Maybe I shouldn't have mentioned it, raised your hopes. Just a rumour.' He grinned and touched his nose, a gesture I knew only too well, that meant he wasn't prepared to disclose those rumours and what went on behind the scenes in Edinburgh City Police was none of my business.

He followed me as I took the bicycle out of the barn, aware that he was longing to say 'You will take good care of Meg, won't you?' I could read it in his eyes as we kissed and said goodbye and it stayed with me. His anxiety haunted me: this moment I was to remember later.

As Thane and I whizzed down the road away from the safety of the Tower and Jack's hand upraised in farewell, I had my first shaft of fear. We were such a happy, united family, but it is in the nature of life that things can change without warning. Could we stay always as we were now?

And I said a little prayer, the bit about 'delivering us from evil', without the least idea then how much it was to be needed.

As Thane and I reached St Mary's Street we could hear the trains rumbling in and out of the station. We could see and smell the smoke, a sight that never failed to excite me and Meg would love it too. What joy trains had brought into all our lives, when I thought of the gruelling days of all those miles jostling about in a horse-drawn carriage.

In the station, our first setback. A forlorn little group waiting for us with the news that Olivia and Faith would not be joining us after all. Vince had received a message via the stationmaster.

'Nothing serious, I hope!'

Vince sighed. 'Faith is poorly. Sick during the night. She has a fever, a slight temperature. Probably nothing to worry about, she has bouts like this often enough, but you know what Olivia is like.'

He was calm about it but I sensed his underlying annoyance. As Faith's father and an eminent physician dealing with royal patients he felt let down that Olivia could not trust him to take care of their own daughter.

'She sends her apologies to everyone. We'd better get going.' With a long-suffering sigh, he signalled the porters to load our luggage.

Mabel sighed too, clearly disappointed. So many years since she and Olivia had met. This was to have been a special occasion, one of the main reasons for her coming all the way to Scotland.

Meg took my hand, whispered sadly: 'I was looking

forward to having a new friend, Mam, specially one who is a sort of cousin.'

She leant close to my side and I felt sad for her too. She had no family but Jack and me. As a tiny baby Meg had no memory of her own mother or, I suspected, of the kindly aunt who adopted her but sadly died when she was three, leaving her in the care, if care could be correctly defined, of a ne'er-do-well uncle who shortly remarried. And that was when I caught up with her.

She was so delighted to claim Faith as 'a sort of cousin', and being well in advance of her seven years, according to the nuns, three years between the two girls I hoped would make little difference.

We walked along the platform where our train waited. Thane was not to have the indignity of the goods van, the rule with normal trains; he was allowed to travel with us.

We were shown into a roomy, well-upholstered six-seater compartment, three seats to a side, Vince and Meg, Mabel and Lily, with the former looking as if she wished her maid could have been accommodated perhaps in the luggage van.

With Thane lying on the floor between us, there was the sound of the engine gathering steam, the creak of wheels, and the excitement of a journey about to begin.

Suddenly a figure dashed along the platform. A tall man, head down, rushing towards the train.

'He almost missed it,' said Vince.

A whistle, the platform slowly vanishing, then Calton Hill and the last glimpse of Edinburgh.

We were off. The great adventure for Mabel and Meg had begun.

Meg had difficulty remaining in her seat, bouncing up and down, staring out of the window. 'Isn't this wonderful, Mam? "Faster than fairies, faster than witches, bridges and houses, hedges and ditches . . ."' She laughed. 'And it's all happening out there, just like he wrote.'

Thane had sat up as if he wanted a look too and she put her arms around his neck. This was her favourite poem written by Robert Louis Stevenson, driven into exile from his beloved Edinburgh by its atrocious weather to die in the South Seas, not from bad lungs but from a cerebral haemorrhage brought about by overwork. That was in 1894, the year before I arrived at Solomon's Tower.

'". . . charging along like troops in a battle, All through the meadows, the horses and cattle . . ."' Meg chanted and I smiled. From her earliest days with us she had loved having poems read to her and could soon recite them from memory.

I looked at her. Where had she inherited so many talents? 'You must be so proud of your little daughter,' the nuns said, 'so well ahead of her classmates.'

Jack's daughter, not mine, and again I thought about her mother. What had she been like? Jack never spoke of her. All I knew was her name, Margaret, the rest of their association contained in a sentence. A barmaid in a Glasgow pub he had picked up one lonely evening. Furious at my rejection, my refusal to marry him, in need of comfort he had too much to drink and went home with her.

The consequence was this gifted child he had barely acknowledged as his own, until after many trials and tribulations four years ago, I tracked her down and brought them face to face. His fears that she might not be his were ended. Neither he nor anyone else could deny that she was his child, his image.

A sigh of relief from me. And since at forty I had a history of miscarriages and could not have a live child, Meg had brought us overwhelming joy.

Still, because it was in my nature to be haunted by mysteries I could not solve, I would have given much to know a great deal more about the distaff side of Meg's origins.

CHAPTER FIVE

The train compartment although comfortable had little room for manoeuvre. Opposite Vince, Mabel and Lily, Meg and I with Thane at our feet and my sketchbook which I never travelled without at the ready. This journey promised sketching opportunities, people and landscapes to turn into paintings when time permitted. Or even a portrait?

I looked at the silent Lily, her eyes perpetually downcast. I hoped she would not mind being drawn and as my pencil flew across the page and her face emerged, I realised I had never heard her speak beyond a whispered yes or no and I wondered if she was English. Mentioning this to Mabel later, she laughed.

'You do ask the oddest questions.' And she shrugged, 'I can tell you nothing about her. She came from a trusted friend, she performs all the duties required of a personal maid and that is all I need to know.'

'Aren't you curious?'

Again she laughed. 'You are such a strange person, Rose. I imagine that her background is very uninteresting and very boring, so I shouldn't let it bother you either.'

But it did, part of my nature as a detective is to want to know everything there is to know about everyone. Jack often found this curious too and raised his eyes heavenward at all my probing and apparently unnecessary questions.

Still, each time I looked at Lily, she seemed more of an enigma, although I doubted if she would have understood the word. When the necessity of finding out who her parents were, and where she came from in a moment of crisis still to come, Mabel wasn't much help either.

Once, finding myself alone with her, I tried a few tentative questions but she merely stared blankly at me and shrugged. Perhaps she was deaf and embarrassed to admit it. That hadn't occurred to me and I mentioned it to Vince, adding: 'And I think she's foreign.'

But his reactions were like Jack's regarding my unpardonable curiosity and, to a certain extent, Mabel's as well. He shrugged and I knew another reason why women's suffrage was so important: that we fought for every woman to have her rights from the poorest servant to the lady in her castle and every individual case was of interest to me.

At my side Meg chanted: '"All of the sights of the hill and the plain, Fly as thick as driving rain; And ever again, in the wink of an eye, Painted stations whistle by . . ."'

And so it was: Perth, Montrose, Stonehaven, a glimpse of the sea and Aberdeen's cold granite, then westwards to Banchory, Kincardine O'Neil, Aboyne. All framed by hazy blue mountains, their nearness an illusion of wine-clear air and, closer at hand whizzing past the window, moors covered in great carpets of unending purple heather. Then like a solemn regiment on guard over the scene, sombre tall dark firs, majestic pines, remains of the vast Caledonian forest that had once covered this land, and nestling almost apologetically along the rail side, delicate silver birches, and dainty larches with drooping lemon leaves.

And everywhere castles. Castles turreted, haughty, lived-in and prosperous. Castles dark, mysterious, enchanted, peeping out of thick woods, where a princess might sleep and dream for a hundred years. Castles ghostly, their roofless crumbling majesty long past dreams of human habitations. It was like some rich medieval tapestry, bordered in the sharp sunlight of a perfect late summer's day.

Meg clasped her hands in delight and pointing out of the window, quoted again from her favourite poem come to life: '"Here is a mill and there is a river, Each a glimpse and gone for ever."'

I laughed. 'Not quite. Here we are!' The train was slowing down.

Ballater at last. Vince folded his newspaper. Mabel opened her eyes. She had not made much of the journey and statue-like at her side, Lily unmoving, unflinching – heaven knows what her thoughts had been about her fellow travellers. Thane stood up, stretched and yawned.

He would not be sorry to get down onto firm ground again.

We steamed into the station, its platform elegant, garlanded by huge displays of flowers as befitted royal connections. This was the end of the line and as we stepped down from our compartment, the train emptied of passengers, most in transit for Balmoral Castle. Around us a vast collection of shrill English voices, the mark of the aristocracy with their mounds of luggage, their servants, and their dogs.

Meg pulled at my arm. 'Mam, I'm needing,' she whispered. No need to say any more, she couldn't make the rest of that journey in such discomfort. Fortunately, no doubt bearing in mind the problem of long-distance travellers and the eleven miles further to the castle, there was a ladies' waiting room with a lavatory. Something of a novelty, but Queen Victoria had had one installed especially for her convenience midway along the railway line to Ballater.

'Come along, hurry!' I said as we ran towards the sign. I hoped there were not ladies already queuing with similar needs. As we approached, one emerged. Meg rushed in while I watched the colourful spectacle of this particular slice of English society awaiting carriages, aware from the *Illustrated London News* that after his morning ride in Rotten Row, the man of fashion was never seen without his frock coat and top hat of pearly grey, carrying stick and gloves. His lady would have an enormous hat on top of her padded hairstyle, her costume bedizened with ribbons, flowers, feather boa and carrying a parasol.

Women's fashions were created in London and Paris,

the styles copied by home dressmakers, using the sewing machines which had come into general use in the late Queen's reign and putting an end to the hard labour of hand-sewing long seams. The coat and skirt were now primarily in evidence, not only for the new breed of working-woman but also for the upper classes. Regarded as much more convenient and sensible when travelling, they had replaced the silk costume with its absurd bustles and hourglass shape.

Trying to keep my eye on Vince and the rest of the party while I awaited Meg's reappearance, I stood on tiptoe. My arm was suddenly grabbed by a large, stout lady, much flustered in countenance.

'Don't stand there dithering, gel.' And so saying, she thrust two large hatboxes at me. 'Give me a hand with these.'

I stared at her. Thanks to my lack of fashion and unconventional attire, I had been mistaken, once again, for a servant.

'My sister, Your Ladyship.' A cold voice and Vince was at my side.

The woman looked me up and down and turning her lorgnette on Vince said: 'Ah, Dr Laurie, I trust you are well . . .'

'Indeed, My Lady. Very well indeed.'

Meg had joined us. Giving a chilly bow and without further introduction, Vince said, 'Come, Rose,' and raising his hat he marched us to where Mabel and her maid waited with Thane.

But his face was flushed, annoyed and embarrassed by my encounter with English society.

'Sorry about that, Vince,' I murmured.

'Don't be silly. Not your fault.' But it was.

'Oh, there you are. What on earth happened to you?' Mabel demanded. 'I thought we'd lost you. In all this great mob, one should take care not to be separated.'

Explanations were made. 'What is the delay?' I asked, having expected a carriage to meet us.

'After coming all this way,' grumbled Mabel. 'This is too bad.'

Vince agreed. 'Tiresome. Typical of HM, I'm afraid. Gather he had a six-pointer in his sights.'

Meg looked puzzled. 'A stag,' I whispered, as Vince went on: 'And of course, every spare carriage would be needed at the hunt.'

It was the usual procedure, one rare quality that the King shared with his formidable mother. Ladies also accompanied the hunt, and although they were not expected to carry guns and shoot at anything, it was an excellent excuse for a picnic and more robust liquid refreshment for the hunters.

Vince remarked to me later: 'HM is a little unreliable as regards keeping appointments. One thing at a time on his mind, that's his rule. Everything and everyone else must await his pleasure.'

We were not the only impatient guests. Yapping pet dogs, growling and barking, strained at their leads to get at one another. As for Thane, no need for means of restraint. He simply walked at Vince's side and it wasn't his reactions to all these dogs that intrigued me, but theirs to him. They looked up at him, most of them being only half his size, yet not a bark out of any of them. If dogs could bow in reverence, that was how their behaviour might best be described.

I was amused and amazed and yet I should not have been for I had seen this reaction from other animals, even the wild white Border cattle. Whatever it was in Thane that we didn't – couldn't – recognise, it was obvious to the animal kingdom.

At last the sound of carriages approaching, a long line strung out with a few motor cars. And one was for Dr Laurie and party. A very large, handsome Rolls thoughtfully provided, behind the driver, seats to accommodate four passengers. And Thane.

There was only room for our hand luggage much to Mabel's distress. She had to accept the reassurance that hers and the rest of ours would be collected by cart and arrive later. She looked with considerable disfavour on my bicycle which was being strapped onto the back of the Rolls and edged away as far as possible from Lily sitting next to her.

'We'll be seeing the castle at last, Mam,' said Meg, seizing my hand in excitement. 'Oh, isn't it wonderful?'

I smiled encouragingly, hoping that neither she nor the rest of us were in for a disappointment. Well, surprises are always welcome and there were plenty in store that only the very unimaginative would have classed under the heading of disappointment.

As we were moving off, Vince said: 'Well done, so he caught it after all.'

I looked across as he pointed to a man who had pushed forward as if to be first in the queue for the carriages. The one who had rushed along the station platform at Waverley as the train was moving off.

Now I had a better look at him. Tall, thin, dark hair that obstinately fell over his forehead, I felt a sudden chill, a flash of recognition. As we moved away and we lost him, I told myself this couldn't be the same man I had glimpsed outside Penby House. I must be mistaken.

Was it merely because any man with a fleeting resemblance to Danny could have this strange effect on me? This longing to return to a past life and a love that was gone for ever.

Feeling guilty and disloyal, I thought of Jack and the weeks ahead without him. I was used to short periods of absence in Edinburgh when necessity led him in pursuit of criminals or as witness in a homicide, but on rare holidays we had always been together.

I would miss him and so would Meg. We could only hope for a couple of days at most where he might make a brief visit when matters at the Central Office were on hold and his absence allowed. I was to realise Meg felt the same when she was to ask with daily frequency: why can't Pa ever be with us? or I wish we could hear how Pa is.

'Shall I send him a letter, Mam?'

I encouraged her to do so, not expecting any reply since he was a poor letter writer, but I was in for a surprise. I had forgotten the bond of parenthood. There were shrill cries of delight at a constant supply of postcards from her pa. Indeed, so often she watched for the postman each day.

I was pleased, although I had never experienced this kind of devoted attention. It was yet another strand in the man I had married, and in all truth, I was content with what I had and happy to leave some areas of his character unexplored. Confident of his love, I was grateful and yet guilty that I could never return it with equal passion, for I had been deeply in love only once in my life and I could never, I believed, recapture that experience.

The fact that a glimpsed stranger could vibrate some chord of forgotten delight was a fatal warning, but it was not until our paths crossed again that I knew, too late, not only unsettling emotions, but also dangerous areas best left unexplored.

CHAPTER SIX

'Wild and yet not desolate'. As the road twisted its way out of Ballater into the mountainous countryside, the late Queen's words in her journal described the scene most aptly. She had loved to draw it, as I did now, as we progressed west along the road with far below us tantalising glimpses of a gleaming river.

At our exclamations of delight, Vince as passenger instead of driver took the opportunity of waxing lyrical and knowledgeable, giving for Meg's benefit a short school lesson in geography:

'This particular quality of Deeside is to combine great heights around the river's source and a gentle broadening in its middle life. And therein lies its enchantment. The Dee falls rapidly from its spring in the Cairngorms, among wildness and desolation, to become the famous salmon river descending amid forests to the fertile lands of the lower Strath; indeed, the area through which it travels to join the sea sixty miles distant at the city of Aberdeen is both Highland, sea coast and plain.'

Pausing to point out a track winding downwards, he continued:

'This no doubt originated as one of the drove roads. The only means of transport from the Highlands, the main road in fact, the only possible link carrying great herds of cattle when they moved down from the north to trysts in the more populated areas.'

'That must have taken a very long time,' said Meg and Vince nodded.

'The herdsmen travelled about twelve miles a day and camped as they could. Many landowners welcomed the beasts for the manure they left behind them. Folk around Balmoral would be well accustomed to these autumnal migrants. Look, some of them are over there.'

To our right, a group of caravans and horses were huddled together in a vacant space, the smoke of their fires rising to greet us.

Vince laughed. 'Gipsies, Meg. The descendants of the herdsman,' and I thought of their less illustrious descendants, the tinkers with their bad reputations who skulked about the outskirts of Edinburgh, as he continued: 'The folk will be watching their own property just as eagerly as they did when the herdsmen were passing by. In the old days it was cattle thieving, a well-established sport of the Highlands and regarded as a natural way to increase their often meagre herds. They were poor men and likely to acquire good appetites as they tramped so it was as well to keep an eye on the poultry too.'

Meg looked back over her shoulder, waving to the little group fast vanishing, some having rushed over to take a look at the motor car speeding past.

'I like gipsies, Uncle Vince,' she said wistfully. 'There is something very exciting about travelling the countryside in a caravan.'

'So speaks the city-dweller!' Vince laughed and took a swig from whatever rich liquid filled his silver hip flask. 'You wouldn't say that if you had to live in it in all weathers.'

'Can I have some of that, please, Uncle Vince?' Meg pointed to the flask.

'No, my dear, not until perhaps when you are a grown-up young lady,' he said, polishing it on his sleeve. 'This contains one of the local products. There is a long tradition of illicit distilling in our glens, a few wily practitioners who escape the net cast by excise officers. However, there is popular local support for the million gallons of whisky – usquebaugh – distilled without licence.'

'Even here?' Meg looked round as if expecting to see evidence of the illegal trade.

'Indeed, my dear, it is unlikely that so remote a district as Upper Deeside, with its high reputation for turning the sparkling water of its burns into something stronger and more invigorating should have been reduced to a wholly meek and law-abiding lifestyle.'

And pointing again. 'Especially as the district is well equipped with those convenient drove roads. Think of it, Meg. In the old days, not so very long ago really, where motor omnibuses now grind to the Devil's Elbow and the Spittal of Glenshee with their tourists, there used to be moonlight flittings, ponies carrying a great convoy of whisky kegs, escorted by Highlanders armed with useful cudgels and the like. And not afraid to use them either—'

As if in timely illustration of Vince's tale, our road was barred not by men with cudgels but by the sudden appearance of a herd of sheep from a well-used farm road. A few bolder than the rest were heading directly in front of us. Our driver leant on the horn with little avail and the farmer's collie dog's retrieving attempts made the sheep even more frantic.

While we waited, not quite patiently, for some sort of order to be restored, the disturbance caused on that normally quiet road had made us the object of some entertainment from the gipsy encampment on the lower reaches of the hill, presumably remnants of those we had encountered earlier.

Now children rushed down to scramble onto the crumbling wall and stare at us, adults followed shouting at them – and at us. I expected all gipsies to be dark and swarthy-looking, like the women who came by the Tower selling clothes pegs and wanting to tell my fortune – 'Ye have a lucky face, dearie' – which I firmly resisted. Now a closer look revealed that although some of the older men were very Spanish-looking with their weathered faces, some of the young women were quite exotic, and many of the children beneath the grime were fair-skinned, sandy-haired like Meg.

One of the men pushed forward to seize a small child who had stumbled and was crying. Tall, thin, with a wayward lock of dark hair tumbling over his forehead. He was at my side of the car nearest the stone wall, gazing down at me.

The man who almost missed the train? My heart jolted as I saw him at close quarters. Would I never be free of men who reminded me of my lost beloved Danny, who in his dying breath had made Jack promise to take care of me? And Jack had done more than that, he had married me. I was his wife now, for better, for worse, for richer, for poorer. And I thought of the rewards. Of Meg, the darling of both our hearts.

The sheep were gone and we were moving on. The man shouted something at Dave, our driver – a gesture which included the motor car and us. The driver shouted back; it sounded like an insult although the exchange had been in Gaelic, I thought.

'Bloody Irish,' muttered Dave as we pulled away.

'Language, driver, ladies present,' Vince reminded him sternly.

'Gipsies, I like gipsies,' said Meg again, looking over her shoulder for a last, fleeting glimpse. She sighed. 'And I'm not scared of bad weather, like Uncle Vince says. You would come with me and live in a caravan, wouldn't you, Mam?'

'Of course I would. But what about Pa – you wouldn't want to leave him behind would you?'

She began to protest that he would come too, of course. But I wasn't listening. My mind was still on the gipsy, shaken by the turmoil of emotions his resemblance had conjured up.

Meg sensed there was something wrong. She took my hand. 'Are you all right, Mam, did the sheep coming at us like that give you a scare?'

'Of course not, darling.' I put my arm around her.

'Patience everyone,' Vince announced: 'Only a couple of miles now.'

The journey was almost over and there was Crathie Church nestling close by a bridge over a tumbling river and we were at the gates to the castle. As we drove through Vince said: 'There are minor estate roads closer to the cottage. Mere tracks for a horseman and not for the likes of us, our Rolls would be seriously offended by potholes and so forth.'

A long drive almost at an end, full of twists and turns past well-manicured lawns and tall trees, so ordered and regulated to suggest the vanguard of an army watching over us. An occasional distant glimpsed cottage.

'Is that ours?' asked Meg.

But it never was until, at last, we glimpsed the turrets of the castle and in the foreground the massive structure of the stables, where Vince informed us some of the former coach houses were being turned into garages, the final destination of our motor car.

'Here we are.' A small cottage close by.

And that was the first surprise.

CHAPTER SEVEN

Facing us, the usual cottage exterior, supported by a rustic porch, a window on either side and two dormer windows above it, presumably bedrooms.

'It is very small,' whispered Mabel anxiously. Handing her down, Vince merely smiled as he opened the door.

That was the second surprise: the tiny rustic cottage vanished as before us a stretch of tartan-carpeted hallway led the way into the two rooms facing each other. Vince opened the one on the left and Mabel sighed with relief.

'Why, it is very much larger than it appeared from outside,' she said as we walked into the handsome dining room with a well-polished mahogany table ready to seat eight people, overseen by a cavernous sideboard stretching the length of one wall and overlooked by what could only be rather obscure family portraits.

Vince opened the door opposite, leading the way into

what would have been once designated as the parlour, opened only for special occasions, weddings, christenings and funerals. Its transformation was an elegant drawing room with plush sofas, armchairs, pretty, small tables and a lingering smell of those expensive cigars.

'Not a country cottage at all, Vince,' I murmured. 'More like a gentleman's hunting lodge.'

Vince looked pleased. 'And there is even provision for dogs,' he said.

'So our landlord knows we have Thane with us.'

'Indeed.' Vince pointed. 'Through the kitchen there, although I believe HM usually keeps his pets at his bedside.'

With a grin, he led us further down the hallway of what was the much-extended interior of a cottage deceptively small from the outside.

At the sight of a well-appointed kitchen, Meg ran towards the sink, turning on its shining taps.

'Running water, Mam, like we have at home.'

'That's a blessed relief,' said Mabel. 'I must confess, I am most impressed, so much . . . grander and more comfortable than I expected.' She smiled at Vince. 'You have done us proud.'

Vince bowed and I learnt later that the alterations had been HM's idea once he became king. He wanted to have a small private place which passers-by would dismiss without a second glance, a mere estate cottage. Only a closer inspection would reveal that as an illusion and that it was three times its original length, embellished with pieces that suggested distinguished origins in Abergeldie Castle.

There were more delights as we went up a handsome

staircase, more to be associated with a Georgian house than a narrow set of steep wooden stairs.

Meg was rushing ahead, opening doors. Two bedrooms overlooking the front and with an uninterrupted direct view towards the castle.

'A thoughtful piece of planning,' Vince told me later, 'so that the occupant could have plenty of warning of any approaching.'

I was making several guesses what kind of warning that might be when Vince decided that Meg and I should share this bedroom with its splendid view, not only of the castle but a good prospect of the surrounding country. What Meg thought was a cupboard was, in fact, a small dressing room containing, of all things, a water closet.

'Isn't this perfectly lovely, Mam?' said Meg. 'And such a lovely bed, too.' And bouncing up and down, 'Plenty of room – you could sleep a whole family here.' Watching her gave me an uneasy feeling of lese-majesty, considering that the bed must have frequently sheltered an occupant not just alone for peace and quiet away from the watchful household and an equally watchful spouse.

Mabel was to have the other bedroom where she indicated that Lily could occupy one of the two attic rooms, invisible from the front and accessible by a ladder, presumably installed for guests' servants and valets.

Vince had his own quarters in the castle assigned to members of the household. In addition they contained his surgery for daily consultations and dispensing medicine for minor ailments. He was also used to being on call if needed by sick tenants on the estate.

Even as he was seeing us installed, two maids were

hurrying across from the royal kitchens with food provided after our long journey. Silently they moved into the kitchen and in due course we were served with soup, venison stew and steamed pudding after which they cleared the table and as silently departed back with the debris of our meal.

'What about Thane?' Meg demanded anxiously.

'Not to worry,' said Vince beaming on us over his cigar smoke, the inevitable and satisfying end to every meal. 'The kennels are across there in the stable block and food will be brought to him. He'll get his share, don't worry, the dogs are particularly well fed.'

A consoling prospect, although the groom was alarmed at Thane's size. 'Like feeding one of the ponies, madam,' he said, looking at the contents of the bowl.

I assured him that would do very well. Thane had quite a small appetite for such a large animal. He was used to sharing our meals at home, but I often wondered if he added to it by other things; I said 'things', trying not to identify them as wild creatures he caught and ate on Arthur's Seat, especially when Mabel put it all into words.

'That dog should be in the kennels. Does he not go out and hunt?'

Mabel always referred to him as 'That Dog', regardless of the fact that he had a name. Patiently trying to explain that he was a hound not a dog was something Meg did regularly but without the least success.

Vince asked: 'Well, how do you like it, Meg? This will be your home for a month.'

'A whole four weeks,' she sighed.

'Yes, right until the Highland Games. After that HM

leaves for London and there is a general exodus of visitors until next year.'

Meg was hugging Thane and conveying this information to him. Vince and I had decided to keep a watchful eye on him until he had time to settle in and get used to the terrain around us.

'He might even be mistaken for a wolf,' said Meg nervously.

'There haven't been wolves in this part of the world for a very long time,' said Vince consolingly, but as he explained to me, there were gamekeepers armed with rifles and a strange, huge, grey animal might provide a target, especially a hound of the breed noted for hunting deer.

We found we were not alone in our fears regarding Thane's well-being when the gamekeeper Aitken arrived to welcome us. Sternly surveying Thane, peacefully stretched out at Meg's feet as she read a book, he said: 'That animal is too big for a house pet, sir, should be kept outside. Could damage Royal property, you know,' he added with a sharp glance around the room for any evidence to add weight to his remark.

Vince said, 'He is used to living indoors, well trained. One of the family,' he added.

Aiken grunted and shook his head. 'Proper place for him is in the stable kennels with the other dogs, sir.' Frowning, he paused and said: 'I have strict instructions that he is not to be let run wild, he is to be restricted to a lead. At all times, sir.' Another look at Thane lying peacefully ignoring him. 'We'll have to see if his presence so close by upsets the other dogs. They'll bark at anything and we can't have the family', with a respectful nod towards the castle, 'kept awake at night.'

Vince gave a solemn assurance on Thane's behalf and Aiken nodded but doubtfully. Taking his leave, he said, 'A word of warning, Dr Laurie. Don't let HM clap eyes on him. What I mean is that if he were to get a glimpse of such a handsome creature . . .' Pausing, he scratched his ear thoughtfully and sighed. 'We don't have any deerhounds and well, you know the rest – if you take my meaning, sir.'

Touching his bonnet he walked away to where his labrador was waiting, chained to the fence. Unleashing it he saluted us solemnly.

'What did he mean by that – about the King?' I asked.

Vince glanced at Thane. 'Come on, Rose, surely you know the royal prerogative. If the King should come and say "That's a fine dog you have there" then he would expect you to curtsey and say "Please, Your Majesty, I would be honoured if you would accept him as a gift".'

Meg who had been listening to this conversation gave a shriek of horror. 'No, Uncle Vince, never!' And with a protective arm around Thane's neck. 'He's mine!' She was suddenly tearful, and Vince said, 'Don't worry, Meg, it isn't going to happen. We won't let it happen.'

I was doubtful about that. Word gets around with surprising speed and we were here for a month. Could we possibly keep his presence a secret from the King?

We had only been in the cottage a few hours and already I could see complications looming on the horizon, especially as next morning I heard a horseman close by.

Looking out of the window, there was the King emerging from the stables on a handsome stallion, his favourite I learnt, to be entered for one of the national steeplechase events. I thought he gazed intently at the cottage. Was he on the lookout for Thane?

I shivered. If one was on the lookout for bad omens, a lad had drowned during the salmon leistering in Loch Muick. 'The river's swift-moving,' Vince told us. 'He stumbled, fell and hit his head. Knocked him out and he was swept away.'

We went to the window, as the doleful procession carrying his body back passed the stables on a litter.

An ominous start to a holiday, indeed. I clutched Meg to my side.

A quiver of fear went through me. It was one I recognise and I would do well to heed. That old warning shaft was never in vain.

CHAPTER EIGHT

The gamekeeper Aiken, whose job I suspected included keeping an eye on us, was being very helpful. If extra provisions were required, a cart went from the stables twice a week into Ballater, and regarding us doubtfully, he added: 'If any of you ladies wished to be accommodated there would be room, a couple of benches.'

A nervous glance at our expressionless faces warned more than words that this would be a bone-shaking experience, and clearing his throat he reassured us that a list of our requirements would receive careful attention.

I smiled and thanked him while Mabel frowned at travel offering possible indignities; Meg and I applauded the idea.

'A day in Ballater. What a delight, shops to explore.'

'And cards to send to Pa,' said Meg enthusiastically.

Mabel merely sighed and our glances swivelled

with hers in the direction of Lily sitting with downcast eyes intent on mending lace on one of her mistress's undergarments. If we expected any reaction from Lily, there was none. What were her thoughts? Did she even hear most of the time, I wondered?

In those first days, the weather was idyllic, with wine-clear air so different from waking each morning to the smoke of a thousand homes in Auld Reekie. What bliss! And we had so much time on our hands, nothing to do but enjoy the mellow sunshine, sit in the garden and read or walk in the pleasant wood full of birdsong.

On one of our walks by the riverbank, we noticed midstream a tiny island with a monument of some kind visible through a clump of trees. It must have known visitors, although not very recently judging by the condition of the small rowing boat for two people moored and rocking gently at the water's edge.

'Someone must live there,' said Meg.

'I think not. It's probably one of the many stones set up by the King's mother to mark special occasions.'

'Can we go across and explore, Mam?' she demanded excitedly.

'Not today, dear, and certainly not with Thane, there wouldn't be room for him and us.'

Meg sighed with disappointment. As usual, everything had to happen in her life immediately. 'Sometime soon, then? Promise!'

First I had to consult Vince, as I had doubts about the stability of that boat in reaching what was in fact a strip of land like a peninsula in the midst of swirling waters.

'You must promise that you won't go there without

a grown-up, then,' I said sternly, fully aware that Meg's fearless approach to adventure might well lead her into danger.

The matter agreed, I gave it no more thought in the following days as we established a kind of routine with all meals provided via the royal kitchens. A somewhat unvaried menu betwixt salmon from the river and venison from the hills.

Mabel spent a lot of time in her bedroom where we were made to understand that she was heavily engaged in writing a speech, a vote of thanks to the Pankhursts for coming north to Aberdeen to address the Women's Suffrage in Scotland meeting. Occasionally she emerged clutching sheets of paper and as she swooned ecstatically over these important speakers I was expected to go into raptures by return at such a privilege.

'Wait until you meet them, Rose, you will know what I mean. They are pure magic, the pair of them.'

I could hardly believe that I was to shake the hands of my heroines, see them in the flesh, so to speak, just days from now and the only excitement apart from the weeks-away Highland Games, an annual event established by the King's mother and open to the public who might come to gawp at the royal family. A rare glimpse of them at leisure, with princes and princesses too.

Meanwhile we were content with our uneventful routine. Meg and I taking Thane for daily walks on a rope until out of sight of the cottage. Once in the pretty woods of the estate he was allowed to roam, watched over by those stern sentinels of tall conifers. One could hardly be frivolous; there was something martial and forbidding by such witnesses of Thane loping ahead of us. Nevertheless we were careful not to be in the open areas, the woods protecting us from the predatory eye of HM out riding. Taking heed of Aiken's warning, I could see endless trouble from that direction but felt certain that we could rely on Thane who would return to our side at the first hint that we were not alone, alert to detecting any sound, human or animal, well before it reached us.

Vince spent much of his free time at the cottage with us, but he was always on call, should any of the royal household or any of the tenants urgently require him to look at childhood maladies, sore throats and accidental injuries sustained by the estate labourers. Fortunately for him and for us they were much healthier than town-dwellers.

Then very suddenly our halcyon summer days that began and ended with cloudless azure skies, with birdsong and bees humming in the hedges, fell flat on its face. Storm clouds roared in and the rain began. And what rain. There was none in our experience to equal this intensity, this Highland downpour, sheets of stinging icy rain which turned our Edinburgh variety into mere drizzle by comparison. Was this the same weather that the late John Brown assured his royal mistress was a 'moist day'? Moist unto drowning, I thought, desperately clutching a book Mabel had insisted I should read, more for education regarding our suffrage movement than for the pleasure of my favourite Jane Austen.

While Mabel retreated and remained in her bedroom with an excellent log fire, refurbished by Lily along with frequent trays of tea carried upstairs, Meg and I huddled close to the peat fire and got out sketchbooks and paintbox. Meg's drawings were to send to Pa. She already showed talent, which she had not inherited from him I thought, as I drew Thane endlessly. So we passed the hours ignoring the rain beating on the windows, and if it ceased even momentarily, opening the door and peering upwards ever hopeful for the merest glimpse of blue in that solid, heavy, grey sky.

On the rare occasions when Mabel joined us, it was to stare balefully at Thane as if the hours spent in her room and the change in the weather were his fault.

'That dog should be in the kennels with the other animals. It cannot be beneficial to the health of any of us, trapped inside all day and having to breathe the same air as a huge dog.'

In response Thane gave her what could only described in human terms a look of reproach.

'Is it worrying you?' I asked. 'He doesn't smell, you know.'

That was true, I rarely bathed Thane or had reason to do so in all our years together. Some mysterious force kept his coat immaculate.

'All dogs smell,' said Mabel loftily. 'Take him outside into the rain.'

I shook my head and asked if Lily had plenty to do to keep busy, since she no longer appeared at mealtimes. When I asked why, Mabel said: 'She has her meals with the stable lads, as is only right and proper.'

I wasn't sure whether the stables quite fitted the description 'right and proper' for a young girl who was possibly foreign and a lady's maid, but obviously Mabel was anxious to spend as little time as possible in her company.

'She is making some new underwear for me – I like lace borders and she is quite good with the crochet hook.'

As for me, used to a busy life, I had to confess that with thoughts of uncertain weather, mostly rain, time was beginning to lie heavily on my hands. The highlight of each day was Vince's visit to check on our comfort, play cards and share our miserable glances at the unceasing rain pouring down the windows.

It continued day after day for a week with determined frenzy, no doubt lasting until Sunday, when it seemed we were expected to venture out of doors in order to go to church.

Although I was not a regular churchgoer in Edinburgh I felt it would be a relief to get out of doors and see something new. An agreeable change of scene, since the cottage's four walls were becoming claustrophobic, assisted in no small way by Mabel, whose presence always managed to include some spiteful remark about Thane.

For Meg's benefit I was forced to appear cheerful. She never seemed bored trapped indoors, and as a condition of childhood, found pleasure in small things, painting and reading, and talking to Thane as if he had become her human playmate.

We were to go to Crathie Church by motor car and in answer to Meg's question, yes, we would see the King and Queen and doubtless some of the royal children.

Meg was beside herself with delight but Mabel opted out of this, much to our surprise, saying stiffly that she was not of the Presbyterian persuasion. She did not elaborate. Was she, then, a Roman Catholic, I wondered? That idea had not occurred to me as religion had never figured among our limited topics of conversation.

However, she announced that she would stay and look after That Dog, adding, with an added flash of generosity, Lily might like to accompany us but would, of course, accompany the other royal servants.

'She is most welcome to go with us,' Vince said.

'No,' Mabel replied firmly. 'That would not be proper.'

Oh dear, such snobbery, and leaving them to argue, I felt irritation rise again. How long would I be able to remain calm and untroubled by Mabel's presence? She got worse by the hour rather than the day, doubtless due to our close confinement, and everything she did and said now seemed like a barb to me.

She was such a disappointment. I had hoped that knowing the Pankhursts she would have fascinating stories about them. Inside gossip, things only told to friends and acquaintances and never made public. But any leads I gave were turned aside. As far as I was concerned I would have to wait impatiently for the day next week when I would meet dear Christabel and Emmeline when they stood on the platform addressing the audience in Aberdeen.

CHAPTER NINE

And so we set off. With the car hood over us we swept through the grounds, out of the gates and across the bridge where lining the road a small crowd eagerly watched us, trying to peer in at the windows, hoping this was a first glimpse of the King and Queen.

Across the road and up the hill to the new kirk which had been dedicated only ten years earlier in 1895. A disappointment in a way and I said I had been hoping for something earlier, a romantic ruin perhaps that had escaped the Covenant. This was Vince's cue to tell us that there had been an earlier building dating back to the seventeenth century which had fallen into disrepair and become too difficult to maintain.

This new kirk with its lofty and beautiful setting amid birch and conifers was a fitting piece of Scottish fabric according to Vince who gets carried away on architectural matters. He sometimes, I felt, regretted his choice of medicine as a career, determined to give me a short guide of Crathie Church.

'Much thought was given to the planning of the present building, white granite hewn from the neighbouring quarry at Inver and roofed in terracotta tiles,' he added proudly. We smiled our appreciation and as we approached, dutifully noting that the central tower with its small spire pointing heavenward was based on native rock.

Clean and shining on the outside, all was pleasantly cordial within. A semicircular apse with the Balmoral pews on the right, the woodwork – which still smelt new – carried the rose, thistle and shamrock with the monogram of Queen Victoria.

As we took our places reserved for the royal household, he whispered that the hexagonal pulpit was made of fifteen varieties of Scottish granite. Princess Louise, Duchess of Argyll had presented a collection of stones from the sacred isle of Iona which were worked into the granite, and the communion table was also of Iona marble. A rustle of silks and footfalls as, around us, the congregation filed into the pews.

'Over there,' Vince whispered. 'That's a monument to Victoria, Princess Royal, later Empress of Germany and mother of Kaiser Wilhelm, to commemorate her engagement to Prince Frederick William of Prussia in a glen only a few miles distant. She was the darling of her father Prince Albert, but alas rumour has it that this was the prelude to a less than happy married life.'

The congregation rose as the door opened to admit

members of the royal family. I am, through force of habit by my career, always conscious of being watched and in this case I looked up and saw the King staring directly across at me. Our eyes met and there was a mere twitch of recognition, for seeing me seated next to Vince and knowing he had an excellent memory, had HM remembered our other encounter in an Edinburgh hotel after he had presided at the opening of a bridge and had Vince as his personal physician in attendance? He belonged to those males who have the ability to strip any attractive young woman naked in a glance as if weighing up her possibilities as a conquest. It had made me extremely uncomfortable. The years had not been kind to him since that meeting; he was larger than life, to say the least.

We stood for the opening hymn and prayers and as I followed the order of service, I hoped that the sermon would not be as long as had been desired and encouraged by Queen Victoria.

It was long enough and Meg behaved beautifully throughout but I was rather glad to hear the announcement of the closing hymn.

The royal party rose and again that rather searching glance from HM as they left. A curtsey from Meg and me. Thanks to the nuns, good manners were part of the syllabus by which their pupils were trained for a woman's only role in life. Indeed it was what their parents paid for, to catch a husband, although as brides of Christ such skills were wasted on the nuns themselves.

Shaking hands with the minister at the door, his prayers for better weather had not been in vain, for there was even a glimpse of blue hastily concealed by burgeoning clouds. Waiting for our motor car, Meg spotted a pretty collie dog, chained and patiently awaiting his owner emerging from the kirk.

Vince laughed. 'That's Biddy, she's the minister's dog. She has to be patient. Did you enjoy the service, Rose?' he asked anxiously.

'It was quite an experience.' I stifled a yawn. 'A rather long sermon.'

He laughed again. 'Pity Biddy isn't like the collie of a former minister. Rev. Anderson's dog was famous as a regular follower of the Sunday service. He followed him up to the pulpit steps and lay quietly on the top step during the sermon, or quietly at least until he decided that time was up and further eloquence unnecessary. He would then stand up, stretch himself and yawn – just like you wanted to do, Rose – I saw that! Anyway, when the Queen came to morning service, Rev. Anderson left the dog at home but she had heard of the collie's habits. Someone had made a sketch of the pulpit with him lying there and she suggested that the minister's dog must certainly not be excluded for her sake. Although she claimed to be a ready absorber of sermons, especially of Scottish ones, she may have valued the dog's services as timekeeper.'

I was looking round for Lily so that she could come back with us in the motor car. And there she was, head down, talking animatedly to a man, a tall man, wearing a bonnet.

'Look, Uncle Vince, Lily's made friends at last,' said Meg.

'A dark horse, indeed,' Vince laughed. 'It is a well-known condition among young females who never have a word to say to their own kind that they prefer to save their sparkles for gentlemen. Ah, here's our car at last.'

As it came alongside it momentarily blocked our view but as the man turned I thought I recognised him as the passenger racing along the station platform in Edinburgh and with those alighting from the royal train at Ballater. Then again, among the gipsies when we were held up en route by the sheep. He seemed to be everywhere. Who on earth was he, this man who reminded me of Danny? And what was his connection with Balmoral Castle?

And more intriguing was the animation of the normally speechless Lily. I decided I must tactfully raise the subject with Mabel when we got back to the cottage but no opportune moment occurred that day.

Then, next morning, not only the hoped-for postcard from Jack, but the totally unexpected arrival of Vince rushing in clutching a telegram. His smile, radiant as the sun that had deigned to reward us with an appearance, put our fears at rest.

'You'll never guess! Livvy's on her way with Faith. They're arriving at Ballater this afternoon.' He was almost jumping for joy and I knew how sad and concerned he had felt at their absence, how much he was missing Olivia, anxious about that frail wee daughter too, when he added:

'Nothing serious with Faith after all, but you know how it is, how cautious one becomes.' And to Mabel. 'Livvy was so disappointed – felt she was letting you down missing this meeting after so many years.'

Now there was a great flutter of excitement at the prospect of the new arrivals. Mabel was cautiously pleased, Meg delighted that she was to see her new-found cousin, confident that they would be great friends and have such fun playing together. As for me, I was delighted at the prospect of being with Olivia again, since we had met far too rarely since I came back to Scotland; a conscientious mother, she was bound by children who she refused to leave in the care of servants so that she could come to Balmoral with Vince and break her journey in Edinburgh.

There was a further reason too, which accounted for her overprotectiveness, when she told me about the other wee girl, who would have been Faith's older sister. Born with some organic defect, she had died just a few months old. Olivia said it was still so painful that Vince would never discuss it, how he felt in a way responsible, that as a doctor with all his knowledge he had been helpless to save his own child.

We naturally expected that Olivia would be staying in the royal household apartments with Vince and when Mabel mentioned this he laughed. 'Not at all. She is quite definite about staying here in the cottage with you.'

Smiles were exchanged. We were immensely flattered at such a decision, choosing the humble cottage rather than the grand castle.

Mabel said in tones of awe, 'Indeed, that is good of her,' while Meg was busy telling Thane how he would love Faith. 'We will have such fun, climbing all those trees, playing games together.'

I wasn't so sure about that. Vince had confided that

Faith was terrified of large dogs and was regarding Thane thoughtfully. I was regarding him thoughtfully for another reason. A new Thane had emerged since we came to Balmoral. He had become a domestic pet, no longer the strange creature more human than canine, and that set me wondering if his magic was related to his mysterious origins, that he belonged to and was controlled by Arthur's Seat. At least Meg had not observed any change in him while I thought of those interminable rainy days when he was quite content to lie at her feet.

By introducing him to another environment, had he reverted to being 'only a dog' as Vince insisted, or 'That Dog' as Mabel described him? I hoped I was wrong, remembering ten years of protection during which he had watched over me and had known instinctively when I was in danger.

At last the sound of the motor car's horn, with Vince at the wheel. We ran to the door as Olivia and Faith emerged. The next moment, we rushed forward, hugs exchanged.

'Rose, let me look at you,' said Olivia. 'You haven't changed a bit since last we met – how long ago?'

Olivia had changed, but for the better, more elegant, more regal and composed, security fulfilled by a happy marriage and motherhood.

Meg had taken charge of Faith, leading her by the hand, and observing them together there seemed little difference in the three years between them. Meg was tall for her seven years while Faith at ten was rather pale and frail-looking. Like her father, I suspected she was never going to grow up to be taller than average height.

Thane was framed in the doorway, tail wagging, a large friendly dog waiting to be introduced. I saw the look of alarm, the hesitancy as Faith looked towards her mother, but Meg held her hand firmly, whispering words of reassurance. A sigh of relief from me, at least, as I saw her tentatively stroking his head, the signal that he was not to be feared.

The ever-silent Lily had been instructed to set the table and prepare tea and as we went inside, Vince marshalled the new arrivals' luggage upstairs. Mabel and Meg and I had the best rooms but Olivia insisted that no change be made.

This was to create problems. Olivia's choice to remain with us in this far from humble abode instead of under the royal castle roof left the only other available bedroom in the attic next to Lily. However, by evening, the two girls, friendship firmly established, had arrived at a solution.

Meg said that her mother and I should share my room while she moved up to the attic and shared with Faith. She did not regard losing the comfort and the magnificent view as important.

Mabel said: 'I am most impressed by Olivia's sacrifice,' having obviously feared that she might be the one downgraded to the attics.

In an aside to me, Vince murmured: 'Mabel hasn't seen the household's quarters or she might change her mind about them. They are rather starkly furnished and quite chilly, the late Queen was a stickler for economy and did not think that ordinary mortals needed the comfort of warm beds and cosy fires.'

He rubbed his hands together. 'Nothing like having a snug little cottage, a pretty little garden and an ancient tree with the right kind of stout branches. Meg is wistful about turning it into a tree house when I have the time.'

At the back of my mind the presence of that great tree, although handsome and sturdy-looking, suggested alarming possibilities for the fragile Faith. As for Meg, she had inherited another of Jack's more dangerous traits. She was utterly fearless.

CHAPTER TEN

Olivia's decision to stay with us was mostly influenced I thought by her anxiety to watch over Faith. We could continue to have meals provided by the castle kitchens, a splendid idea initially but there were complications. Even moving dishes very swiftly across the short distance, food tended to be lukewarm by the time it reached the table. As neither Mabel nor I were enthusiastic cooks, we were coping with that quite well but Olivia decided that she would prefer we made our own meals.

'Faith can be difficult about food, she doesn't like meat and has other fads, like all little girls.' Olivia paused and smiled at me encouragingly for support that I could not give her. Meg had been brought up from her first days in Solomon's Tower to eat the same meals as we did. This was something Jack insisted on. He had no time or patience for faddy eaters.

Olivia's other reason was that she adored cooking and confessed that she read recipe books like other women of her acquaintance read romantic novels. 'I never get the chance at St James where everything is provided by a very efficient kitchen staff,' she sighed. 'So this is such an opportunity.'

We couldn't deny her that and Mabel for one was very pleased and offered to help. Living alone, she said, was so dreary where meals were concerned and Lily, we gathered, was not particularly accomplished in that area either. I occasionally lent a hand, although the two ladies provided a surprisingly excellent cuisine which also met with Faith and Meg's approval.

So a daily routine was established. Provisions such as vegetables would come via the kitchen gardens, meat (mostly venison) and fish (mostly salmon) from the larders. The two maids we had met on arrival, Jessie and Yolande, whose exotic name and dark good looks hinted at more romantic forbears than Royal Deeside, would look in each morning, sweep floors and light fires when appropriate, as indicated by the weather. They would also carry off our not inconsiderable laundry, thanks to the addition of another female and a small girl to our regular change of linen.

We had no facilities for washing clothes at the cottage, not even the sight of a drying line. A mass of underwear conspicuously blowing in the wind would, I fear, have lowered the tone of the estate and have been distinctly frowned upon by 'higher' authority.

It was decided that we should all go to Ballater, not only to pick up some special ingredients for Faith's diet but also several crucial necessities her mother had omitted through their hasty departure.

Vince reassured her that as Ballater shops were used to coping not only with tourists but also with the castle itself she would find all she needed. In an aside to me, he whispered: 'Typical. Livvy's not used to travelling alone. She needs me at her elbow saying "have you remembered so-and-so, be sure to pack this and that".'

Mabel, overhearing, nodded in agreement and said to Olivia: 'It is so essential to have one's personal maid and a comprehensive list on even the shortest stays away from home, my dear.'

Olivia laughed. 'Not I, Mabel. And I do not need a personal maid. I can manage perfectly without one. Besides I am frequently on my own these days with Vince up here in royal attendance.'

Mabel sighed. 'All those children too.' (As if there were thirteen, not three.) 'No wonder you prefer to remain at home.'

As we prepared to leave, she said: 'Lily will be coming with you. She will be needed to carry all our purchases.'

By which 'our' not 'your' indicated that Mabel intended availing herself of the opportunity of some personal shopping.

'Surely you intend coming with us?' Olivia said.

Mabel shook her head, insisting that she would be quite content to remain with the two girls, especially as she had notes to add to her speech of thanks to dear Emmeline and dear Christabel at the Aberdeen meeting, adding sternly, 'While you are pouring over your shopping lists,' making that particular activity sound very frivolous, like an admonishment, although on further questioning Lily was to be sent in search of lace and wool for Mabel's embroidery, which we had yet to see in evidence.

Olivia was charmed by Ballater and the shops, most of which carried By Royal Appointment signs. Lily received polite directions from shopkeepers where her mistress's requirements could be obtained and an hour later Olivia and I adjourned with our shopping to the nearest hotel for afternoon tea.

As we waited to be served, we realised that this was the first time we had been on our own together and I was curious to learn how she had reacted to this meeting with her old school friend. I asked: 'How do you find Mabel?'

Olivia thought for a moment before replying. 'She isn't at all what I expected from her letters. I know that does happen quite often and a person can change over the years from the one you imagined you knew so well, and quite a stranger emerges.'

Pausing she sighed. 'It's as if we have to get to know each other all over again and there are certain limits to conversations about schooldays. So remote and far away, now like part of another world, especially as we both seem to remember happenings that were so important at the time, that the other has forgotten completely.'

'What about her suffrage involvement?' I asked.

Olivia shook her head. 'It was barely mentioned in her letters. Most were about the books we were both reading, and in her case, about her travels.' She frowned and added, 'Strange, she doesn't seem at all as I remembered her from our schooldays. Quite mannish, somehow.' Then apologetically, 'Not in appearance, of course, but that rather aggressive manner.'

As I listened, I felt that Olivia was disappointed in this long anticipated reunion when she added: 'I do hate having to confess this, Rose. It does seem disloyal. I feel mean, especially when she has come so far, all this long way just so that we could meet again.' She sighed. 'And she seems to have a genuine fondness for me.' A depth of feeling I gathered that Olivia was finding it difficult to reciprocate.

It was time to pay the bill. We had asked the driver Dave to draw up outside the hotel. I looked across the square and saw Lily. She was talking to someone taller than herself, the shadow of a man I couldn't see distinctly, a shadowy figure hidden by the trees. But there was an urgency in their conversation; he put a hand on her arm as he walked away, as if he sought to detain her.

'Ready?' said Olivia. Dave had arrived, standing alongside the motor car which had drawn some interested attention and comments from passers-by.

As he saw us seated on board, I looked across the square but Lily had disappeared.

I asked Dave had he seen her but he shook his head and said slyly: 'Seems she had a chap to meet, madam. Saw them walking away while I was taking a breather half an hour ago.'

'Someone you knew?' I asked eagerly since logically this must have been a local man.

He shook his head. 'Seen him around the stables.'

I was taken aback. So the ever-silent Lily had hidden

depths and had got to know some lad when she had her meals there.

I said to Olivia, 'I wonder if it's the same fellow we saw her talking to outside Crathie Church.'

She shook her head. 'Whoever it was, Mabel will not be pleased.' Then laughing, she added, 'Well, good luck to her. It's not much of a life for a young girl being lady's maid to Mabel.' But looking around, her frown indicated that she should not have kept us waiting.

Curiosity aroused, I said to Dave: 'What was he like, this fellow?'

Dave looked at me, also curious that I should be interested in a mere maid's fancy.

He shrugged. 'Tall, thin, dark, youngish – maybe a ghillie or one of those gipsies we have about here,' he added darkly. 'She should be careful, they're a rum lot.' He paused. 'Do we leave without her, madam?'

Olivia and I exchanged glances. This was a quandary and what were we to say to Mabel? However, at that moment, Lily appeared hurrying towards us, mumbling apologetically about having problems matching madam's wool.

That was a lie and I wasn't listening. I gave her a hard look, as she sat eyes downcast, clutching the small packages. As we moved off towards the Balmoral road, I was unable to shake off a growing chilly feeling of unease, certain that I had recognised the description of her male companion.

A ghillie? Dave's description also fitted the traveller on the train to Ballater, the man in the gipsy camp who had taken such an interest in our passing. But what was the connection, what was his interest in the ever-silent Lily? I had to find out!

Another thought, almost incredible. Could he be her lover? Was he in fact the gardener I had glimpsed at Penby who had followed her all the way to Scotland? Was she the reason for his presence, keeping an eye on her? I found that difficult to convince myself, even my flights of imagination failed to reach such heights, although I had often heard from clients with unfaithful husbands that it was often the maid, 'the quiet plain unobtrusive maid', who had fatally attracted them.

And our journey over, watching her trailing towards the cottage, remembering the somewhat sad and pathetic figure who regularly trailed a few steps behind Mabel's regal figure, I thought, surely not Lily.

CHAPTER ELEVEN

Vince had been busy in our absence. We were to take the girls to Braemar Castle on the neighbouring estate, home of the once powerful and still extremely rich Farquharson clan. Vince wanted the girls to see a 'real' old castle and they were very excited at the prospect.

The present laird's younger brother had been at Edinburgh University with him and was in residence at the castle meantime, with his wife and two little girls.

'Is there a ghost?' Meg demanded eagerly.

Vince laughed. 'Not that I know of.'

Meg looked disappointed. In her opinion no castle was worthy of the name unless it had a bloody history and a ghost roaming the battlements or disappearing through the bedroom wall.

I smiled, feeling sure she felt let down by her own home in Solomon's Tower whose ancient history, long lost, belonged to a Scotland once described as 'theology tempered by murder', a time when a permanent building for domestic use and peace was not encouraged among wild Highlanders raised from their earliest years on hot tempers and cold steel.

We had our own strange history full of unsolved mysteries. One day when she was older Jack and I would show her the 'secret room' and tell her how we had discovered it.

When I mentioned that to Jack, he said to wait – he didn't want her having nightmares. I thought that for all its doubtless violent past, the Tower felt safe enough with the comfortable reassurance that had there been any spirits lurking, then Thane would have let us know. He would have been aware of them and reacted as all animals did to supernatural presences.

The approach to Braemar Castle was all that visitors could wish for and certainly a more romantic prospect at first sight than Balmoral. It was almost miniature by comparison but much more ancient, dating from the seventeenth century and replacing the original eleventh-century Kindrochit Castle, stronghold of the Clan Farquharson when castles were built for defence. Indications of its past turbulent history lay in the grim gun loops still visible on the walls. The once protective moat had long since disappeared, but inside the castle remained the grim bottle dungeon which had awaited luckless prisoners.

The girls were shy with their new companions but that soon wore off as we heard their trills of laughter, being escorted round the dark corners and scampering up the spiral staircase.

Persuaded to stay for supper, since the four were now quite devoted companions and the grown-ups were getting along splendidly, we travelled back in the glowing twilight when all the trees seemed asleep, according to Meg, who had been placated in her appeal for ghosts. There was a spectral piper and a clash of steel could sometimes be heard on the battlements, as well as a baby crying.

As the girls had explored the castle with their new-found friends our hosts had given us a guided tour at a more leisurely pace. Suddenly I was face to face with the portrait of a young man in eighteenth-century dress. That black hair and white skin I found so attractive, a compelling rather than merely handsome face, full-lipped with a quizzical almost familiar smile, oddly like the ghillie I had seen at Balmoral.

Our hostess saw me looking at him. 'A sad story, his bride is one of our ghosts. A younger son, they had not long returned from honeymoon and she woke up – alone. She couldn't find him anywhere in the castle and, certain that he had abandoned her – it was well known that he had a mistress pre-marriage – she believed that he had returned to her. Well, the silly girl, broken-hearted, feeling betrayed, committed suicide. Of course, he was distraught when he did return home, not guilty on this occasion – perhaps. But he soon married again, an heiress this time.' She smiled. 'We are lucky to live now. Marriages were not for love in those days, it was a matter of dynasty, providing an heir,' she laughed, looking out of the window at her own daughters playing a noisy game together.

After the castle the cottage seemed remote and unassuming. Thane greeted us wildly as if we had been absent for days rather than hours. He seemed relieved at our presence as Mabel, seated by the fire, informed us that she had returned some time ago.

'Returned from where?' I asked, as she had declined the invitation to accompany us for afternoon tea, claiming she had one of her rare headaches and needed extra rest to be fit for the Aberdeen meeting. The malady which had apparently been shadowing her for several days certainly accounted for her odd reclusive behaviour.

'In your absence I decided to attend that informal suffrage meeting in Ballater after all.'

This was the first I had heard about any meeting and felt somewhat slighted. She might have mentioned it, knowing that I would have wanted to be there too. She must have seen my look of disappointment and added hastily: 'The local ladies were simply anxious to set the stage, so to speak, for the meeting with the Pankhursts. As a matter of fact, they approached me some time ago, when they knew I intended coming to Scotland. They wished me to be included, as a special friend of dear Emmeline and Christabel.'

She sighed and eyeing me almost apologetically, added, 'It would appear they believed that the expertise of an English lady would keep them on the right lines.'

So that was, according to her, how they had expressed it as she went on: 'I must confess that I had dismissed the time as inconvenient and it was a last-minute decision to go. I decided on the pony trap, my favourite means of travel from childhood days, known then as a governess cart.' Pausing, she smiled. 'I was, of course, offered a carriage when I approached the stable boys with my request.'

I was wondering about that headache so suddenly relieved, as she continued: 'I assured them that was out of the question. I had no desire to appear "grand", so to speak, arriving by carriage. I wished my attendance to be as simple as possible and wished to put the good ladies at their ease right from the start.'

She added: 'I made sure That Dog was carefully secured in the cottage and decided to take Lily with me, that she might be of some use on the journey.'

Doing what? I wondered, failing completely to see her in the role of an ideal travelling companion. I was curious to know how she had responded to making the long drive, twice in one day, doubtless left outside to sit in the pony trap until her mistress re-emerged.

Mabel stared at me when I asked her. 'Oh, she didn't come after all, complaining about a sore stomach, something she had eaten over at the stables. I wasn't very sympathetic, I'm afraid, and just left her here.'

Poor Lily. 'How is she now?'

Mabel shrugged. 'I have no idea. I needed a new petticoat trimmed with the lace she brought back from Ballater. When she'd finished that, I expect she was well enough to wander over to the stables, ungrateful girl.' She sounded bitter.

I was not to be put off. Remembering the Ballater encounter I said: 'Has she got a young man over there?'

Mabel's expression of amazement suggested had I asked if she had grown wings. She laughed shortly. 'I have absolutely no idea about her personal life, nor have I the slightest interest in her comings and goings. She is merely a servant and as long as she attends to her duties efficiently that is all that concerns me.' The look she gave me suggested that she found my interest in Lily quite extraordinary.

'Will you be well enough to go to Aberdeen?' A blunt 'yes' was the response to Olivia's question and her anxious attempts to offer Mabel advice and medicaments for the headache were ignored.

Olivia always roused the best in everyone but when later I asked Mabel if she was feeling better, she shook her head, sighed deeply and seemed at pains to distance herself from our chatter. Perhaps because that headache which she had dismissed had returned. I observed that she seemed particularly on edge.

My curiosity about the day's events went unappeased. I had expected an enthusiastic account of the informal meeting, but apart from the hour we were to meet the ladies, she replied to our polite questions with a mere yes or no.

But I was certain that something had happened in our absence at Braemar to upset her.

CHAPTER TWELVE

And so we departed for Aberdeen the following morning, Mabel, who seemed to have recovered, in moderately good spirits. There was an air of excitement about attending a women's suffrage meeting with the famous Pankhursts.

We couldn't all go and Olivia, despite being sympathetic to the cause, elected to remain with the children in the cottage. She would have loved the chance of a visit to Aberdeen and waved us off wistfully when the motor car arrived to take us to Ballater. From there we would proceed with the local suffrage ladies in a large automobile, the envied property of the wealthy husband of one of them, which must have put Mabel's patronising attitude of being considered 'grand' slightly out of countenance.

After being politely introduced, I let their

conversation drift over me, happy to enjoy those next few hours. The weather promised to be kind, calm and sunny as we approached the city, driving through the leafy twisting roads towards the growing suburbs of Banchory, Peterculter, Culter, Bieldside, Cults and the more modest streets of Mannofield. Then Queen's Road, with its handsome mansions for merchants made rich from shipbuilding, fisheries and the like during the late Queen's reign. Mansions architecturally turreted had sprung up like miniatures of Balmoral Castle, with a national desire for a lifestyle in imitation of their Queen. For less well-off or aspiring citizens, the suburbs owed their properties and prosperity to the railway trains carrying holidaymakers to fashionable Royal Deeside, and an ever-growing demand for guest houses en route.

As we approached our destination at Cowdray Hall in Union Terrace, I wondered at the choice of venue since a meeting with the Pankhursts sounded important enough to qualify for the Assembly Rooms on Union Street.

As we alighted from the automobile, a few ladies were carrying banners with suffrage slogans and a small crowd had gathered, presumably from the national press's account of Pankhurst notoriety. But at second glance, the choice of venue became obvious.

Trouble was expected. I knew enough from Jack's experience of political meetings in Edinburgh to understand that a decision had been made on high that the main street should be avoided as a potential danger spot. To put it plainly, police were everywhere, outnumbering the onlookers, mostly mounted on their splendid, glossy well-trained horses who knew exactly what was needed to control and deal with unruly mobs and potential rioters.

I looked around apprehensively. I did not like those police horses that began stamping a little, great horses that by merely nudging could crack a rib or severely injure anyone in their path. And mingling with the small crowd some better-dressed men suggested policemen in plain clothes ready to move in smartly on any emergency.

As we trooped up to the entrance, the crowd's murmurs intensified with growing hostility. I was aware of rude catcalls from the flat-capped workingmen who formed the majority of the onlookers surging forward. Obviously they did not believe in votes for their women and wished to remain the absolute rulers of their households, however poor they might be.

I was glad to get inside with the door closed.

The first surprise was that there were no Pankhursts in evidence. No dear Emmeline or Christabel on the platform and it soon became obvious from a few tentative enquiries that Mabel had made an error. But she stood her ground, saying she had been misinformed. She had been told definitely to expect them.

I felt bitterly disappointed, and as I listened I wondered – had they ever intended being present? The meeting was opened by the chairman of the local group and though absent in body, Emmeline Pankhurst was certainly present in spirit.

Two dedicated ladies, passionate to the cause, mounted the platform among cheers from the audience and the atmosphere was thick with Pankhurst messages and quotations.

'We are here not because we are lawbreakers, we are here in our efforts to become lawmakers. The argument of the broken window pane is the most valuable argument in modern politics, for there is something that governments care for more than human life and that is the security of property, so it is through property that we shall strike the enemy. We urge you all to be militant each in your own way . . .'

I was well acquainted with their sentiments, knew them by heart from my addiction to the extensive suffrage literature, and so on and on for a very stirring hour, ending with questions from the audience. I felt delighted to be with so many women, sisters in spirit, who shared my belief in the fight for our future and the certainty that we must win in the end, yet unable to shake off the feeling of being let down somehow by the Pankhursts' absence, and the feeling that this meeting was something of an anticlimax. I looked round the tightly packed audience mostly composed of women, as one might expect, with a few men looking sheepish as if they had been dragged along unwillingly by wife or sister, their distressed expressions saying they would rather be anywhere but sitting in Cowdray Hall at this moment.

A depressing sight, indeed, and I realised we had a long way to go before men could be persuaded that we women were their equals and had the right to vote for who should govern our country.

The speakers brought the meeting to a close with a blessing, one of Emmeline's: 'Trust in God – She will provide!' That brought a laugh and plenty of cheering.

I nudged Mabel encouragingly, certain she would have something to say but she merely shook her head.

'What about your speech, your vote of thanks?' I queried.

'Not appropriate, Rose,' she whispered.

Feeling that someone should say something, I stood up and introducing myself as chairman of the Edinburgh branch, I thanked the ladies for their well-informed and excellent talk, how inspiring it was to all of us, and so forth. I ended by asking that the good wishes and firm resolve of all Scottish women who believed in the importance of our movement be conveyed to Mrs Pankhurst.

As we were leaving, it soon became obvious that despite her claims to be a dear friend of Emmeline and Christabel, no one knew or had even heard of Mabel Penby Worth. They regarded her with polite but vague smiles.

I was glad to leave the meeting and, waiting for our motor car outside, where police and crowds had thankfully vanished, Emily Dickson, a quite gentle-seeming woman despite her platform performance as a passionate speaker, came over to hold out her hand and thank me for my vote of thanks.

'Mrs McQuinn,' she said using my professional name which I still used despite my second marriage, 'I have heard of you and the excellent work being done by our sisters in Edinburgh.' Flattered indeed, I was aware of Mabel at my side, edging forward and longing to get in something about Balmoral Castle and our stay there.

I felt sorry for her, so sadly deflated. After all her boasts about her friends the Pankhursts, not even a chance to read that prepared vote of thanks she had worked on so assiduously since our arrival at the cottage.

As Emily Dickson left us, we adjourned with our Ballater companions. We all felt we deserved a break and decided to take tea at the hotel across the road. After a delicious but brief afternoon tea, as we were discussing our share of the bill, a waiter came forward, touched my shoulder. 'Mrs Macmerry?' he whispered. How did he know my name, I wondered? 'A gentleman wishes to speak to you in reception. If you will follow me.'

Mabel, who was deep in conversation with one of the ladies, hadn't noticed any of this and I whispered: 'Won't be a moment.' She nodded, presuming I was excusing myself to go to the lavatory.

Completely mystified, I followed the waiter. And there leaning on the counter—

'Jack! What on earth?'

He kissed me and grinned. 'I told you I might be in Aberdeen and here we are.' He pointed to a nearby table and the unmistakable presence of my old antagonist, Inspector Harvill Gray, late of Edinburgh City Police and, much to my relief, recently promoted to Grampian as chief inspector.

'Is this a reunion of some sort?'

'Not quite, just a bit of police business.' And his lips closed firmly, a remembered gesture. Whatever his reason, he wasn't going to tell me. 'I guessed you would be here at the meeting.'

'Are you coming to Balmoral?'

He shrugged and said cautiously. 'Maybe, but not today.'

A glance towards Gray who saw us and acknowledged me with a brief nod.

Apparently we weren't going to join him. Jack took my arm and was ushering me back in the direction of the restaurant.

'How's Meg – and Thane?'

'In splendid form, they're loving Balmoral.'

Jack nodded. 'That's great. Take care of her.' I wanted to know more, but Mabel and the ladies had come into reception. Our automobile was waiting.

Jack led me to the step, kissed me again. 'See you soon – hope to have a day or two up there on the strength of this visit.'

'What visit?'

He bowed a farewell to the ladies and Mabel asked: 'Isn't he coming with us?'

I shook my head and realised I didn't even know whether he was heading back home or pushing on elsewhere. It was all very frustrating but one thing was obvious. The meeting between Jack and Gray was no accident.

Suffragettes? Or something to do with the 'rumour' I remembered Jack mentioning before we left Solomon's Tower?

At my side, Mabel said: 'I must write to dear Emmeline, tell her how we missed them both.' I nodded absently, my tangled thoughts still on that brief meeting with Jack. 'You would have so loved meeting dear Christabel,' she added with a sigh. 'A truly wonderful young woman, a noble creature . . .'

And so on and on. It had been a long and oddly frustrating day, not quite the return journey I had imagined, full of eager, excited talk about meeting the esteemed Pankhursts. Instead the ladies were silent, obviously very weary as we travelled back through the growing dusk. We were all relieved to reach Ballater where we left the automobile and bid our companions goodnight. Dave was sitting patiently at the wheel of the motor Vince had sent to collect us.

I was glad to be back.

CHAPTER THIRTEEN

The next day Olivia had decided that the girls might enjoy visiting Vince's quarters in the castle. Meg immediately asked if I could go with them.

Olivia laughed. 'Of course she can, dear. Your mam is always included and Miss Penby too.' (The agreed form of address from the girls – she was Mabel to the rest of us.)

I shared their excitement. This would be the first time I had been inside the castle since our arrival. There was only one problem – Thane. For obvious reasons he could not come with us and we were being very careful at keeping his presence unknown to the King, which meant restriction to discreet walks in the woods near the cottage well out of range of the castle.

Meg was disappointed, so was I. There seemed only one solution. 'It's only for a few hours,' I said. 'I'll stay with Thane. I can visit it with Uncle Vince some other time.'

Mabel, overhearing this conversation, said firmly: 'You must go, Rose. That Dog will be quite safe with me.'

This generous offer was quite unexpected knowing how Mabel felt about Thane, but before Olivia and I could protest it was greeted by the girls as a great idea and a great relief to Meg in particular. It hadn't escaped my notice that she spent a lot less time talking to Thane now that she had Faith as her dearest friend and the two girls were inseparable.

Still, I never liked leaving Thane with Mabel, who had added: 'Lily will look after us.' That seemed a forlorn hope indeed, but as I was being urged on every side, I could not refuse without rather pointedly suggesting that Mabel was incapable of spending a day on her own and looking after That Dog.

The royal household quarters had been severely upgraded since the Prince of Wales became king, and he had speedily demolished evidence of his mother's sentimental attachment to clutter, in particular to that associated with her long-term widowhood. The modernisation in no way indicated the grandeur of the castle, which was something of a disappointment to Meg whose imagination had soared to lofty ceilings, panelled walls and turret rooms. Vince's apartment, however, was modest, comfortable and most important, warm. Dismissing the late Queen's firm belief that chilly rooms and cold beds were bracing and good for the soul, the King, who liked comfort for himself and everyone else, ruled that rooms with generously heated coal fires were *de rigueur* for his family, their guests and for the servants too. It must have been a great relief for Queen Alexandra – not to mention her ladies-in-waiting, whose pale-mauve complexions and constant shivering both indoors and out had been ignored by the late Queen and regarded as a necessity of character building.

Leaving his rooms, we followed Vince out into the sunshine, across the lawn and into secluded and private flower gardens, as well as the vast walled kitchen garden which supplied all the vegetables and fruit throughout the seasons.

Then an unexpected delight for the girls. Turning a corner we were face to face with the Queen, walking with two of her ladies, one of whom acknowledged Olivia. Her name was Alice von Mueller and we were destined to have a closer acquaintance later.

Vince bowed, we curtseyed.

The Queen paused. 'Ah, Dr Laurie, good day to you.' And smiling down at the two little girls, 'Enjoy the sun, my dears, while it is shining.' As she walked on, taking her companion's arm, she seemed to have a slight limp.

The girls were quite ecstatic. 'Mam,' said Meg in tones of awe. 'That was just like being presented at Court, wasn't it? And she called us "her dears".' We laughed. It had certainly made their day.

'Such a nice lady, Aunt Rose,' said Faith.

'I thought she looked a little sad,' said the ever-perceptive Meg.

I said nothing, I didn't envy her her crown or her husband.

Spending the day with Vince was a rare pleasure. After a splendid lunch we played croquet on the lawn. Tea and cakes were served to us, rich chocolate cakes with lots of cream; the girls were enchanted by such delights, and when darkness fell, they groaned, giving us appealing glances. They were in no hurry to return to the cottage.

And that gave Olivia one of her brilliant ideas. 'Let them spend the night here, Rose,' she whispered. 'I'm sure nightgowns can be provided. It would be such a thrill for them, wouldn't it, Vince?'

Vince frowned. 'A splendid idea, but remember, dear, some of the household folk are looking in later to meet you.' And turning to me, 'Just a small social gathering but if the girls are bedded down, why don't you stay, Rose? Have some refreshments with us before returning to the cottage.'

I was easily persuaded and Vince's 'neighbours' as he called them were pleasant, jolly folk. Two were from Edinburgh and we had much in common. They were intrigued to know that my husband was a detective and asked if I ever heard details of Edinburgh crimes, especially murder.

Vince listened with an amused expression. My profession had not been mentioned. 'What would they think if they knew?' he whispered, refilling my glass.

One of them did. The lady I had seen with the Queen that afternoon who knew Olivia. I was enjoying myself. This was a rare treat. The refreshments provided were all that could be desired. Especially the wine. And that was my downfall.

I am not used to wine at home in Solomon's Tower. Alcohol plays a very small part in my life, reserved for special occasions of celebration. But among the merry chatter, the pleasant company, the local gossip of the other royal servants, I allowed my glass to be refilled rather too often.

Suddenly I came to my senses. I must leave immediately while my legs would still carry me back to the cottage.

I refused Vince's gallant, but I suspected reluctant, offer to leave the jolly company and escort me back the short distance, insisting that I would enjoy the walk. Indeed, that was my purpose, breathing the night air with its faint breeze to clear my head. Besides, I had little time on my own just now, and accustomed to a more solitary and active life, the chance of a pleasant moonlight stroll, thinking my own thoughts, at that moment appealed as a very welcome interlude.

At the door, Vince put my light jacket about my shoulders and kissed me goodnight.

'Sure you will be all right, Rose?' he asked anxiously. 'Quite sure?'

I smiled confidently, not to give him the slightest idea of my limited capacity for intoxicating wines from the royal cellars. 'Of course, dear. Just a few steps, really.'

I breathed deeply and then the fresh air hit me. I was floating above the ground. So romantic too, with a moon riding high above the clouds. I wished Jack had been with me as I waved to Vince who was lingering at the door. As it closed I knew I had made up my mind. The short distance to the cottage was not nearly enough to enjoy the beauty of such a night. So humming a tune from a popular song one of Vince's friends, who had a fine voice, had been singing at the piano, I decided to extend my homeward walk and take the longer way round through the trees where I believed there was a woodland path.

And that was my second mistake. I had walked no more than a hundred yards when the track vanished. The sky, or rather what was visible through the treetops, had clouded over, the moon had disappeared and as that tall forbidding army of conifers closed in on me I knew I was lost.

I have absolutely no sense of direction and there was nothing to indicate where I was heading. Jack laughs at me. 'But seriously, in your profession it could be the difference between life and death, never knowing which way to turn when you are being pursued by a man with a gun. Do I need say more? I'm surprised you've survived so long. You must have a guardian angel.'

Remembering Jack's warning, trying to think clearly through that wine haze was little help and that guardian angel was having a holiday. Perhaps I could retrace my steps. I turned round knowing only one thing for certain, that idiotically, within a few hundred yards from home, I was well and truly lost in a thick forest with trees growing so close together that there was no possibility in the darkness of finding a path, or regaining the path I had travelled so far, if one existed.

Even the moon had deserted me. It was up there somewhere hidden by the tall treetops with only a brief glimmer as racing clouds obliterated its faint beam.

I stood still, momentarily breathless. I had to think of something. In despair I looked around again. What was the point in walking ahead? That was useless, even dangerous when I no longer knew where I was going or if it was the right direction.

Suddenly the absurdity struck me. Here I was lost somewhere on the royal estate surrounded by civilisation, people everywhere within walking distance, I could even hear the faint clip-clop of carriage horses on the Deeside road beyond the river but I might as well have been in the deserts of the Sahara.

And although it was hardly the time for frivolous thought that I might be in a serious situation, the wine effects had not yet worn off completely and I had an attack of helpless giggles. But my legs were letting me down; walking on this pine-scattered floor was like carrying lead weights, quite exhausting and treacherous.

I must stop. Wait for a moment, rest – and think what to do next. I leant against one of the inhospitable trunks, but its sharp bits digging into my back denied any possibility of relaxation.

Now the silence was invaded by intruders gathering around me. The small secret sounds of the night, the scuffles and twitches of a broken branch as an unseen army of small animals busied themselves about their nocturnal business. At least they knew where they were going and they had better eyes than mine. Another of my problems is that I have no night vision. Perfect eyesight by day but blind as a bat in the dark.

At my back, the spiteful tree trunk was urging me on. I walked a few steps and knew it was hopeless to proceed, perhaps the effects of the wine were wearing off and no longer bolstering my courage, all I felt was a great desire to sit down and close my eyes for a while. To sleep or weep for the predicament in which I had found myself, and for which I had no one to blame but my own stupidity.

Going ahead, stumbling through the forest was useless. It was like being trapped in a maze and there was only one sensible but unpleasant solution. Sit it out. Find a place and rest there until dawn shed some light on the way out.

A flicker of moonlight, not much but enough to spot a clearing and kick a pile of soft pine leaves against a nearby tree trunk. Running my hands down it suggested a smoother, more friendly one than the last.

I had never been afraid of the dark. Until this moment. In the stillness, I became aware of more sounds, a bird's alarmed cry, an owl's hoot, a spine-chilling scream from some poor creature caught by a predator. All far away, but closer at hand again those small scuffling, snuffling sounds.

Then the distant sound of a shot. A broken branch, more like a ghillie out after rabbits – in the dark? After that, I thought I heard the distant sound of dogs barking. Did that indicate the royal stables or were they wolves?

I listened again, imagination invaded by thoughts of a wolf pack, their eyes glowing through the dark, picking up my scent. No, no, absurd! I had been assured the last wolf had been killed a long time since. What about foxes then with their sharp teeth? I thought of my extremities being nibbled by foxes as I slept. Deer, what about deer? Would they attack? Or would they be more scared of me than I of them?

I wrapped my jacket more closely about me and too afraid to close my eyes now, I kept listening to the silence. A new sound that obliterated the panic of foxes or that imaginary wolf pack.

Running water, rushing water indicated a stream or a

river somewhere quite close at hand. I must be near the Dee. I stood up. Could I reach it? An encouraging sound but common sense told me it was folly to try, dangerous to follow, stumbling about in the dark. I was suddenly too weary, too tired.

I sat down again. Got to make the best of a bad job and grateful that it was a windless night and not raining, I snuggled into my thin summer jacket, closed my eyes, said a prayer and settled to await first light.

I awoke with a start. For a blissful moment thinking I was in my own bed and had had a terrible nightmare. I listened.

Breathing, definitely human, laboured and close by.

Then I knew I was not alone.

CHAPTER FOURTEEN

I was not alone. A man was bending over me, a dark shadow against the pale moonlight. I could not see his face clearly, but I heard his voice.

'Lost your way, miss?'

Oh, thank God! One of the forest rangers, a ghillie more like. As he moved I heard the metallic sound as he removed the rifle from his shoulder. 'You know you'll be catching your death lying there.'

He sounded amused, a smiling voice. A shaft of moonlight touched his face as he put down rifle and satchel to unroll something. A rain cape, a man's, smelling of sweat and cigar smoke. He was going to smother me.

I sat up, alarmed, stifled a scream, fought it off.

He laughed. 'What's wrong with you? I'm not going to hurt you – trying to help. You're half-frozen.'

A tall man towering over me. His accent, not local Deeside, more Highland or Irish. The moonlight filtering through the treetops had vanished but not before there was enough to reveal a glimpse of his face. Pale, with that wayward lock of dark hair. So like Danny's.

I came to my senses. This was the man I had seen talking to Lily in Ballater. Our driver Dave thought he was a ghillie, had seen him hanging about the stables. What a relief.

'Are you hurt, miss?' Solicitous, anxious to help, to reassure.

I jumped to my feet, wobbled a bit and he caught me, held me firmly by my elbows for a moment.

'Steady now, miss.'

'I am quite all right,' I said coldly and handing back the cape. 'Thank you, but I don't need it.'

'Sure now? What happened to you, did you faint or something?'

I was now standing feeling the cold without the warmth of his arm around me. I said firmly: 'Of course not. Just got lost, that's all. Took a short cut in the dark.'

He had the grace not to laugh. 'A short cut? At this time of night? And where was it you started from? Do you remember? The gipsy encampment is a fair distance away in the dark.'

'I am not a gipsy,' I said shortly. 'I came from the castle, my brother is a member of the royal household. I was at a party—'

I stopped – why was I telling him all this, excusing myself?

But he had moved closer. Tall, over six feet, wide-shouldered, he blocked out what little light there was and dwarfed my less than five. He towered over me and leant forward, that damnable forelock almost touching my face. Oh no, not damnable, that other dear memory.

He sniffed, took a deep breath and smiled. 'Been drinking? And too much of it for a lady at that party, I'll be thinking. Not used to it are you, miss?' His smile was faint reproach. 'And they go rather heavily on the wine and usquebaugh up yonder at the castle.'

He paused, hands on hips, regarding me. 'Newcomer, are you?' He didn't wait for a reply, shook his head. 'Have to be on your guard, know what you're doing, until you get used to it, miss.'

I was cold, tired and the last thing I wanted was a moral lecture on the dangers of alcohol.

'Perhaps you would be good enough to tell me where I am,' I said stiffly in my best Edinburgh accent, so there could be no mistaken identity about gipsies and putting him in his place.

'I can do that, miss.' That suppressed mockery again. 'You're in the midst of the estate forest running down to the banks of the river.' And no longer teasing, patient now: 'And where is it you wish to go, miss? Back to the castle, is that it?'

I ignored the 'miss' as I had ignored the gipsy implication. A horrid but familiar error by strangers at first meeting. I thought of the aristocratic lady in Ballater station. My mop of unruly yellow curls now about my shoulders, wildly tangled. My lack of any dress sense that would be regarded not as unfashionable but as distinctly unconventional.

It wasn't the man's fault. Ten years ago in 1895 when I first came to Edinburgh my self-styled designation: 'Lady Investigator, Discretion Guaranteed' had caused initial problems. Although to all accounts, mostly flattering, I had changed little since; my appearance sadly belied my forty years.

I said: 'Not the castle, if you please. I am staying in a cottage near the stables with my family and my little girl,' I added pointedly.

'And you are on the right track of it, I'll see you onto the path over yonder. Follow it, comes out right by the gates. It'll be daylight soon; you'll see the castle so you won't get lost again. Come along, miss.' And, smiling, he took my arm gently and led the way, a short distance through the trees towards the sounds of the swirling, shining river growing steadily closer.

I was lost for words, a whirlpool of emotions like that river surging inside me. Tired, cold and hungry, but most of all, overwhelmed by the sinister almost supernatural feeling that this man was no stranger to me. I knew him already. Knew that he could lock me into his eyes, not like Danny's, not deep-blue Irish eyes, but even in that faint, early light, a strange luminous amber. Eyes I could drown in, fall down, down into a magic world like Alice-in-Wonderland, a world I had lost long ago.

We had set foot on the path, straight ahead, before us the swift-moving river.

'Over there, see—' he pointed. There was enough light now for the grey outline of the stables. 'You'll be back at your cottage directly.'

He bowed. That was somehow familiar too. 'I'll bid you good day, miss.'

I thanked him, walked a few steps, but when I turned for a last look, he had disappeared, swallowed up by the tall trees of the forest.

I heard dogs barking as I approached the cottage, dogs I had nearly mistaken for wolves during the night, although I could not have been more than half a mile off course. How was I going to explain what an idiot I had been, getting lost in the dark less than a mile away? Thank heaven Meg and Faith had stayed at the castle.

I opened the door. Thane was already there waiting to greet me and Mabel appeared in her night robe, staring down the stairs.

'Where on earth have you been, Rose? That Dog has been going mad all night, flinging himself against the door, trying to get out.'

I was stroking his head, as he leant against my side. I could sense his relief that I was home and safe. That he was trying to tell me he knew I was in danger, he had tried and failed to reach me when I needed him.

'I knew I mustn't let him out, but I didn't know what had got into him, going demented like that,' Mabel was saying indignantly, 'Keeping the whole place awake. Couldn't sleep for the noise. He should be trained not to bark—'

I cut her short, murmured something consoling to her. But I knew perfectly well what had got into him. I hugged him under her disapproving tight-lipped gaze. Thane always knew when I was in danger, now here at Balmoral, as he had in Edinburgh for the past ten years. We still had our strange telepathy that I felt had been transferred to Meg but no, the bond was still there.

And if Mabel had let him out of the cottage, I would no longer have been lost in that black forest all night. He would have found me and led me safe home through the darkness.

'What happened to you, Rose? And where is Olivia?' she asked rephrasing her original question. 'I was told you were just going there for tea,' she added indignantly.

So I told her that Olivia had decided the girls should stay and that when they went to bed, there had been a little party for some of Vince's friends to meet Olivia. She presumed that I had stayed the night and I saw no reason for complicated explanations as she didn't seem particularly interested.

As I made my breakfast she went up to her room and didn't appear again until lunchtime. Nor did Lily put in an appearance, so I felt rather guilty that having been disturbed by Thane's barking during the night both had decided to return to their beds, and that Lily, who normally made Mabel's breakfast, had been instructed that she was not to be disturbed.

I would have liked to follow their example, almost too tired to eat or even stay awake, but I rallied enough to take Thane out for his morning walk in the woods. He showed none of his usual eagerness to run ahead and I regarded him anxiously. He didn't seem himself, shivering and staying close to my side.

'Missing Meg, are you?' He regarded me gravely,

that almost human questioning glance, and then the rain began, a sudden sharp shower and we headed back.

I went upstairs. Mabel was in her bedroom. I thought I heard her voice raised, haranguing Lily, no doubt, who never spoke above a whisper.

I slipped quietly into my bedroom, fell on the bed and slept. Deeply but not particularly peacefully, troubled by weird threatening dreams, none of which I was to clearly remember except that my rescuer had a leading role, but whether as hero or villain never became certain.

CHAPTER FIFTEEN

I was wakened by the sound of voices. Mabel's and that of Aiken; gruff, deep and very carrying.

I went downstairs feeling drugged with an ominous feeling of dread, the lingering shreds of bad dreams. Aiken leapt to his feet, touched his bonnet in greeting. I could see from his expression that there was something amiss. The purpose of this visit was not to bring any good news.

He was looking hard at Thane, then clearing his throat he said sternly: 'We have had complaints, madam, from the castle, indeed from the highest,' he added, bowing his head reverentially, 'if you get my meaning. The kennels were very noisy last night. Their Majesties were disturbed, and children were awakened.' He shook his head. 'This behaviour of the kennels is quite unknown. The dogs are very well-behaved animals, carefully chosen and trained, but they were at it all night, barking and howling.

Something started them off. His Majesty was most upset,' he added gravely.

And so was I. I guessed that Thane had set them off, his panic about me had spread to the other canines and so they wanted to be out too, on the trail, searching. Oh dear, this was awful.

Aiken was saying: 'This is very serious, madam. As you know, I have done my very best to keep His Majesty unaware of your dog's existence. Dr Vince was most adamant that the presence of such a handsome, unusual beast would be kept as unobtrusive as possible.' He stopped, sighed wearily and I realised what a can of worms I had opened. My innocent visit to the castle, staying on for that party, drinking too much and getting lost, had not only endangered myself, but put Thane's future in peril.

As Aiken prepared to take his departure, leaving me to brood on how I had let everyone down, emotions in turmoil, my thoughts flew to Jack. If only he were here, when I needed him most, his expert knowledge dealing with this very nasty situation. Clever, wise Jack would know exactly what to do next.

Mabel set about preparing a meal, which rather surprised me as she rarely ventured as far as the kitchen sink let alone the stove.

'Where is Lily?' I asked. 'Is she ill?'

Mabel scowled. 'I haven't the faintest idea. I haven't seen her all day. Perhaps she has eloped with one of those stable boys.' She gave a dismissive shrug. 'I have had more than enough of that girl, I can tell you. Totally unreliable and not a word of gratitude for being here, sharing the cottage with her betters. She seems to think she is on holiday too and can neglect all her duties. I can tell you, Rose, I have had enough. Enough! When she does appear, I shall send her packing, and without a reference either.'

I was delivered from Mabel's further tirade about the delinquent Lily by the arrival of Olivia and the two girls. A great fuss was made over Thane by both of them. Olivia was delighted at the amazing transformation in Faith during this holiday.

She took me aside and said: 'Faith is so fond of Thane, she has quite got over her terror of all dogs, large and small, and we have had to promise her a puppy when we get home.' She stopped and sighed. 'And that will not be long now, Rose. Just a few days.'

I had forgotten theirs was to be a brief visit. 'We will miss you. Must you go so soon?'

She smiled sadly. 'I'm afraid so, Rose. I have a lot of commitments linked with living in St James's. Ladies committees, that sort of thing. I even have a fashion show to organise, a charity event.' She looked over at Faith playing happily with Meg. 'And Faith too. She must get back as she goes to boarding school this term.'

'She is so young. Are you sure you want her to leave home?'

Olivia shook her head. 'Not I. I would be more than willing to keep her with us, send her to a local private school. She is rather shy but she would soon make friends of her own age, I'm sure of that.'

I had no doubt of that either, watching the friendship blossom so rapidly with Meg.

'The trouble is that she's an only child, really – her

brothers are so much older and Vince believes that the experience of boarding school will be the making of her.'

Reading between the lines I suspected that Vince was also considering it was time to cut those apron strings, as well as her mother's perpetual fears for her health. As he said to me later, 'All will be taken good care of in an excellent school for girls like Faith. The one we have chosen has a most reliable reputation.'

Listening to Olivia and watching the two girls, I said: 'Meg will miss her, they've grown close in the few days together.'

Olivia smiled and sighed. 'Cousins, too. So nice. Will you be sending Meg off in due course?'

I shook my head. There was no possibility. Even if we could afford it I could not see Jack ever agreeing to that and in truth we both wanted Meg coming home to us at the end of each day. When she outgrew the convent there were splendid schools for girls in Edinburgh.

I had made a pot of tea and called upstairs to Mabel. There was no reply and I decided that having had a broken night with Thane and the noisy dogs next door, she had probably taken the opportunity to recover her lost sleep.

As we sat at the table with the regular supply of newly baked scones from the castle kitchen, Olivia said: 'Did you get home all right, by the way? Vince was anxious about you.'

There was no point in lying to save my face, so I told her how I had got lost but a kind ghillie had set me on the right road. I omitted the horrid details that I had been in that beastly dark forest all night and as I was skimming the surface, so to speak, I wondered why I was not telling the whole truth, but then she did not know the details about those earlier encounters with my strange rescuer who reminded me so of Danny.

At that moment, I had no wish to start explaining it all to Olivia who would have been rather embarrassed, I felt, by such a confession. So, let him go as an unknown ghillie. And I still didn't know his name.

Olivia was saying. 'I came to look for you later at the party and Vince told me you had left.' Pausing, she regarded me thoughtfully and said, 'Before we leave, there is someone who wants to meet you. Someone who believes you may be able to help her,' she added gravely and I thought, Oh no, not a prospective client, surely. Not at Balmoral.

'Alice von Mueller. You may remember her, she was with the Queen when we met them in the gardens.'

All my attention had been on curtseying and I had only the vaguest memory of a lady accompanying her.

'Alice looked in to our party, but you had rushed away. She is English. Her husband is a very high official in the Kaiser's government, a remote cousin of the Kaiser. We have friends in common and occasionally meet them at St James's.' Smiling at me expectantly, she added: 'I said I was sure you would have a word with her.'

I could hardly refuse but I guessed already that her problem, whatever it was, sounded well out of my territory. Straying husbands, thieving maids, fraudsters. Royalty indeed!

Olivia was aware of my cautious expression and said: 'It is only advice she needs – desperately, I gather.'

'How did she hear about me?'

131

Olivia shrugged. 'Overheard some friend of Vince's talking about Edinburgh crimes and your famous father Inspector Faro having been Queen Victoria's personal detective and that you had followed in his footsteps. I gather there was some mention of you being here on holiday.'

Dear Vince, I thought, how did he manage in the realm of patient confidentiality? He certainly couldn't keep any family secrets.

'Anyway,' Olivia said. 'Please say you will see her. I do like her, she's a nice person, but alas, we do not care for her husband. Arrogant army man – very Prussian.'

Even as I agreed, I admit reluctantly, to meet her I was already filling in some of the details. An unhappy marriage, I had a lot of those in my logbook, with an inevitable love affair and the complications that could bring. Like blackmail. That was the most popular.

CHAPTER SIXTEEN

A meeting was speedily arranged; Olivia worked that way. Alice was to come to tea. At first glance, she was pretty and elegant, but not much past forty, already somehow withered. Sadness shone out of her like a beacon.

After a quick introduction, in the carriage that had set Alice down at the cottage, Olivia gathered up the two girls for a visit to Ballater.

'Shopping,' she said apologetically. 'Things to take home, you know.'

I was alone with my guest and decided to call on Lily to make tea since Mabel wasn't in evidence. We saw little of her, upstairs in her room or away each day in the pony trap following the progress of the shooting. Although only ladies specially invited were welcome to join the King's party, Mabel's father, she told us, was a keen sportsman and as he had no son, decided to bring up his only daughter with an heir's accomplishments. One being that she was a crack shot with a rifle and this holiday provided the somewhat wistful enjoyment and excitement of watching the shooting from a safe distance.

This new preoccupation had completely obliterated her obsession about the Pankhursts. Perhaps their failed visit to Aberdeen was at fault and she felt let down and dear Emmeline and Christabel were hardly mentioned any more.

Excusing myself, I went up to the attic, but Lily's room was empty, her basket of sewing abandoned. She probably took full advantage of her mistress's absence to visit the stables and I for one did not blame her.

Alice was sitting by the window exactly as I had left her. Thane had introduced himself and she was stroking his head. We exchanged some remarks about the weather as I prepared tea. We could hear the guns far off, the sight of an occasional bird that had escaped.

Alice said grimly, 'I find it a rather horrid sport, I'm afraid. My maternal grandfather was a clergyman' (I later learnt he was an archbishop) 'and I was brought up to respect the lives of all living creatures.'

'Thane would agree with you.'

She gave him a tender glance. 'He's a lovely dog. You are lucky. All we have are huge gun dogs at home. They have to be useful, not meant for a lady's lap.'

'Shooting is a man's thing, the sport of kings.'

'And decidedly so with Edward. His father set the pattern.'

Edward? Oh, she was talking about HM.

She ignored the scones and Dundee cake, and merely

took a few sips of tea, pushing the cup aside. Leaning forward, she said: 'It is so good of you to see me at short notice like this, Mrs—? I beg your pardon, I don't know your name.'

'Just call me Rose,' I said hastily. I had no idea how to address German aristocracy. I was hoping she would enlighten me.

Alice nodded. 'There is no one else I can talk to except Olivia. She is so very understanding and has my confidence. She thought you might be able to help.' A deep sigh. 'I am utterly distraught. You see, my husband is taking my children away from me and I don't know how to stop him.'

Neither did I. Husbands still had absolute rule over their children's custody in a separation, a law that would continue until it was changed and women had the vote and some say in parental rights.

Feeling gloomily that this promised to be a difficult session of only negative advice, I poured another cup of tea. She gestured refusal.

'Would you care to start at the beginning?' I said gently.

She sighed, removed her bonnet, a shower of blonde curls in much better order than my own unruly locks. That was all we had in common. She had an inch on me in height and I had maybe a few in years.

'As Olivia may have told you—'

I held up my hand. 'Olivia has told me nothing of you or your circumstances, believe me. She is expert at keeping confidences.'

Alice sighed. 'I was forced into marriage by my father, who was an ambassador to Germany. Hermann had seen me at a reception where I was accompanying my father. I was aware of his interest, watching me, he was attracted although I decidedly was not. At that time I had other plans, and besides he was nearer my father's age than mine.

'I dreaded what was to happen next. He asked for my hand in marriage and I did not dare disobey. I was afraid of my father, a man of formidable will with a temper to match it. He threatened to lock me in my room until I agreed.'

It wasn't a story completely unknown, where rich and powerful men ruled their daughter's destinies, girls put up for sale in the marriage market to the highest bidder.

'I knew it was useless to refuse so I decided to make the best of it, assured of the good life and benefits awaiting at the German court, for Hermann was not only a relative of the Kaiser but also a close friend.'

She sighed. 'I told myself that I was fortunate. I had always hoped to marry while I was young and I wanted children. Apart from the lack of the grand passion, Munich was full of exciting events and the ancient schloss was beautiful. I would adore adding a woman's touch and I must confess I was more in love with my surroundings than my husband, although I had little to complain about then. He was always generous.'

She paused. 'However, I had not long been married when I discovered that he intended cutting me off from my home in England as soon as possible and from all things English. I had learnt German and he would not allow me to speak English, nor our children – they would be punished if he overheard them speaking that hated language. As the years passed I realised it was a kind of madness. The Kaiser had been very fond of his grandmother Queen Victoria and even rushed to her bedside when she was dying. When Edward came to the throne in 1901 it got worse. Hermann maintained that his way of life as Prince of Wales made him unfit to ever be a good king and he, as well as many other Germans, believed that the Kaiser had an equal claim to the English throne and that Victoria should have named him as her heir instead of Edward.'

This was certainly a new version of the history of Victoria's numerous descendants who occupied the thrones of Europe, as Alice watched my expression and continued, 'It sounded mad, I was quite aware that this was an insane idea, but there was no reasoning with him and he began to include me in his hatred of all things English, and I suffered from that. Worse, he turned the children against me and made them hate England too.'

Tearful, she paused and shook her head. 'He succeeded with my beloved Dietrich, our only son, ten years old when he sent him away from home – from his mother's malign influence, he said – to be educated at a military college. They will turn him into a soldier to prepare him to fight the English when the time comes.'

I knew I was listening to a sad story but also that there was nothing I could do except put on the kettle again, deciding that she must be thirsty.

Thane sat up sharply. I thought I heard a noise. Mabel or Lily must have returned – at the worst possible moment.

I opened the door but the hallway was empty. Alice was ready for the next instalment and there was worse to come.

'A small boy taken from his mother's love and caring, but that was not enough for Hermann. He has also removed our two young daughters, sent them to be educated by a governess with the children of his mistress.'

She must have seen my look of surprise, and smiled bitterly. 'Oh, I wasn't shocked. I learnt early in our marriage that it was the done thing for a married man of high standing to have a mistress – at least one.' She paused, took out a handkerchief and applied it to her eyes.

It was my turn to speak, to offer words of reassurance. Did I know of anything, or of someone in Scotland who could help her, especially as she was still a British citizen, to prevail upon her husband and let her have her children restored to her?

I expressed my sympathy, she certainly needed all of that, but I told her there was nothing I could do and doubted whether any Scottish law could help her or any other. Laws had been made by men since civilisation began and they had seen to it that they were biased in their favour.

I tried to add tactfully that this sad situation was out of my field of activity as an investigator. However unjust it seemed, a husband's rights over his wife's property included all rights over their children and there was no law to forbid a father from poisoning his children's minds against their mother, sending their young son to military college and their daughters to be educated with his mistress's governess.

Alice was tearful; she clenched her hands in a gesture of hopelessness. 'Thank you for listening and for wasting your time. I just had to talk to someone and you were my last, my only hope. The Queen has been very understanding, she knows all about difficult husbands.' She leant forward confidentially, 'Edward has a mistress, you know.'

I did know – and more than one – as she went on: 'You have been very understanding too,' and when I apologised once again for being unable to help or indeed, offer any useful advice, she shook her head, 'It has helped, just to unburden myself. Hermann can forgive Scotland, his hatred belongs to England. Balmoral is exempt; he is here for the shooting. I must stay but God knows what will happen when we get home.'

I wanted to hear more but our interview was cut short by a distraught Meg who burst in on us. I had not heard the motor, besides they could hardly have reached Ballater yet.

Alice stood up. 'I must go.'

She cut short my apology to her and my suitable reprimand to Meg. 'Perhaps we can meet again later?' The anxiety in her voice made that urgent and imperative.

CHAPTER SEVENTEEN

'What happened? I demanded. 'Did the motor break down?'

'No, we never got there. Faith was sick in the car, she's gone back to the castle with Aunt Livvy—'

Meg's tears were in full flood. I put my arms around her. 'No need to get upset, dear. Uncle Vince will soon make her better.'

She pulled away from me. 'I'm not worried at Faith being sick – it's . . . it's because she'll be going back to London – leaving us.'

She made it sound like the end of the world as I suppose it was, to her, for there followed a vast number of suggestions why she and Faith should not be separated, none in the least feasible or credible.

No, Faith could not stay here with us without her mother. No, her father was much too busy to look after her.

'Then can she come to Edinburgh and live with us?' Meg pleaded. 'I've told her all about our Solomon's Tower, and she says she would love to come.'

'And well she may, dear – to visit us,' I added sharply. 'She knows she will be very welcome to come for a holiday any time.'

Meg bit her lip. 'I don't mean that, Mam. I mean to stay – for always,' she added impatiently.

'No, dear. She cannot do that. She is still a little girl—'

'She will be eleven next year!'

I ignored the interruption. 'Until she is older she needs to be with her father and mother – they would miss her dreadfully, think how you would—'

'No, they won't,' she interrupted. 'They're sending her to boarding school.'

'That is not quite the same thing,' I said wearily.

But Meg refused to be placated. The demerits of boarding school came into it somewhere and so it went on and on between us, Meg putting forth ideas, trying to wheedle some sort of wild agreement. Finally, because I was tired and irritable and still feeling the effects of my nightmare hours in the dark forest, I lost my temper with her.

'Do stop talking nonsense, Meg. Please be sensible about this and stop making silly suggestions. Faith must – like you – stay with her parents in her own home.'

'I don't think my suggestions were silly, Mam. Faith is my cousin, the only close kin I will ever have unless you and Pa are ever going to give me a brother or sister. I keep on hoping every day.' She paused and gave me a hard look; waiting for the explanation I could not give her that her hopes were in vain. She sighed. 'I have got the nuns praying for one—'

That smote me to the heart, as did her tear-filled eyes as she ended: 'It's not like you, Mam. You're not like this, usually we can talk together, tell each other everything. When I tell you things that bother me, you always know what to do. I can rely on you for everything.' She shook her head sadly. 'Not this time, though this is the most important thing that has ever happened to me. I want my cousin, the only relation I will ever have,' she repeated heavily, 'to live with us.'

And taking Thane, out she went, her back straight, cold and defiant. And left me feeling that I had let her down and for the first time ever we had come near to quarrelling.

But that wasn't the end of my miseries. Worse was in store.

We had another visit from Aiken and at the sight of him coming up the path the next morning my heart sank. Was this more bad news for Thane, for bad news seemed certain by his grim expression.

'Thought I should tell you, madam, there's been another tragedy.' He sighed deeply. 'The Dee has claimed another victim.'

I wondered what he was talking about.

'Poor young lass drowned. Found by one of the ghillies walking his dog this morning.' He shook his head and sighed again. 'They're making enquiries. Been a bit bashed about, poor craiter, river's rough there, boulders, ye ken. Och well, we were all expecting it,' he added glumly.

'After yon wee lad drowned the very day you arrived.

We all ken that the Dee claims three a year.' And pointing in the general direction of Crathie Church: 'It's there written down in the parish records, generations back, and aye, in the kirkyard for all to see their graves.'

At my look of surprise, he said patiently, 'The Dee tends to ferocious flooding after the snow melts on the Cairngorms or at this particular time of the year after long spells of rain. Folk hold their breaths waiting for the worst to happen. "Blood-thirsty Dee Each year needs three, But Bonny Don, She needs none".'

As an epilogue to this grim piece of folklore, he went on, 'Aye, that great flood back in '29 is well remembered for its ravages. The Queen herself had to be reminded of the Dee's menace when one of the local lairds lost a bairn. Spares nobody,' he added glumly, 'high or low.'

I needed no reminder of how we had seen from the windows the sad procession carrying a drowned lad from the river. The memory still chilled me. An omen somehow that all was not going to be the happy carefree holiday we expected. And a sudden grim thought, a reminder that had I pressed on through that dark forest where I heard its enticing gurgling waters, I might well have been its third victim.

I was soon to find out that my intuitive feeling of disaster had just begun.

Vince arrived back with Olivia and Faith who stayed outside with Meg, whispering to her volubly and darting angry looks in my direction.

Faith seemed none the worse for her sickness and Vince shrugged off my concern.

Olivia said: 'A pity, but it sometimes happens. Just

going over these rough roads in the motor, I expect.'

However, one look at Vince's face as he silently led us into the kitchen and closed the door signalled some catastrophe.

'You had a visit from Aiken, telling you that a girl has been drowned.' I said how awful and he went on: 'I was called in. Nothing I could do. She'd been in the water for about two days.'

Olivia said, 'Such a dreadful tragedy. Have her parents been notified?'

Vince said nothing; he was looking at Mabel who had just come downstairs. 'Where is Lily just now?'

'Upstairs in her room, I expect. Is she needed?' Mabel sounded slightly disapproving as he said: 'Ask her to come down for a minute, if you please?'

'Why do you want her?' But before Vince could reply there was an interruption as Meg rushed in demanding glasses of lemonade. Playing on the swing had made Faith thirsty and yes, they were both hungry, as usual.

Olivia attended to this and Vince continued to regard Mabel who had not answered his question. 'Please, Mabel.'

She sighed and rose from her chair as if this request required too much effort.

Meg had sat down at the table and with Faith prepared to do full justice to a plate of scones as she chattered excitedly about a hedgehog with five little babies they had found beneath their incomplete tree house – likely to remain that way now, but our recent disagreement over her plans for Faith's future were momentarily laid aside.

Vince interrupted. Still watching Mabel, he touched

Meg's shoulder. 'Do something for Miss Penby, please dear. Save her legs and run upstairs. Ask Lily to come down.'

'Of course, Uncle Vince.'

Mabel resumed her seat, murmured: 'Much obliged.'

We were silent, what did Vince want with Lily? I hadn't seen her all day but that was not unusual. She was removed from us as much as possible, Mabel reminding us that Lily was her personal maid and that she was not to consider that she was here to run errands and make cups of tea for the rest of us. She had duties to perform each day and Mabel saw that she was kept fully employed.

And Lily certainly made herself unobtrusive. A silent creature, she made no noise as she moved, flitting in and out of the cottage, so pale she looked bloodless, a large humanised moth.

We heard Meg run upstairs to the attic, the opening and closing of a door and a minute later she was back with us, alone. She looked at Mabel apologetically. 'She isn't in her room, Miss Penby, it is quite empty.'

Vince looked enquiringly at Mabel who shrugged. 'Thank you, Meg.'

'Can we go out again, Mamma?' said Faith. 'We are playing a fine game.'

At Olivia's nod of assent the girls rushed out. Mabel sighed deeply. 'She must have gone for a walk, for a little fresh air as she calls it. And of course,' she added heavily, 'did not think it necessary to ask my permission or even inform me of her intentions, which no doubt takes her in the direction of the stable boys. Her behaviour grows daily more intolerable. Impossible ever since we got here.

Seems to have got the idea that she is on holiday too—'

Vince cut short the tirade, said gently: 'May I ask you, Mabel, when did you last see her?'

Mabel shrugged, an irritated gesture, and he said quickly: 'Today?'

She frowned. 'No. That is precisely what I am telling you about—'

'Yesterday?' Vince put in.

Ignoring the question, Mabel said crossly: 'Oh, she comes and goes these days, seems to have forgotten I pay her wages. She does as she likes. I do make allowances, I do not want to be a stern employer but she had better smarten up when we get home or I will be looking for another personal maid.'

Vince leant across, touched her hand. 'I'm afraid you will have to do just that, Mabel.'

She looked confused, angry as if ready to say that it was no business of his. 'Indeed?' she said coldly.

Vince sighed. 'Yes, indeed. I'm sorry to have to inform you that we believe the girl who drowned is Lily.'

A horrified exclamation from Olivia. Mabel put her hand to her mouth, gave a sharp scream. 'Oh, the silly creature, did she go and fall into the river?'

'We don't know the details,' Vince said slowly.

'Are you sure it is her, then?' she asked.

'She has been in the river for at least twenty-four hours. There are obstacles: rocks, dashing turbulent waters. I will spare you the details, but when I was called in to examine the body, I recognised her.' He paused, bit his lip. 'I am afraid this is not very pleasant for you, Mabel, but she has to be officially identified.'

147

'I thought you said you recognised her,' Mabel said coldly, aware I thought of what was to come when Vince said:

'That is true, but the identification must be made by you as her employer, for the fiscal's records and so that her family can be informed.'

'I don't see the necessity,' Mabel protested. 'Surely identification by a doctor such as yourself is sufficient?'

Vince shook his head. 'Not for legal purposes, I'm afraid. That is your responsibility.'

This statement put Mabel into a wearisome argument with him until I intervened and said that I would go with her. She seemed surprised and grateful for this offer.

I did not add that I had looked at many dead bodies in my life. Before those cases in my Edinburgh logbooks, during my ten pioneering years in Arizona, there were Apache raiders in Arizona, scalped soldiers and massacred women and children. A drowned girl would not have any terrors or qualms for me.

CHAPTER EIGHTEEN

We set off across the grounds to a small building, possibly one of the ice houses for storing venison and game birds, taken over to serve as a temporary mortuary. Inside there lay Lily, her head bandaged, her face only marginally paler, hardly more colourless in death than she had been in life.

It was a sad and tragic business and I fought back tears for the poor girl, surprised to see at my side, how admirably well controlled were Mabel's emotions at this bitter waste of a young life. I took her arm gently. Was she feeling guilty that she had not been kinder?

As we emerged, she took a deep breath of fresh air. I was wrong. She merely shrugged: 'Foolish girl getting herself drowned. And what am I to do for the next few weeks without a maid, might I ask?'

I suspected that inconvenience troubled her most. Did

she really expect an answer to that heartless question? We returned in silence to the cottage and as I lay awake, I wondered if Mabel slept much that night.

Vince was waiting with Mr Green, introduced as a member of the household in charge of such matters as accidents on the royal estate. One look at Mr Green whispered policeman to me although he was in plain clothes, slightly more formal than a ghillie, denoting a notch higher in the Balmoral echelons.

He produced an official-looking notebook and invited us to sit at the table. Vince joined us as his presence was necessary. Meanwhile Olivia tactfully removed the girls to walk in the castle gardens and since dogs would not be allowed, except for the royal pets, Thane was left with us. He did not look happy, confined to the cottage without his companions and I noticed Mr Green eyeing him warily as I produced refreshments and he got down to the sad business of details about Lily from her employer. As my presence wasn't needed, I decided to remove myself from the scene. I knew nothing about Lily, not even her surname and neither it seemed did Mabel.

Mabel looked distinctly thoughtful even hesitant.

'Lily? Lily . . . ?' She frowned. 'White, I think.'

An interesting and apt surname that fitted her description like a glove. Mr Green was saying to Mabel: 'You will, of course, be informing the young woman's family of their sad loss.'

I left them to it, went upstairs and a few moments later I heard Mr Green and Vince leave, then Mabel's footsteps on the stairs as she went to her room.

The sound of voices outside. Olivia came in alone and

we sat down to discuss the appalling tragedy. How had it happened? Neither of us able yet to take it in, shocked that such an accident could have occurred.

Our speculations were interrupted by a knock at the door. Probably Mr Green wanting more information.

I opened the door to Vince. At his side the man I least wanted to see, Chief Inspector Gray. His rather cold bow indicated that the feeling was mutual.

Olivia was introduced and, about to depart into the garden, received a charming smile from the inspector who requested that she remain. He indicated seats around the table and I guessed what was to follow. Although Olivia might be ignorant of the procedure, Gray's presence struck a new light on the tragedy. He was not satisfied with Green's report on the accident. His questions would follow a regulated pattern. Where were each of us at the estimated time of Lily's disappearance and subsequent death?

He looked at his notes. 'Miss Penby Worth?'

The door opened. Mabel had seen him arrive with Vince and, being introduced, she somewhat reluctantly took a seat at the table. Gray began by offering sympathy to all of us for this very unfortunate occurrence on our holiday and, while I was wondering what on earth was a chief inspector of police doing at Balmoral asking questions about a guest's drowned servant, he opened a notebook, turned to Mabel, repeating Mr Green's opening line, that she would be informing Lily's family of their sad loss.

Mabel's face was expressionless. 'We require some details for our official records, madam,' he said quietly.

She stared at him as if this was some outrageous request

and said stiffly: 'I have already told Mr Green all I know.'

Gray shook his head. 'Which, alas, is not quite enough, madam.'

Mabel sighed. 'And what further details do you require?'

'The usual ones,' Gray explained patiently. 'When did you last see . . .' and pausing to consult the notes 'Miss White?'

Mabel came back promptly. 'Some time after I returned from Ballater. Yesterday afternoon.'

'At what time would that be precisely?'

'I haven't the slightest idea,' she said coldly.

'None at all?' Gray obviously thought this odd and, placing his fingertips together, regarded her thoughtfully. It was not my place to jog Mabel's memory but I thought I had heard her go upstairs while I was having tea with Alice von Mueller.

Mabel shrugged. 'I gave her some sewing which I needed urgently. She went up to her room.'

Gray stood up. 'Which I should like to see, if you please.'

'There is nothing of interest, I assure you,' Mabel protested.

'That is for me to decide, madam.' And I remembered hearing Mabel's voice haranguing Lily. I made to follow them but a stern frown from Gray indicated that this was not wanted.

'The inspection of Lily's room must have been very cursory,' Olivia whispered as we heard their footsteps descending the stair a few moments later, Mabel looking rather flushed and angry as Gray motioned her back to the table and took out his notebook.

'I will try not to detain you much longer, madam, but I require some details of the deceased's next of kin. Presumably this will be her parents, so we need their names and addresses.'

'I have not this information at hand, I am afraid, nor have I the slightest idea about her parents. This is not usually regarded as important when employing a lady's maid. However, I will look into it when I return home and inform you in due course,' she added with an air of finality and sat back in her chair. Gray's prying questions seemed to have offended her.

The inspector nodded, put down his pen. He was annoyed, that faint smile a dangerous expression that I knew of old. 'How long was Miss White in your employ? And presumably she came to you with some references, madam?'

'Not at all. She came to me – oh, two to three months ago through a friend whose recommendations I trust entirely. I did not deem it necessary to request more than that, indeed it would have seemed rather an insult.' She sighed. 'However, in the present circumstances, it seems regrettable since the girl was unreliable and indeed, rather foolish.'

Gray pursed his lips. 'The girl was sadly drowned,' he reminded her. 'And now, madam, we need these details immediately. We cannot proceed without them.'

I had been watching him as he conducted this interview. His surprise arrival was bothering me. Too fast for him to be summoned from Aberdeen, he must have been at the castle already. A coincidence? An unlikely guest? I must ask Vince.

Mabel was staring out of the window as if she hadn't heard his request. 'I will, of course, pay for her funeral. I presume she can be buried in the local cemetery.'

Vince who had been silent throughout interposed: 'Not without a proper identity, Mabel. A death certificate bearing date of birth and so forth. We have to know more than her name,' he added gently.

Gray regarded him gratefully, before turning again to Mabel. 'Perhaps your friend will provide us with the details we require.' And picking up his pen: 'Her name and address, if you please.'

Mabel smiled. 'That, alas, I am unable to give you at present. Lady Frances is travelling abroad for her health for several months, precisely the reason for sending Lily to me.' She shrugged. 'I'm afraid I haven't the faintest idea of her present whereabouts. I imagine she is travelling somewhere on the Continent at this moment, possibly in Switzerland or Germany.'

Gray nodded. 'Your friend's family will perhaps have details. May we have their name and address, if you please?' he added patiently.

Mabel certainly was not pleased. She said coldly. 'Her family have a place in Sussex, but Lady Frances severed all connection with them some years ago. They wished her to make an unsuitable marriage. She refused. She belongs to the race of womankind who live and travel alone,' she added proudly. 'Lady Frances is a very private person.'

I wondered if their link was the suffrage movement.

Vince and the inspector were exchanging grim looks as well they might. If this Lady Frances was the only one with any information about Lily, it might well take some considerable time to track her down or wait for her return to England. And doubtless the two men were thinking: what to do with the body in the ice house meanwhile?

Gray turned his attention to Olivia and me. 'As this is a somewhat unusual case, it would be helpful to know when you last saw the young woman.'

So we were required to provide answers to questions more usually supplied as alibis in the case of a homicide. Did Gray have reason for suspecting that Lily had not met an accidental death, that she had been murdered?

He turned to Olivia. 'Mrs Laurie?' his smile a gentle disguise.

She shook her head. 'I haven't seen her for a couple of days, but that isn't unusual for she spent most of her time attending to Miss Penby Worth.' She nodded towards Mabel. 'As a lady's maid she had much to keep her busy attending to her mistress's needs. She was not expected to be available to the rest of us.'

Mabel had made that very plain I decided, as Gray turned to me. 'And you, Mrs Macmerry?' He had made the transition very smoothly from Mrs McQuinn to my second marriage.

'I can only endorse Mrs Laurie's statement, Chief Inspector. I have not seen Lily either, although I heard Miss Penby Worth talking to her when I was going upstairs to my bedroom.'

'And when would that be?'

'The day before yesterday – in the afternoon.'

Gray thanked us, briskly closed his notebook, and said he might need to talk to us again. After he left Mabel, went quickly to her room without a word, leaving me to wonder once again what her feelings were at this deplorable tragedy which she seemed intent on regarding as merely an annoyance; that she had lost her lady's maid – a matter of inconvenience. Was she further dismayed, at this moment considering the consequences that Lily could not be laid to rest until the absent Lady Frances provided the required information? Or that the inspector's interest suggested the poor girl might have been murdered?

Olivia said, 'What she said about this reclusive friend who was Lily's previous employer – don't you think it is extremely doubtful that they'll be able to trace her? And frankly, if she shares Mabel's feeling and regards servants as an impersonal commodity, then it's very unlikely she'll have any knowledge of Lily's parents or background either.'

I agreed, and looking out of the window, Vince and Gray were talking earnestly, their heads turned in the direction of the stables. Was that the next direction of their enquiries?

CHAPTER NINETEEN

Olivia went out to join the two girls and Thane in the garden. 'Time for a walk.' And to me: 'Coming with us?'

I shook my head. Suddenly the enormity of Lily's drowning overwhelmed me. I needed help to sort out my confused thoughts. I must talk to Vince. I was unlucky, wrong in my assumption that the stables were Gray's destination. As I opened the front door he was coming through the gate.

'Ah, Mrs Macmerry, I have observed that you have an uncommon interest in this enquiry.'

'No more uncommon than would seem natural for a girl who has been living in the cottage with us and has unfortunately drowned.'

His lips tightened. 'Perhaps I should make it clear to you that the police are quite capable of clearing up this unfortunate incident and any interference by a private investigator will be severely dealt with as unwarranted interference.'

That said, the warning made, he touched his hat and, turning left, hurried in the direction of the stables. He had certainly made his view clear but, had he known me better, would have realised that he had made it obvious there was, in this 'unfortunate incident' as he had called it, more than a mere death by drowning. And that would make me all the keener to carry out an investigation of my own.

Vince hadn't waited for him at the stables. As he was leaving I caught up with him and said: 'If you're heading back to the castle I'll walk back with you. We need to talk.'

His wry smile said that he knew what I had in mind. 'Has it occurred to you that Lily might not be English?' I asked.

He thought about that. 'She always seemed reluctant to speak, is that what makes you think she was foreign? I've never had anything beyond a yes or no.'

'Nor I. And considering her somewhat nomadic previous employer, as described by Mabel, could not this Lady Frances person have picked up Lily on her travels?'

Vince nodded. 'True. It is often the way these days, when regrettably we British pay our servants a mere pittance, foreign incomers, often refugees, are glad to work hard for little more than food and a sound roof above their heads.'

'I find it quite extraordinary that in Lily's tragic death, heart-wrenching even to those of us of who hardly knew her, Mabel could be so disinterested in the background of one who was her personal maid.'

Vince merely nodded and stared ahead, his mind elsewhere. I knew him of old. There was something that he wasn't willing to discuss after Gray's inconclusive interview with Mabel.

Seeing Vince, withdrawn, silent, I felt a sudden ominous chill. It was one with which I was painfully familiar. It told me a lot, the presence of a mystery, of unanswered questions and, most fearful of all, regarding the unknowable Lily White, who was she and had her death been accidental?

We had reached the castle and as we entered the gardens Vince prepared to take his leave. 'Tell Olivia I may be late, I have things to do.'

I put my hand on his arm. 'Is there something wrong, Vince?'

His laugh was mirthless. 'You may well ask. Only a drowned girl, the maid of one of my guests. As if that wasn't dire enough, a guest in HM's cottage. Aren't there enough complications, Rose? Don't you see them looming ahead?'

I had to confess that I hadn't until then realised that there were issues regarding Lily's death involving Vince too as he said:

'I'm not satisfied, nor I think is Gray, with this abysmal lack of information about Lily. There is something wrong here; I feel it in my bones. And we have to keep this low key, Rose. As far as HM is concerned, it must never appear to be more than an accident.'

I looked at him and he went on: 'Surely you can

159

understand the gravity of the situation from the King's point of view? This was not a tenant on the estate, it was a stranger, a stranger unfortunately who was living in his private cottage. The servant of a guest of his household physician in whom he has the utmost trust,' he added heavily.

'Are you suggesting, then, that it might not have been an accident?'

He sighed. 'Think of the complications if that was so. He has foreign visitors, royalty from Europe and beyond, with half the aristocracy of Great Britain, all here for the shooting. Some of them have wives and families with them. Imagine the panic if it came out that there had been a murder, even if it was only a servant,' he stressed the words bitterly. 'And what if it got into the newspapers? "Murder at Balmoral Castle!" Think of that, the press would have a field day.'

He sighed. 'What if she didn't accidentally drown? Mabel has no satisfactory explanation for why the girl was wandering away on her own by the river. What if she was lured there, killed first and her body thrown into the water with a forlorn hope that it would drift away for ever, by someone who wasn't aware of the unlikelihood of that.'

At my questioning look, he said: 'All the signs suggest that if this was murder it was by someone who was not acquainted with Deeside and the river.' Again that bitter laugh. 'Think what headlines that would make. There's another possibility too, Rose.'

'You examined the body.'

He looked unhappy. I knew what was worrying him

when he said: 'She had been battered by the currents and the rocks, but the injury to the back of her head was not consistent with tripping and falling face forward into the river.'

I thought for a moment. 'Was she shot?' I had another swift vision of my rescuer in the dark forest with his rifle and the gunshot I had heard shortly before he appeared, as Vince shook his head. 'No. There was no bullet wound. That would have remained in her skull. Most likely a piece of wood.'

We were both silent, then I said: 'So it could have been murder. And you would have kept it quiet.'

He sighed. 'We might add rifle butt to the blunt instrument. Thinking of an attacker with the shooting parties. All of those gallant sportsmen, some of them keen as mustard to bring down a bird or two but a bit useless with the guns. What if it had been one of them, one of HM's aristocratic guests, head of a foreign power?' He shuddered. 'The consequences are horrendous. Look, I must go.'

'Why is Gray so interested in the stables?'

'So you saw that – nothing escapes Miss Sharp Eyes.' He laughed. 'Mabel knew nothing of Lily's personal life. Gray's theory – remember he's never the one to think the best of anyone – is that she was probably a whore under that quiet exterior. Jack would tell you, there's plenty of them in high places as well as the kitchen. What if she had struck up an affair with a stable lad?'

I shook my head. I couldn't imagine Lily having sex appeal, but that was a secret chemistry only a man could

161

detect. 'Wait. I have one more quick question. Is Gray staying at the castle?'

He frowned. 'What makes you think that, Rose?'

'Well, he is obviously lurking somewhere in the neighbourhood . . .' I paused to let that sink in, 'or how did he appear so quickly after Lily was discovered?'

Vince shrugged. 'He has business here.' The same words Jack used when he wasn't prepared to say more. I was not to be put off.

'About Lily?'

'No.' Sharply but not sharp enough.

I persisted. 'Something at the castle, then. Someone pilfering the silver. It's a long way from Aberdeen, the last time I saw him with Jack.'

Vince turned, looked at me sternly and sighed. 'If I don't say something to keep you quiet I know you won't let it rest. Jack didn't say anything to me.'

'What, about rumours?'

He sighed, perhaps a sigh of relief. 'There are always rumours, Rose, and precautions must be taken, especially at this time of year, the shooting season. So many different nationalities all crowded together. And God knows they are all related by courtesy of the King's mother who provided for most of the thrones in Europe.' And when he added 'There are always dangerous people' I thought of the Kaiser and Alice von Mueller's strange story.

'Like assassins,' I said gently.

'Who knows, Rose. We certainly hope not. And there's nothing definite, just rumours that we always have to be on our guard.'

'And nothing to do with Lily?' I persisted but I didn't

162

get an answer from Vince. The nurse appeared from his surgery, he was urgently needed.

I was walking back very thoughtfully when Olivia and the girls appeared having left Thane at the cottage and decided to come and meet me. Meg and Faith were full of what they had seen, what I had missed on their woodland walk, normally so uneventful.

Today they had seen a deer herd, squirrels that were quite tame, and some of the royals fishing in the river, on and on. Enough to keep Olivia unaware of my silent preoccupation, for I had much to mull over concerning my conversation with Vince.

When we reached the cottage Mabel wasn't in evidence. I made tea and took it upstairs to her. She was sitting by the window, staring across towards the woods. Was this just the aristocratic stiff upper lip and she was upset too, with delayed reaction? As she turned to face me, her expression was no longer defiant. She looked scared and I had another thought to add to my misgivings.

If she knew something more about Lily that she wasn't telling us, was she thinking that her own life might now be in danger?

I considered Lily's possible murder. According to Vince the body had been in the water for about two days but Mabel was certain that she had been missing not more than a day.

Then I remembered my rescuer near the river where her body had been washed up, rifle slung over his shoulder, and I returned again to the gunshot I had heard. The time fitted. Had I been in the presence of a killer and had a lucky escape?

But why Lily? Her presence, so insignificant that none of us noticed her in life, now loomed ominously large in death, regrettably, as far as Mabel was concerned; one she was determined to regard as an unfortunate incident, not as murder but as an inconvenience to herself.

I wasn't satisfied and neither I suspected was Inspector Gray. We hadn't seen the last of him by any means as later that evening he was back again asking more questions.

CHAPTER TWENTY

Olivia had sent the girls up to bed and Gray took a seat at the table with us.

'We need to ascertain who was the last person to see the young woman before the accident.' A question that to my ears again sounded familiarly like the preliminary enquiry in a murder investigation. Neither Olivia nor I were sure of when we had last seen her, used to her flitting silently to and fro in the cottage, ignoring us and never indulging in any conversation, however trivial, that might have been remembered. But we both knew that it was Mabel the inspector had in his sights, failing to understand that the girl had been her personal maid and, with all that implied, must have had a daily routine.

All I remembered was that Lily didn't go out with Mabel in the pony cart because she wasn't feeling well. And that was while we were at Braemar Castle two days ago. That was the last thing I recalled, although I had heard them after that, talking upstairs with Mabel haranguing Lily as usual. I could not swear that was only yesterday and neither could Olivia.

Gray seemed to think this very odd, until we explained that as Lily was Mabel's maid we did not expect her duties to include waiting on us, beyond obliging with an occasional cup of tea or, when Mabel was absent with us at some grown-up function, looking after the two little girls. In retrospect now, this latter made me very fearful for their safety.

Everyone was being questioned. Gray insisted that, secretive by nature, Lily was a young woman, after all, and using phrasing more delicately for our benefit, he suggested as he had done to Vince that she might have been enjoying the attentions of some young man unknown to us. He had obviously profited by his visit to the stables.

I didn't see her in the role of a flirtatious tease or a seductress, but following Gray's philosophy, boys would be boys too. Mabel immediately endorsed that Lily had visited the stables frequently.

'On the slightest excuse. I had to reprimand her on several occasions when she should have been attending matters relating to my toilet and wardrobe,' Mabel added grimly.

And so began the wearisome prospect of Gray interviewing any whose path Lily might have crossed in the faint hope that she might have told someone her life story. This included our two daily maids; the exotic gipsy-looking Yolande and Jessie in the slender hope perhaps that Lily might have shared girlish confidences with them.

They shook their heads. 'Never spoke a word to us.

Thought a lot of herself, she did. Head in the air, went on as if she was too good for us, being a lady's maid and all that.'

Olivia said hopefully that maybe she had made a friend among the stable boys, one who had been bold enough to pierce that secretive shell. I felt this was a waste of time. I had my prime suspect. The mystery man of the dark forest, my rescuer with his rifle.

I put this to Vince later, carefully omitting that incident and merely remarking how I thought I had seen Lily in conversation with him in Ballater, and that Dave our driver saw them together.

I added: 'Remember, the same man who almost missed the train in Edinburgh and was at the gipsy encampment?'

Vince, baffled for an instant, shook his head. 'Oh him, one of the ghillies,' was his only reaction as if this was quite insignificant.

'Does he work on the estate somewhere? I met him in the forest and he was carrying a rifle.'

'When was that?'

'Two days ago. The day Lily disappeared.'

Vince thought for a moment. 'The same man you *thought* you'd seen a couple of times. Come on, Rose, what's the connection – only that you've got a good memory for faces.'

I could hardly explain without telling him the reason was that at first glance he looked like Danny. That would sound so absurd, this painful reminder, no longer mentioned between Vince and me since Jack and I married. The past had ceased to exist; it had been very carefully laid in the grave beside Danny.

Vince was frowning. 'Oh, I expect this fellow will be questioned with everyone else.'

I couldn't understand, it seemed that he was the obvious person, the prime suspect. I went back to the Ballater incident. 'The way our driver Dave said it, rather coyly, seeing them together, I wondered if they might be lovers.'

'Really?' Vince sounded interested. 'Did Dave know him?' he asked.

'No, but he said he'd seen him around the stables and the description sounded like him.' As I repeated it, Vince smiled, a little wearily, I thought. 'Tall, thin, dark hair! Looked like a gipsy.' Vince laughed. 'Come on, Rose, that could apply to half the young men in Deeside. Pure coincidence.'

In my experience coincidence is never pure but there was no point in arguing. Vince was saying: 'HM had a word with me this morning. He is, of course, seriously concerned, as am I, about the fact that the girl was living in his private cottage. You know how anxious he is not to let that get abroad and I was made to feel somehow that it was my responsibility to sort it all out. Clear the path, as he called it.'

He laughed bitterly. 'He trusts my discretion. He reminds me constantly that Inspector Faro was his mother's personal detective and how she valued him. He saved her life once or twice, as I expect you know. Anyway, seems to think I helped Stepfather in some of his cases and that I might have inherited some of his genius. He is now seeing me in that role. Which is, I'm afraid, too big for me.'

A good doctor but a poor actor, I thought. That was

true. But the role wasn't too big for me, I was used to solving crimes – Lady Investigator, Discretion Guaranteed, crimes small and large, and that included murder.

I decided I would say no more, keep it from Vince, go undercover as it were, and find the answer to Lily's death, for I was certain that this was no accident.

I had not a great deal of time either; we were to return to Edinburgh after the Highland Games at Invercauld, the climax of the royal season. Olivia sadly would have to miss it; as well as her pressing London engagements, she had a family wedding, a Gilchrist niece getting married in Surrey, that she could not cancel. At her side Faith constantly bemoaned having to be parted from Meg, while Olivia's patience wore thin.

'After all, Faith knew that we wouldn't be here all the time with you,' she shrugged. 'Of course, she didn't expect her cousin Meg, so much younger, would turn out to be a soulmate.'

I sympathised since I got plenty of the same kind of moans from Meg. These domestic issues were all very trying as I had additional very real fears of my own about those Games and the opportunity they would provide for Lily's killer on the loose among all those illustrious guests.

But I was no longer free to pursue my investigations as I might have been in Edinburgh. Here I had family commitments, of the most pressing kind. I was a mother now. I had a seven-year-old to take care of, my first duties were to her, and I must never forget that with Faith gone Meg would need me to share the hours of her lonely days.

I had also expected Mabel to take her departure with Olivia, sharing the long train journey back to London, since her main reason for coming with us had been, as well as the women's suffrage meeting, to be reunited with her old friend. Some tactful hints that she would miss Olivia were dismissed with a sad shrug but she showed not the slightest inclination to cut short her holiday. She was clearly enjoying herself and had adapted to the lack of a personal maid, quite content with daily expeditions in the pony cart, either following the guns or into Ballater. Never the easiest or jolliest of companions, here she would remain with us until the holiday ended and Vince saw her safely onto the London train.

Then suddenly we heard from Vince news that we had been dreading and everything else was momentarily swept aside by another crisis looming. A crisis closer to my heart and to Meg's than even her distress at Faith's imminent departure. On our doorstep this time, the secret of Thane's presence was out.

The King knew we had a magnificent deerhound, more than usually large for the breed. And he was very interested. That was all that had been said, but it awoke volcanoes of terror.

CHAPTER TWENTY-ONE

We decided that this information must be kept from Meg. Vince hoped that with the Games looming, the King might be too busy and that by the time he remembered about the deerhound, it would be too late and we would be back in Edinburgh, with Thane safe to roam again on Arthur's Seat.

That proved to be a forlorn hope, however, and we were fated to have a quite unexpected encounter. From the cottage we often had a fleeting glimpse of HM riding out of the stables, if we were up and about early enough each morning. A creature of habit, he normally followed a set daily route around the estate which we were careful to avoid, regarding our little wood as quite safe, the only place where we exercised Thane each day, completely cut off from any view from the castle.

We had got to know it well and Meg was intrigued by

the tiny island mid-river with its monument, and each time we passed the wee anchored boat she reminded me that I had promised we were going to row over and explore.

'We can't take Thane,' I reminded her again. 'He is much too large, we would capsize. And you are never to go without me. Understand?'

The boat looked very old and fragile but I was determined to take it out and test its safety before risking Meg, especially as there had been wistful hints of a picnic with Faith before she left, arousing fears that Meg with her sense of adventure might persuade Faith to tackle it on their own.

Meg had decided that the folly was set up by Queen Victoria over a graveyard for her beloved pet dogs. I thought that improbable but it had that touch of sentiment and romance that she enjoyed, always preferring real stories rather than Grimm's fairy tales.

Suddenly Thane rushed back to us and took his place at our side.

We felt the ground shake, birds happily chirping in the treetops took off into the air with startled cries at the sound of horse's hooves and the jingle of harness.

Two horses appeared. There was no mistaking the rider in the lead. Meg and I curtseyed, expecting him to ride on, but the King reined in, looked down not at us but at Thane at our side, fearing for our safety, not his own.

'That is a very fine animal,' said the King to his companion, presumably an equerry. 'Bring him over.'

The man dismounted and came over to us. Thane

was stiffly on guard as the man approached. The equerry looked at me and said sharply: 'Why has he no collar?'

'He never wears a collar.'

'That is surely most unwise for a valuable animal,' was the disapproving reply. 'No lead either, I see, and that is a requirement on the estate.'

Ignoring that remark, I said: 'He is very obedient and will go with you if I tell him to.'

There was nothing I could do. Meg was at my side, trembling, her grip on my hand painful. Thane was looking at us both, hesitating.

'Go with him,' I said.

Thane trotted off looking offended, his backward glance at us anxious as the King dismounted.

Meg whispered: 'Why did you do that, Mam? You should have told him to run away. Hide among the trees!'

'Shh' I said. The King was examining Thane, his head, flank, ears and mouth were explored by what seemed expert hands. Through all this Thane stood alert, his head averted, and if a dog could be said to signal displeasure, he was doing so. The King of England was just another human and he was fussy about being handled, much less being touched, by strangers.

The King looked up and spoke to the equerry who signed to us to come forward. It was no more than a few paces but it felt a lot further.

Again we curtseyed and he looked up from handling Thane as if aware of us for the first time. We weren't important.

'He is your dog?'

'Yes, Your Majesty.'

'How old?'

'About ten, Your Majesty.' A wild guess since I had no idea, only that he had been with me for ten years. I could only pray that an advanced age might put the King off the idea of owning such a dog.

'Indeed? Remarkable, he looks quite a young animal.'

Turning from stroking Thane's head, he looked up at me, a flicker of recognition in those hooded eyes. 'Ah, my physician's sister, is it not?'

'Yes, Your Majesty.'

He nodded towards Thane. 'We like your deerhound. He would fit excellently into our kennels. He is without doubt the best specimen of his breed that we have encountered,' he added approvingly.

A pause as he regarded me, smiling expectantly. I made no move and the pause became longer than was polite, as I knew and he knew what was next. What was expected? That I should curtsey again and say: 'I would be honoured if Your Majesty would accept him?'

But I was damned if I would! Meg's grip on my hand was imploring. I was so angry. Who had invented this ridiculous archaic custom by which a monarch had the right to claim everything he clapped eyes on? I wasn't having any of it, it belonged to the Middle Ages and this was the twentieth century and I was a suffragette.

The King's regard was very hard now, his smile growing thin. He wasn't used to being kept waiting. His equerry was staring at me, frowning, shuffling his feet, an impatient throat clearing.

'Your dog, is he not?' the King asked again.

Suddenly Meg stepped forward, curtseyed and put a hand on Thane's head.

'No, Your Majesty. He is my dog. I cannot give him to you' – she choked on a sob – 'you can put me in the Tower of London if you wish, but you cannot have my Thane.'

Her voice broke, her courage failed and, kneeling, she flung her arms around Thane. But she wasn't finished with the King yet. She looked up at him. 'Your Majesty has a lot of dogs, but I have only Thane and he would die of a broken heart if we were parted.'

The King was taken aback; his open-mouthed equerry broke the silence, murmuring about extraordinary behaviour to me as if I was a very lax parent, adding something about the presence of royalty.

But the King cut him short, held up his hand. He looked at Meg for a moment, as she clung there holding onto Thane as if her life depended on it. He smiled thinly. 'We would not dream of depriving you of your dog and he has an excellent name. Did you know that Thane is the word used by the ancient kings of Scotland?'

The equerry whispered, twittering, and the King said sharply: 'Nonsense, Charles, besides we have no suitable bitch of his breed for mating.' Remounting, he looked down at Thane regretfully. Puzzled he shook his head. 'And we have no idea where we would find one to match him.'

As they rode off, Thane gave what was an almost human sigh of relief and we all went home to tell a shocked but relieved Vince of our encounter.

Meg was smiling now. 'He is really quite a nice man, your king, Uncle Vince,' was her verdict on the incident.

When Mabel heard, declaring Meg's behaviour quite disgraceful and hinting that she should be punished, she was also surprised that anyone, especially the King of England, could seriously want That Dog.

CHAPTER TWENTY-TWO

Now that crisis had been dealt with I knew I could delay no longer. I must leave Meg with Thane and Mabel and set off immediately if I was ever to solve the mystery surrounding Lily's death, whether it had been an accident, or whether, as I firmly believed, she had been murdered. And I had only days left to do this, even though I was acting against Vince's wishes, Inspector Gray's stern command and with precious few clues to follow.

The first place to begin was also the nearest. The stables where, according to Mabel, Lily had spent many of her leisure hours.

My entrance caused a little stir and not just among the horses. Unlike Olivia and Mabel, who were very definitely upper-class ladies, the appearance of this small woman with unruly yellow curls and a rather untidy gown raised considerable doubts as to whether the situation demanded the manner appropriate for what the stable lads had been brought up to regard as their betters. There was an air of uncertainty. Was I to be treated as serving maid or lady?

I remembered that first occasion when I had called in to enquire about a pony trap for the girls to discover that Mabel had the only one available. One lad bolder than the rest made up his mind, sallied forth and gave me an impudent stare. Another lad nudged him, winked and said: 'Go to it, Bobby.' Bobby had the look of a wide boy eyeing me up and down, considering his chances as he would all females from sixteen to sixty. A Casanova born in the wrong century and the wrong society to wreak havoc in female hearts, he was doubtless the lad Mabel had seen talking to Lily. Doubtless he had taken her on too.

Later, reporting my interview with Bobby to Mabel, she sighed wearily and said: 'I dare say she would be delighted, grateful to have any fellow give her a second glance.'

'Oh, I think it was perhaps more than that.'

On this occasion the lads came forward and stared at me again, uncertain.

'Where is Bobby?' I asked.

Jock, the older of the lads, came closer. Weather-beaten with a skin like crinkled leather, the result doubtless of forty years in charge of the stables, he shrugged. 'Where is he? Who knows, miss? (I left that misstatement uncorrected) A right chancer, that one.'

'Did he say when he would be returning?'

Jock stared at me. 'No. Just walked out. Here today and gone tomorrow. Typical of lads these days. Not like when I was young and loyal to the family—'

My mind was racing. Two days ago, around the time Lily was drowned. Was Bobby her killer? I interrupted: 'Did he say where he was going?' I smiled, trying to make it sound like a usual polite enquiry, but Jock wasn't fooled. He frowned, gave me a hard look. Why did this woman across at the cottage want to know Bobby's movements? A bit old but you never knew with Bobby. His glance suggested he was calculating if I was one of his tarts.

I knew what he was thinking and decided immediate explanation was needed. 'It concerns Lily, the young girl who drowned. Just talking to people who knew her, like Bobby,' I added lamely.

Jock nodded. This seemed to satisfy him. 'We dinna' ken all that about the lad. Came from over Ballater way. Beater first, for the shooting, when he was about twelve. His mother was a servant up at the castle. He was adopted as a bairn—'

Now that was an interesting link to follow but I didn't want his life story which, having won Jock's confidence, I felt might be lengthy.

'Was he friends with Lily?'

Jock paused and laughed. 'Friends? Is that what you ladies are calling it now? There's no word like that for Bobby, not with a lass. Ask the lads here.'

One of them listening, stopped polishing the harness and grinned. 'Not with Bobby. It was all or nothing. A leg over—'

Jock coughed, threw an embarrassed glance in my direction and the lad stopped, flushed, and resumed polishing the saddle with great vigour. Here was a reason for getting rid of Lily. Had she regarded Bobby as her

179

chance to escape from Mabel, form a new life? And had he lost his temper at that suggestion and killed her?

Jock had turned to another lad who had been on the fringes listening to the conversation. 'Pete, you kenned Bobby more than the rest of us. This lady wants to know about him and the poor lass that drowned.'

Pete came forward nodding eagerly. 'Ye ken, Jock, we all saw them at your seventieth birthday party.'

Jock took up the story, grinned. 'Aye, aye, loads of ale and other things too, ye ken.'

I suspected drugs too, as Pete went on: 'Right enough. Seems the lassie didna' understand what we were saying. Only came in a lot 'cos she liked the horses, talked to them.' He shook his head. 'Bobby didna' understand a word of it. Like foreign, it was.' That didn't surprise me. The locals were used to speaking Gaelic and I found the Aberdeenshire dialect when they reverted to it for my benefit completely baffling too.

'Aye, Bobby thought he'd made it with her, that she was maybe from one of yon places abroad, ye ken,' said Jock.

'Austria, the Lipizzaners,' the knowledgeable Pete nodded. 'Where they breed them special kind o' white horses.' He shook his head. 'Aye, kenning so much about horses, I said it was a pity they didna' employ stable girls here.'

'We wouldna' get much work done, I'm thinking,' said Jock and raucous laughter met this remark with all its possibilities where lascivious lads like Bobby were concerned.

As for me, I was getting nowhere fast, and trying to

sound casual I asked if they knew where he had gone.

Jock shook his head. 'Bobby could be very secretive-like, didna' say all that much about himself 'cept when he was bragging about all the girls he'd had. He was aye after the main chance, ye ken.'

'Was he upset about the girl drowning?'

Again Jock shook his head. 'Could be. But not what you might call heartbroken for a lass he had been courting. All he said if I mind it right was "Too bad. What a waste of a good—"' He stopped, blushed at the word he had bitten back, forgetting that I might be a lady.

'Does his mother still work up at the castle?'

Jock looked vague. 'I think she left a while back, found the work too hard for her. Chronic rheumatism, and all the early mornings, the stairs and them cold corridors.'

I asked for her name and he grinned. 'Mrs Biggs. Bobby liked his surname, said it fitted him – in every way, ye ken.'

Thanking them for their help, I left with great dignity and a feeling that without doubt my interest would continue to be a talking point and a matter of some speculation.

I was certain Bobby's sudden flight was connected with Lily. Either he had killed her or her killer suspected that she had passed on to him some dangerous information. Anyway, I had gained something. I had a name. Would Mrs Biggs be a large enough needle to find somewhere in a haystack in Ballater?

Mabel was sitting at the window reading a book about the suffrage movement she had brought with her. I wondered if she still felt a bit let down now that the speech she had worked on for the Pankhursts' welcome had not been needed after all.

She looked up and said: 'I saw you coming out of the stables.'

It was a question really, so I told her about Bobby and Lily and what the lads had told me. She nodded absently, didn't seem interested, keen to get back to her book.

I said I thought I would go to Ballater and hoped that a woman who had been a servant at Balmoral Castle would be remembered.

And I got some help from Mabel. One of the suffrage ladies had also been a servant and might possibly know a Mrs Biggs. A forlorn hope maybe, but it was a beginning and I was ever optimistic – having started from less in some of my past, most successful cases, I knew the value of tenacity.

Mabel offered to take me in the pony cart next day, but I declined. Time was vital and with the address of a certain Mrs Semple I set off on my bicycle. Fortunately it was a pleasant afternoon. I loved the feeling of warm sunshine and no disagreeable wind to hold me up. The wheels turned smoothly as the miles disappeared and I gave thought to what lay ahead supposing I met Mrs Biggs and Bobby.

I had established a certain set of rules in my profession. If you want information it is important at that first meeting to put your prospective client at his or her ease. Never pitch yourself too high. Thankfully my unfashionable appearance gave me an air of informality. I flattered myself that it gave clients confidence and I could drop a notch further when necessary. I can speak upper-class Edinburgh but I have a less formal accent for all occasions which I used in Arizona where Danny and I frequented the saloons in the company of cowmen and prostitutes, the latter from whom I learnt some remarkable self-defence which I had used to good effect when necessary.

I was lucky at Ballater to find Mrs Semple at home. She recognised me from our meeting in Aberdeen and, too polite to ask why, said yes, she remembered Mrs Biggs from the days they were servants together. A very nice woman, and yes, as far as she knew she was now living at Crathie. There were not a lot of houses and she should be easy to find.

Politely declining the invitation to tea and doubtless satisfy her curiosity regarding my mission, I remounted my bicycle and set off, thankfully with the wind at my back, on the few miles back to Crathie. Deploring the fact that I had probably passed by her door en route to Ballater, luck was with me and the first person I encountered was the local postman walking along the road past the church.

He pointed to the cottages just above us. 'Mrs Biggs? Aye, number four just along there, second house,' he replied, eyeing me curiously and with not a little envy, I fancied, obviously not used to seeing a young woman riding a bicycle that would have made his life very much easier.

The cottage, small and neat, was one of six with a splendid view towards Lochnagar. Thanking him and following his directions I tapped on the door, holding my breath. Would she be at home?

The door opened. 'Mrs Biggs?'

An immediate explanation for the reason for my visit was not necessary. As was the custom, I was first politely invited in; the bicycle parked outside her immaculate garden frowned over doubtfully as a possible blot on the landscape.

The interior of the pretty, ivy-covered cottage lived up to what one might expect, the smell of lavender polish over well-cared for sideboard and table, handsome home-made rugs, embroidered antimacassars on armchairs and plump needlepoint cushions. Exclaiming over them in the course of conversation I discovered that Mrs Biggs had been no ordinary servant but a favourite needlewoman to the late Queen.

I was not the only visitor. She was having tea with another lady from our Aberdeen meeting, Mrs Rayne, who welcomed me and began by asking after Miss Penby Worth. She sounded rather in awe of her but both ladies, as I joined them at their afternoon ritual, were more than a little curious about the purpose of my visit.

I had to think of a good reason swiftly. A quick think provided the answer. I turned to Mrs Rayne. 'This is a most fortunate coincidence, but it is you, Mrs Biggs, I wished to consult. You see, since we have been staying in a cottage on the Balmoral estate, my little daughter, Meg – she's seven – is very interested in horses and I believe your son Bobby, having worked in the stables, is an expert.' (Nothing like a bit of flattery.) 'They tell me he has moved on but I would like a word with him as I wish to purchase a suitable pony for her.'

It all sounded a bit lame to me but Mrs Biggs seemed quite impressed. She beamed at me. 'You're in luck, Mrs Macmerry, Bobby is at home right now, has a new situation down south, but came to see his mum first for a wee visit.' She added fondly, 'He's such a good lad.'

Mrs Rayne took the hint and rose politely and said to Mrs Biggs: 'Thank you for the tea, my dear.' And to me, 'Please remember me to Miss Penby Worth.'

There followed a few quick words about the next suffrage meeting, in whose house and what time and I looked round the walls at a collection of photographs, some family and some suffrage, a banner in the hall. If you were a Roman Catholic you had a photograph of the Pope but for a member of women's suffrage it was Emmeline Pankhurst.

As the door closed on Mrs Rayne, Mrs Biggs called: 'A lady to see you, Bobby.'

Bobby peered out of the kitchen where he had obviously taken refuge from his mother's visitor, his anxious expression going over what new misdemeanour was being brought to his door.

His smile was a question, that curiosity wiped out completely when he realised who I was and that I was from Balmoral.

'Mrs Macmerry is here to ask you about horses, dear. She wants a bit of help buying a wee pony for her little girl. You'll be able to tell her all about that, I'm sure,' she added proudly.

Bobby gave me a quizzical look, smiled at his mother, and giving her a hug, he seized his jacket from the chair: 'Have to go now. Couple of lads to see at the pub. Be back later.'

I thanked Mrs Biggs and said goodbye. Bobby closed the door behind him, no longer the vibrant wide boy, and seized my arm firmly. I indicated my bicycle.

'Did you come all that way on that thing?'

Not waiting for a reply he frowned, looking over his

shoulder nervously as if his mother might be watching. 'Now what is all this about, missus?' That backward glance confirmed one thing. He was scared.

'Your mother misunderstood me—' I began.

'She does that a lot,' he murmured. 'Go on.'

Wheeling my bicycle, keeping pace with him, I said: 'I'm enquiring about Lily.' He paused, his step had faltered. 'Lily?' he said.

'Yes, you remember Lily. And the policeman who came to the stables.'

At the word 'policeman' he suppressed a shudder as I went on, 'They have to have some details, you understand. Name, address and so forth of her parents.'

'Couldn't the woman she worked for, that friend of yours, tell them that?' he said impatiently.

I wasn't prepared to go down that tedious road. 'You know what employers are like,' and aware that he probably didn't, I went on hastily, 'As she seemed to be friendly with you, I wondered if there was anything extra you could tell us about her. And as I was heading this way—' I lied.

'I know nothing,' he interrupted. 'Hardly knew the lass.' He stopped. 'Is that all?' he added firmly.

It looked like the end of our talk. I said: 'I gather you have a better job to go to. Better prospects ahead than the stables at Balmoral.'

He looked rather sick. 'Who told you that?'

Ignoring that question, I smiled. 'Why else would you leave?'

He stopped, rubbed his chin and said coldly: 'I was told to leave, day before yesterday.'

'Dismissed, you mean?'

'No, nothing like that. I was – warned off.' He sounded angry, indignant now.

That was a surprising piece of information. 'By whom?'

He shook his head. 'Don't ask me. Someone high up, I was given a message, handed ten quid and told to go and not to ask any questions.' He took a deep breath and sounded scared as he added, 'Said I wouldn't get any answers.' His voice rose. 'Just leave. Leave now, if you know what is good for you, that's what they said.' He paused 'Otherwise—'

'Wait a minute. Who were "they"?'

'Don't know. A man. Kept out of sight.'

'Anyone you would recognise? What he looked like.'

He laughed. 'Have a heart. It was dark, I was coming back to the stables.'

'You must have some idea what he sounded like.'

He shrugged. 'Taller than me, hoarse kind of posh voice. Think he had gloves on when he put the money in my hand.'

I stopped and looked at him. He was telling the truth, no doubt about that, and he was still scared. I said slowly, 'So you were threatened.'

He nodded. 'Exactly. So I packed my gear and went.'

'But that is terrible,' I said.

'It's terrible, missus, to have your throat cut – or, like Lily, be found drowned.'

'You don't think it was an accident?' I asked quickly.

He laughed harshly. 'Don't ask me to answer that one, either.'

'Hey, Bobby!' Two lads were approaching and I knew

I would get no more information. But as I rode back to Balmoral, I had sufficient to confirm my suspicions, although no one else would be willing to believe me, not even Vince.

I was certain after meeting Bobby that he had not killed her, their brief relationship had meant no more to him than any of the other one-night stands with willing females that made up his love life. He would have simply laughed at her suggestion of a permanent life, of marriage based on their slight intimacy, told her not to be daft and walked away.

But to someone, Lily as Bobby's lover had suggested that his continued presence at Balmoral was dangerous. I didn't imagine for one moment that someone was a jealous colleague in the stables.

The fact that he had been warned off by a man 'with a posh voice' had sinister implications. I was now certain that Lily's death was no accident. It had been carefully planned.

But why? For every murder there has to be a motive and that I was determined to find out. After all, ten pounds was a hefty sum of money, a small fortune for a stable lad to clear out and keep his mouth shut.

CHAPTER TWENTY-THREE

Only a few days remained before Olivia and Faith were to travel back to London by sleeper on the royal train to prepare for the imminent family wedding and a very tight schedule indeed.

Before they left us, however, Vince decided that no holiday for them would be complete without a visit to Loch Muick and a picnic at Glas-Allt-Shiel. He would drive us in one of the motor cars, followed by ghillies lured from the guns ostensibly to fish for trout, which were prolific in that area of the Dee at this time of year. The holiday was made all the more memorable knowing that the King and his entourage were also at Glas-Allt-Shiel.

Having considered this as a family outing I was surprised that Olivia's friend, Alice von Mueller, was to come with us.

'I was sure you wouldn't mind,' said Olivia. 'She is so lonely and unhappy, I thought it would be a great treat for her.'

'Of course, she's most welcome,' I said and Olivia looked relieved.

'She did so enjoy meeting you.' The anxious look that accompanied it, hinted that Olivia had not given up hope that I might be able 'to do something for Alice's problem'.

Without wanting to be heartless, unhappy marriages weren't in my territory. I had met quite a few potential clients in Edinburgh and had to turn them away. A counsellor wasn't quite the same as a detective. Advice – and I gave the best I could – was not the same as solving a crime. And I could only offer my services if a crime was involved.

I tried to explain this to Olivia – without success, I'm afraid – who viewed a cruel husband from the security of her own loving relationship with Vince. She had a tender heart for lost causes and made friends easily; friends like Mabel, who I suspected only she could understand and who was, quite frankly, something of a trial to the rest of us.

Mabel had shuddered at the very idea of a picnic. As for the idea of a row on the loch, greeted with cries of delight by the two girls, that did not tempt her in the least. She would remain in the cottage with That Dog. Her decision was a relief as I had been wondering what to do about Thane. We would only be gone for a few hours but I was nervous about leaving him behind with the ghillies, as he was too large to go out in the rowing boat. I felt grateful to Mabel, as with the addition of Alice, Vince driving with her and Olivia in front, Meg, Faith and I in the back seat, a huge deerhound would have been unmanageable.

The weather was perfect and augured well for our planned day as we were greeted by a beautiful morning, a sheer blue sky. The road was rough and narrow in places, but not too difficult given the good weather we had that day. A few unexpected swerves had us clinging to the sides of the motor which, however, kept its equilibrium and behaved well in the circumstances. But I did tremble to think what it must have been like on horseback or in a pony cart just a few years ago when, in those sudden fierce Highland storms, the rain fell not vertical but horizontal.

Another curve and we got our first glimpse of the loch. According to Vince, who had visited it many times, in its variety of weathers it looked either noble or sinister.

'Muick in Gaelic signified darkness or sorrow,' said Vince. 'Stepfather knew it well: on one of his cases when he was the Queen's personal detective at Balmoral, he saved her life here from an assassin.'

I had a sudden cold feeling as he said: 'You probably know all about it.' I shook my head. Although Vince had often assisted him through the years, Papa never talked to us about his cases, especially any that involved royalty. His discretion was absolute.

The Queen had loved Glen Muick. I quoted from her journal: 'The scenery is beautiful here, so wild and grand, real severe Highland scenery with trees in the hollow. We had various scrambles in and out of the boat and along the shore, saw three hawks, caught seventy trout. For an artist the scene so picturesque, the boat, the net, the people in their kilts in the water and on the shore. The ghillies steered going back and the lights were beautiful.'

I had to agree with her, breathing in that clear air, her account sounded as if it had been penned just yesterday.

'You should see it from the other side of the glen,' said Vince. 'It's even grander, stretching away up to a great chasm filled by the waters of the loch. One can agree with "severe", and in weather not ruinous to the view "solemn and striking" may seem adequate.'

He laughed. 'A recess for those who like the bare bones of the heath rather than the prospect of Nature feathered and furred.'

The Queen had decided soon after leasing the original Balmoral from Sir Robert Gordon that it lacked the sufficiency of solitude. Noticing a lone cottage far up the glen in the wilderness beyond Birkhall, she considered that it had potential as a habitable shelter when the passion for still more privacy or even more strenuous exploration was upon her. The replenishing, its enlargement by a wooden addition, was followed by another small house a few yards away. This outpost nine miles south-east of the castle, on Abergeldie land, was called Alt na Guisach, after the name of the burn which poured down from Lochnagar to join the River Muick.

Our destination was closer. Glas-Allt-Sheil, 'cottage of the grey burn' or 'the widow's house', was built by the Queen after Prince Albert's death when she could no longer bear to stay at Alt na Guisach with its happy memories of their times there together. Of more modest proportions with fewer rooms, it was useful for access across some very rough country rising behind. Glas-Allt-Shiel lay at the remote end of the loch where the burn runs in from the White Mounth, snow-capped before autumn, in the midst of a few sheltering trees and a little wooded promontory running out into the water surrounded by precipitous rocks.

As rugs were spread on the ground for our picnic, a group of ghillies were disappearing towards the fast-flowing river, nets in hand. In kilts and bonnets, and in their midst a tall, dark-haired man, hatless. My heart signalled his presence even before my eyes, and I wondered again about the story of John Brown and the Queen. Was it a myth as I realised I was seeing Glen Muick exactly as she had a generation ago? This was the land where time left no mark, with stones and boulders older than recorded history.

There were abundant trout in the loch still and present-day midges too, which would be equally troublesome in the evening, by which time we would have completed our day's activities and be on the way back to Balmoral.

After we had consumed the contents of the picnic baskets, salmon sandwiches, fruit and Dundee cake, it was time to take the boat out on the loch. I was glad to see Alice laughing, looking happy and relaxed as we marched down to the promontory, the boat which was quite large swaying slightly as we clambered aboard. The once empty blue sky was now occupied by a few fleeting clouds and a slight breeze ruffled the water. That was enough to cause me some concern as Vince took his place alongside the rowers while I sat with Olivia and Alice, the girls running forward to the bows, shrill with excitement and utterly fearless.

As we steered away from the shore, I gulped and took a deep breath. I have faced many terrors in my life and learnt to cope with them in the wild west of Arizona, but neither Apache raid, arrows or bullets scared me more than moving water, the fear of drowning.

Everyone, they say, has an Achilles heel. And this is mine. My recurring nightmare. Despite Orkney ancestry and an allegedly selkie great-grandmother, the natural ability to swim had been left out of my inheritance. Yet a possible storm on the loch had taken me by surprise. I had no unpleasant memories from childhood of crossing the notorious seas between Orkney, where Emily and I lived with Granny Faro after our mother died, to Edinburgh and summer holidays at Sheridan Place under the care of Papa's excellent housekeeper, Mrs Brook.

Curiously enough my sea crossing to Orkney a year or two back, which I had anticipated in terror, was like a millpond. Perhaps travelling across smooth Orcadian waters was a blessing in my inheritance from Sibella, my great-grandmother.

Now as Meg and Faith beckoned us to move forward and feel the spray, I put on a brave smile. They were enjoying it, as were Olivia and Alice, no qualms or uneasiness in either of them. They did not seem to notice or feel alarmed that the sky had lost its tranquil blue and dark clouds were overhead. Vince, too, was enjoying himself with the other three rowers, sharing a joke.

I looked over the edge, the waves were gathering

around us, swirling, reaching out. The boat leapt suddenly and Vince shouted: 'Sit tight. Nothing to worry about.'

One of the ghillie rowers grinned. 'There's a storm approaching, ladies, but don't worry we are quite used to it and this wee boat can cope with anything.'

His companion grinned and nodded reassuringly. 'You are quite safe with us.'

I didn't believe him for a moment. We were now some distance from the shore, the idea being to row to the top of the loch as far as Birkhall and back again, a two-hour journey.

And I knew I would never make it. I felt my stomach heaving, delicious salmon sandwiches about to put in another appearance. In a few moments I was going to be very sick indeed. And that would not be the end of it; as well as disgracing myself and making everyone feel uncomfortable, this nauseous condition would continue until I stepped back on dry land back again.

Olivia's hand was on my arm. 'Are you feeling quite well, Rose?'

'No. I feel very ill indeed.'

'Oh, then we must go back immediately, get the rowers to return, Vince—' she began.

He did not hear her against the creak of the oars, but the girls turned their heads, regarded us, frowning and I knew I could not do this to them, spoil their day.

'No, Olivia. Just seasick, I'll manage.' I tried to sound cheerful.

She stared into my face. 'My dear, you've gone quite green.' She stepped forward, clinging on to the side and spoke to Vince. He turned and I heard her say: 'You must tell the rowers, we have to return, Mrs Macmerry is unwell.'

Cries not of sympathy but bitter disappointment from Meg and Faith, resentful looks too, I fancied, at the odd ways grown-ups could behave. I had ruined their day, this and not the picnic was what they had really been looking forward to.

It was Vince's turn to look anxious.

'No,' I said firmly, 'just put me ashore on the shingle over there and I'll make my way back to Glas-Allt-Shiel. It isn't far.' I pointed. The chimneys of the house were still faintly visible.

'Are you sure?' asked Vince.

I nodded and he asked the rowers who were resting on their oars waiting for a decision to be reached: 'Can you do that?'

'Aye, Doctor.' One pointed landwards. 'Over there. There's a wee sheep path to the top.' But Vince was still uncertain. He looked at me anxiously.

'I'm a martyr to seasickness, Vince, but all will be well once I'm on dry land.'

He glanced at Olivia. The two girls looked close to tears of disappointment. In something of a quandary, he nodded: 'Very well, if you're absolutely sure.'

As the rowers turned the boat and headed towards the strand, it was Olivia's turn to look uncertain, as she shaded her eyes to regard the tall cliff standing a hundred feet high above the shingle. Sheep were grazing on the top.

'Will you be all right, Rose? Are you sure – it's very steep?'

'Don't worry,' I said to her. 'You heard the lad say there's a sheep path.'

There was no evidence of that as the boat approached the rock-strewn shore and it did look alarmingly steep at closer quarters, a cliff towering above us, seven hundred feet and rising sharply.

But I had no option now, feeling increasingly sick, with an alarming headache of mounting magnitude. I knew the symptoms, my stomach still remembered them again from the two terrible sea voyages on the big ship back and forth from New York to the Clyde. Once to go out and join Danny in the 1880s, and back again, to return alone without him ten years since.

I looked again at the high cliff. I would rather risk the invisible sheep path than feel that death would be too good as I did at the moment, aware that I could not contain the contents of my stomach much longer.

I looked at the others in the boat as it bobbed up and down like an enormous cork. They were unmoved; I was to be alone in my predicament. Oh, the shame of that in front of them all. A precarious walk up a cliff path was nothing by comparison, the easier by far of two evils.

The boat slid towards the beach with its dark brooding cliff hovering above, even more threatening than it had looked offshore. The rowers knew the area around Glas Allt-Shiel well and amid reassurances said that I must take extra care as the path was very narrow.

'If you're afraid of heights, don't be tempted to look down back the way you came.'

His companion nudged him, a warning that he was being tactless.

Olivia steadied me in the swaying boat as I removed my boots, preparing to wade ashore. Meg was watching, biting her lip.

'Shall I come with you, Mam?'

What a sacrifice! It took some effort but I managed a confident smile. 'Of course not, dear. This will pass.' She looked up at the cliff and shivered. I could see it scared her. She didn't like heights.

'See you back at Glas-Allt. Enjoy the trip,' I added. The boat ground onto the shingle and as Vince lifted me over the side, the bile rose into my throat and I prayed that I wouldn't be sick over him, then and there.

On a nearby rock, I waved to them as I sat down and put on my boots again, watching the boat turn back into the swirling waters waiting to engulf them. It looked dreadful and I fought mounting urges to be sick just watching them, suddenly fearful for their safety and for Meg, fearless, heedless of danger, very much her father's daughter. I groaned. If anything happened to her . . . and what of Jack, heartbroken for all time, when I had promised to take care of her?

Even as I tried to banish such thoughts, the boat had become a tiny bobbing object only occasionally visible, rocking and rearing above the waves, growing smaller, almost indistinguishable from the waters of the loch.

As I began my climb I was soon aware of my own danger for the first time. The narrow path worn by the sheep occasionally disappeared completely or came perilously near the edge of the cliff with only feet between me and a rapid descent onto the rock-strewn beach below. I decided not to look down again, once was enough for vertigo, another kind of sickness eager to take over as my main concern. Above, the path turned and twisted like a drunken man's progress. Seemingly endless, it was often slippery with sheep droppings, another hazard to be avoided.

I stopped to draw breath, no sign of the boat any longer. As my path veered to the left I hoped it was just out of sight, hidden by sea spray and not under the waves. Far above my head, I heard an ominous rumble. A deep, sharp rumble of falling stones. I stepped aside, flattened myself against the shelter of the protective cliff wall.

And not a moment too soon, for it no doubt saved my life as I watched the shower of large stones bounce off my path and thunder down to the shore.

Horrified, I realised had it not been for my swift movement I would have been carried with them. Heart pounding, I was afraid now to resume my perilous journey, for the path in front of me was also partially blocked by the fallen stones which I would have to negotiate. What if this was just the start of an avalanche? What and how had it started? An animal, one of the sheep – and yet another more terrifying thought – a human?

Had someone from Glas-Allt tried to kill me, aware that I was getting too close to Lily's killer?

Another sound, more stones, more in the path ahead, so I was trapped. I crouched flat against the cliff face, considering how I could possibly continue my upward journey, my legs shaking now. Obviously the person, for person it must be, was pushing the stones over the edge and my only hope was to stay rigid against the cliff. But how long could I remain there and who on earth could ever come to my assistance?

I tried to negotiate one of the larger stones in the path and suddenly realised that my presence was known. A face looked down from above, the top of the cliff, some twenty feet above, a face growing quite familiar now.

My rescuer from the dark forest and my executioner.

CHAPTER TWENTY-FOUR

'Stay where you are, miss. I'll come down and give you a hand. Are you hurt?'

'No. Just petrified!'

'Wait. Don't move. I'll explain.'

I hoped it would be a good explanation as I heard another ominous rumble, and minutes later the rest of the tall figure of my rescuer edged down the path, a hand held out for me to grasp. A strong, warm, somehow reliable hand. As I clung to it, he said:

'Follow in my footsteps and I'll see you safe to the top. It isn't far now.'

His hand was like a lifeline, I had to trust him. At last, breathless, the flat top of bitten grass. Around us the sheep darting away.

'There go your beasts who started the avalanche, two of them were fighting and dislodged the stones.'

Was that the truth? I had to believe it. 'Thank you,' I said and he released my hand. 'How did you know there was anyone on the path?'

He grinned, pushed a strand of dark hair off his forehead. 'Saw you leave the boat. I was wondering about that. Not a good day for a row on the loch. Those sudden squalls can be very nasty. Blowing hard and I could see the rowers were having a job pulling against it.'

As we walked towards Glas-Allt, I saw that there were a lot more gathered than when we had set off in the boat. The fishers had been increased by some of the sportsmen who had abandoned the guns to fish for trout instead. They were distinguished by their tweeds and their hats – popularly known as 'deerstalkers' – from the kilted ghillies.

My rescuer did not adhere to either sportsman or ghillie, informally dressed, hatless in breeches and jacket. The sportsmen had gathered outside the hut, relaxing after their fishing efforts with a long line of trout strung across the veranda.

Even at a fair distance the air was heavy with cigar smoke and the pungent odour of whisky, useful also for keeping the dreaded midges at bay, although it was early in the day for their onslaught.

The King was with the fishermen, seated on the veranda, easily spotted in any crowd, a large, regal and commanding presence, suddenly just a man enjoying a joke and a drink with his friends and doubtless a few foreign princes who were distant relations. I recognised one of them, Graf Hermann von Mueller, Alice's husband who I had seen walking with her in the gardens. He looked genial enough, hard to believe that he treated her so cruelly.

There were no women present, this was an entirely male activity and as I hesitated, my rescuer, tall at my side said: 'You're still a bit shaken, aren't you? Scary thing to happen.' He was warm and close, a supporting arm which I no longer needed but was in no hurry to decline. He took out a flask.

'Here, have a dram, well known for its restorative powers.'

I lifted it gladly and he watched, those strange amber eyes on me, as I drank.

'What on earth made you leave the boat, miss?'

So he had seen it all. I felt a shiver of fear, realising that this had also been his opportunity to get rid of the woman who might be dangerous, for even if he denied all knowledge of Lily I was still certain that if he had not killed her, then there was some connection.

What if the gardener I saw at Penby and this man were one and the same, could he have been her lover and pursued her to Scotland? Her interest in the Lipizzaner horses and her reluctance to converse with us hinted that she might be foreign. My mind raced ahead. Perhaps there were more sinister depths to her death, she'd been sent here on a secret mission.

As we neared the veranda, I shied away from the idea of joining this male enclave with explanations of my presence. And as my rescuer also had an uncanny aptitude for reading my mind, he was aware of that and said: 'Perhaps you'd rather return to the cottage?'

I nodded gratefully and he smiled. 'Very well. Allow me to escort you.'

'Are you sure?'

'Of course I am sure or I wouldn't have offered. Excuse me one moment.' A bow and he walked swiftly to where the main group of sportsmen were gathered. Gestures and nods indicated messages to be passed on. Then he was back again and leading the way to where the motors were parked and stable boys looked after the horses.

'Do you drive?'

He shook his head. 'Not one of my accomplishments, I'm afraid. But over there, look – there's Dave snoozing at the wheel. He'll take you safely home. There's plenty of time, his services won't be needed for a while yet.'

Dave bolted upright and saluted him as we approached. A word and we were installed in the car.

I felt an apology was needed to my travelling companion about taking him away.

He laughed. 'Not at all. My work's done for the day and as I don't enjoy cigars and bad jokes, all of which I've heard before, I'm glad of an excuse to leave.'

We sat in silence after that, the return journey seemed a lot shorter than when we set out this morning. Perhaps that was because I enjoyed the presence of this man, warm and strong and close, especially on the swerves of the motor, which brought us into even closer contact. I liked his profile too, now that I had a chance to study him near at hand, the straight nose, the firm chin. I was beginning to like everything about him and not only because at first encounter he had reminded me of Danny, of a life and a love lost for ever.

But the possibility that he was Lily's killer I could not shake off. Intuition played an important part, a useful accessory to a career as a successful detective. That much I had inherited from my father, Chief Inspector Jeremy Faro.

All my intuitions were basic and the evidence pointed strongly in his direction. There was something alive and dark and threatening swirling unseen below the surface of what appeared as a pleasant summer holiday on a royal estate. That something I must unravel. Even if it proved him guilty.

What if he had already tried and failed to kill me once that day and the sheep's activities causing an avalanche were an invention? However, for the precious moments of that drive back through Glen Muick in a smiling landscape calm and beautiful in the late afternoon, I was willing to suspend my suspicions that I sat by the side of a ruthless killer, who might well strike again.

CHAPTER TWENTY-FIVE

At the cottage Mabel had watched my arrival from the window. Thane leapt out to greet me. His almost human look of concern reminded me of an anxious parent for a missing child. That he had been aware of my danger was confirmed when Mabel grumbled: 'That Dog has behaved in the most incredible way ever since you departed. Wanting to get out. I knew I must restrain him since that was expressly forbidden,' and eyeing him at my side: 'He is the most spoilt animal I have ever seen.' That said she asked where were the others and why had I come back alone?

There was no point in dissembling. I told her the truth, that I was a martyr to seasickness. She shrugged. 'It was your own fault then for agreeing to accompany them. Besides, picnics are an intolerable waste of time and effort and the maximum in discomfort. All that sitting around on damp grass, having to eat without proper implements, fighting off insects.' Another shudder.

I took Thane for a walk and talked to him. At least he seemed more understanding than Mabel. Had he been afraid for me? Again that look of concern. 'I wish you could talk and answer me, Thane. It has been the one important missing factor in our life together. And at this moment there are so many missing clues regarding poor Lily that I am sure you could help with.'

We had just returned ahead of Vince. Leaving Olivia and the girls, he was driving Alice back to the castle. Leaning out of the motor, she asked anxiously how I was and assured that I had completely recovered, she smiled.

'You look yourself again,' she said and stretching out a hand she added sadly, 'I had hoped for a long talk today but the opportunity never came. Perhaps we can meet again before you leave.'

I was sure by her anxious look that the long talk would be a repetition of her problem, which she hoped in vain I would be able to solve, but I gave the polite response expected.

Mabel had made a pot of tea. She had found herself quite accomplished at minor kitchen tasks without a personal maid. 'I suppose I had better get used to it,' she grumbled with a long-suffering sigh and as we ate a swiftly prepared meal of ham, sausages and eggs for the hungry homecomers, they wanted to know what had happened to me. Leaving out alarming details of the avalanche, I explained that one of the ghillies had brought me in a motor car driven by Dave who had passed on the information to them when he returned to Glas-Allt-Shiel.

Meg and Faith were ecstatic about the row on the loch, all the things they had seen, herons and a golden eagle and all manner of wading birds. 'It wasn't nearly as bad as you imagined, Mam. The storm only lasted minutes and after that it was quite smooth. You really would have loved it, you should have stayed and we would have looked after you.' And taking my hand, 'We missed you.'

Everyone was tired and Olivia reminded Faith that it was bedtime. Tomorrow they would be travelling back to London to prepare for the family wedding. Faith, reminded of their departure, was again near to tears at leaving Meg, only the prospect of that bridesmaid's dress awaiting made her smile.

I felt sad at them leaving so soon, as Olivia insisted that Jack and I and Meg must come to St James and enjoy all the marvels London had to offer. At that moment it was as remote as the prospect of visiting another planet and although in retrospect I had spent far less time with Olivia than I had hoped for, my sadness was nothing compared to Meg and Faith, who parted with tears shed, promises of everlasting friendship, with letters and as many visits as they could possibly fit in.

A story I had heard before, it was also the story of Olivia and Mabel to some extent as they again parted outside the cottage where Vince awaited to drive them to Ballater. The same promises that they must have made many years ago, and I wondered if both of them had felt let down at the meeting they had looked forward to for so long. They had a walk together most days, when the weather was fine, but from my conversations with Olivia I gathered that their meeting had failed as the joyous reunion those letters over the years had anticipated.

Vince returned from the railway station looking rather bleak too but with stiff upper lip intact. He was used to longish separations from Olivia, Faith and the boys. He merely looked sadly round the now so empty cottage to where Meg was sitting tearfully with her arms around Thane, her accusing wounded looks in our direction blaming us for taking her best friend away.

As Vince departed I suspected that Meg was gearing up for another impossible argument about Faith staying with us, so I went upstairs to my bedroom, made some notes about the visit to Bobby and settled down until supper time to finish off the drawing begun on our train journey to Ballater.

It was of Lily sitting opposite, remembering that I had hoped to give it to her as a present. Perhaps if we found her parents I might send it to them, as offering it to Mabel might be regarded as a merely tactless reminder. I sighed; it belonged among my many other sketchbooks containing portraits and drawings from over the years – some happy times, some sad – an ability, Jack said, which was quite remarkable since I was able to draw from memory.

'You should have been an artist,' he said. 'It's a great gift.' I smiled wryly; the only use it had been to me was in my profession, remembering faces and being able to reproduce them as Jack now did with such ease, his new toy a photographic camera.

There was still no word from him, but that was not

surprising. We had said all the things to each other that mattered, but those daily postcards to Meg had become less frequent. I had hoped there would be one that would have cheered her up, now that she was very low in spirits, feeling the whole world was against her.

I was finding problems watching over Meg allied to the role of a detective with a possible murder to solve. There was no one I could turn to except Vince, with whom I must discuss my visit to Bobby Biggs, although I was pretty sure what his reactions would be. Perhaps that's why I put it off.

I was right about that. If I expected to be applauded for my actions I was sadly mistaken. Even as I began I could see from the way his face closed in at the mention of Lily that he did not approve. Even before he sighed and said sternly: 'You put yourself to a lot of unnecessary trouble, Rose. Why on earth don't you just enjoy the holiday, this unique opportunity of a cottage at Balmoral that I was able to arrange for you? Everyone has been most accommodating, all meals prepared for you once more if you wish, since Olivia, who enjoyed the role of chief cook has left us. You have everything that I had negotiated for you,' he repeated reproachfully.

'Dear Vince,' I said, 'Please don't think for a moment that I'm ungrateful.' I paused. 'It was all going so well until Lily—'

He held up a hand, but before he could utter more than a murmur of protest, I went on: 'There have been developments. The stable lad, Bobby Biggs, was threatened.'

He looked at me. 'Wait a minute. What do you mean, threatened?'

'Warned off. I don't suppose you know or realise the significance of that?'

And as I told him the exact words from my meeting with Biggs, I expected a reaction, natural curiosity, but his expression never changed. He merely sighed.

'Aren't you even just a little surprised?' I asked indignantly.

'No, Rose. I'm merely thinking the obvious.'

'The obvious?' I repeated.

'Yes, Rose. Don't you see it yourself?' he added patiently. 'That was the prepared story he was telling everyone. If you searched his employment record, you would find that Biggs had committed some misdemeanour which had upset a person in authority.' Pausing he shook his head. 'That sort of thing will not be tolerated here—'

'To the extent of having his life threatened?' I interrupted. 'That person must have been very high in authority.'

Again Vince sighed wearily. 'All I meant is that he overstepped the mark. The moral standards are very high for even the most menial in royal employ. They have to be. And it's fairly clear from your talk to the stable lads that he fancied his chances with the ladies, and the likelihood is that he made some improper advance to one of the maids up at the castle. A complaint was made and as it probably hadn't been the first time, knowing the lad's character, he was dismissed.'

'With ten quid in his hand,' I said slowly, 'that's a lot of money.'

Vince smiled. 'Not at all and not a bribe. A year's wages, Rose, and rather generous in the circumstances, if you consider it.'

We went on walking, silent for a moment. Suddenly I decided to tell him about the man I had seen when we went to collect Mabel at Peebles and then seeing him again and on the Ballater train.

'Could you be sure of that?' Vince interrupted. 'There was a man working but he was some distance away. I certainly would never have recognised him again.'

Although I was no longer sure, I was reluctant to admit that.

'I have very good eyesight and an excellent memory, never forget a face. It's an essential in my profession,' I reminded him. 'If this was the same man, then he followed us to Scotland.'

Vince was silent. He studied me, frowning, then said quietly. 'You could be mistaken, Rose. The man on the train, who I think is one of the ghillies, maybe reminds you . . .' He paused and eyebrows raised, added casually, 'A slight resemblance to someone?'

'So you've seen it too.' I had a heart-sinking feeling, knowing he meant Danny but would never say so.

He smiled sadly. 'It is not unusual, a medical fact indeed, that when one loses someone close, particularly in tragic circumstances, in the depression that follows, a patient shows a tendency to imagine strangers who bear a slight resemblance to convince themselves that their loved one is still alive.'

'I am not imagining that,' I said indignantly. 'I know Danny is dead. I saw him die – to save my life. Remember!'

My voice broke and he put a comforting arm around me. 'I know, I know, Rose dear. He is dead, but not for you, not ever. You'll keep on seeing him. The Penby gardener was the first and the ghillie fellow who was on the train—'

'What is his name?'

Vince frowned, thought for a moment, shrugged and said. 'Not sure. Brown, I think.'

I laughed. 'Mr Brown and Mr Green, very colourful names for those working at the castle. Are we to meet a Mr Blue, Red and Yellow and even Orange – we already have – or had – a Miss White.'

Vince didn't think it funny. 'Brown is very common hereabouts, the name the Highlanders adopted when their clans were sequestered.'

A moment to let this information sink in then he said sharply: 'Take my advice, Rose, that part of your life is ended for ever. Be thankful you have a husband like Jack, who understands you so well, and don't go chasing a ghost of the past.'

This was the nearest Vince and I had ever had to a disagreement, but worse was in store.

'And I must beg you, Rose, for my sake if not for your own, if there is any mystery regarding Lily or anyone else for that matter, it is not yours to deal with, and by mystery I mean meddling in affairs that don't concern you. Remember you are on royal property, the rules are different here and your actions could well endanger my future too.' And reminding me again: 'You are my guest and I am responsible to HM for you. And if you do something to offend him, then I will suffer too.'

At least there had been no repercussions over the King's interest in Thane and Meg's spirited reactions, as Vince went on: 'In the nature of my situation here it follows that I am trusted implicitly not to introduce anyone who might be a troublemaker.'

I wanted to ask if the description 'troublemaker' could also apply to a killer, but we were interrupted by one of the footmen hurrying towards us.

Doctor Laurie was needed urgently. There had been a scalding accident in the kitchen to one of the maids.

CHAPTER TWENTY-SIX

Next day Jack walked in unexpectedly. No letter, no warning. He wanted to surprise us, having a few days respite after being in Aberdeen for what was proving to be a very complex and exhausting investigation regarding a criminal organisation in Edinburgh with links in other cities.

I had been so looking forward to seeing him and so had Meg, although maybe not quite so much as me. Thanks to Vince, she was making new and exciting friends and yesterday had been to a children's party up at the castle. Several of the young royals were present including the King's grandson Edward, son of the Duke of York. She said he didn't join in the games and added scornfully that he thought a lot of himself and was at the age when boys didn't like girls very much.

But to return to Jack's unexpected visit. As ill luck

would have it, on the morning before he arrived, having been given a lift from Ballater railway station, I realised I was feeling distinctly unwell, in for a horrendous cold, or even the dreaded influenza. No one else had it, thank goodness, and heaven knows where I picked it up. I rarely take ill but when I do the symptoms make up for that rarity in their severity. A streaming nose, a violent headache equal I was sure to any of Mabel's, who eyed me with anxiety, perhaps touched with resentment since the province of severe headaches was hers alone.

There was nothing I could do but retire to my bed with lemon drinks fortified with hot toddy or medicinal whisky, keep out of everyone's way and hope to sleep myself better. I did not want to pass it on and if I was thankful for anything, it was that the delicate Faith had gone home.

Jack came upstairs and took one look at me. Sympathy tinged with irritation, I suspected, as if I had got the damned cold just to be awkward.

He sighed; he had so many plans for the precious few days together. However, he soon came round to forgetting all about me lying in my sickbed upstairs by spending every moment with Meg. I heard their voices from time to time, merry laughter drifting upwards, while I could hardly raise my head and felt that death would be too good.

I was just beginning to recognise signs of survival when Jack was about to return to Edinburgh, the carter giving him a lift into Ballater for the train next day.

Apart from sitting at my bedside and chatting for a

while after Meg went to bed, we had had no time together, as I insisted that he sleep in the bedroom Meg and Faith had shared, which considering my state of health, did not grieve him in the least.

As I rallied on his last day, it was imperative that I talk to him. I had a lot to tell.

'Anything interesting happen?'

'I expect Vince has told you about Mabel's maid?'

The two men had spent convivial evenings downing drams together by the sounds of laughter drifting upstairs.

He nodded. 'What a tragedy. Mabel must have been very upset.'

It wasn't like that at all, I realised, the version he got from Vince. 'Did Vince tell you that it might not have been an accident?'

Jack groaned and patted my arm. 'He said Rose thought it might not be and I thought, "There you go again." Typical. You can't resist it, can you? Here for a holiday and you seize on a drowning as suspicious circumstances.'

He laughed and regardless of any lingering germs, gave me a hug. 'Darling Rose, all you get when you have time on your hands is an overactive imagination.' I began to protest vigorously. Only that morning, hearing male voices in the garden had revealed below my window, Jack and Vince in deep conversation with Inspector Gray.

When I asked why Gray was here, Jack shrugged. 'Just a private matter.'

'Staying at the castle?'

'I believe so.' And that indicated the private matter concerned the royals.

'Someone stealing the spoons?' I said lightly, aware that Inspector Gray's presence meant considerably more than that; it suggested matters of deep concern to the state.

Jack smiled and said hastily: 'Nothing to do with us, love.' And eyeing me steadily with what I knew well enough to be a warning look he went on: 'Whatever you're thinking, love, just forget it, please. You're not here for a murder investigation, even if the girl's death wasn't an accident, it's none of your business or mine. They have a very efficient division, I'm sure, dealing with such matters.'

And suddenly, because I was being misunderstood again, I wanted to tell him about the Penby man, or Mr Brown as Vince had called him. But I was trapped. If he asked me why I was so interested, I couldn't say it was because he reminded me of Danny.

Danny was the forbidden subject, it still hurt him to be reminded that Danny was the love of my life, my first love and that he believed he could never be more than second best.

And yet I had learnt to love Jack, I owed my survival to him in tricky situations back in Edinburgh where my investigation into a murder case had gone seriously wrong.

In all relationships someone once said: 'There is one who kisses and one who is kissed.' Jack knew which was his role. He loved me with a depth of passion I could never return and it had made him happy that after years of saying 'no' I had married him, although he protested at the time it was only for Meg's sake to give her a mother. I insisted that it wasn't, I had given him my word, and my solemn promise in those wedding vows, that I loved him.

We were happy, the three of us and I thought that was all that mattered.

Now, as he was leaving, I wished I could gather up Meg and we could go back together. But Meg had another party to go to and she had made a new friend, Rowena, whose mother Yolande worked in the kitchens and, with Jessie, brought us our daily meals and did our laundry. The exotic Yolande was a real gipsy. Meg was very excited about that.

And then there was Mabel to contend with. What to do about her? After the disappointment of the Aberdeen suffrage experience, when she had hoped to meet the Pankhursts which was her main reason for coming to Scotland, it would have been reasonable to expect that she would have wished to make the long journey back to London with Olivia. But it had obviously never occurred to her to cut short the Balmoral holiday, which had been a happy coincidence, and it would have been hardly tactful or polite to suggest it when she seemed quite content to remain with us until after the Highland Games and then return to London on the train via Edinburgh.

Alone with her most days, she was not the most engaging of companions by any stretch of imagination, a rather dull woman, self-centred to the extreme, a law unto herself, who I knew not one whit better after three weeks living under the same roof than I did at our first meeting. Always polite, our conversations were negligible and mostly concerned with day-to-day domestic matters. She no longer talked of dear Emmeline and Christabel and seemed to have forgotten all about them, although her reading matter was still devoted to books about the movement.

After Olivia's departure when we had been somewhat relieved to revert to meals delivered from the royal kitchen, never fond of walking, Mabel either spent time in her room reading or on most days with the pony trap driving around the estate, following the shooting party or driving into Ballater. I suspected that she was a lonely person when in a rare moment of confidence she said it reminded her of the governess cart of her childhood, and when she suggested that any time I wished I could accompany her into Ballater, I felt rather guilty as, thanking her, I declined since I had my bicycle.

Perhaps it was the symptoms of the cold that had struck me down, but after Jack left I was unhappy, ill at ease and homesick for my own home, for Arthur's Seat and Edinburgh. Suddenly I felt confined by this cottage holiday, which instead of a month of easy, happy, carefree days enjoying a new experience, had seen a tragic accident to one of our party, which I still believed was murder. I had almost quarrelled with my beloved Vince, and Jack's hoped-for visit had seen me laid low with an atrocious cold and fizzled out like a damp squib.

Meg, however, with all the resilience of childhood seemed to have forgotten her heartbreak over cousin Faith and had found an exciting new friend, off each morning to play with Rowena. We hadn't met as yet but Meg whispered proudly that although Rowena lived in the royal household her mother was a true Romany and they had once lived in a caravan.

Thane had also been temporarily abandoned in her new regime, which was not a bad thing. I had no means of knowing how he regarded this temporary desertion. He did not reveal any sign that he had lost Meg and merely returned to being my shadow, my loyal protector.

But even in the brief time we had left, the holiday had its surprises and some grim events lay in store.

CHAPTER TWENTY-SEVEN

My thoughts were never far from Lily's death, where every instinct as a detective told me this was no accident whatever they wished to pretend, and any reasons for upsetting the royal shooting season's apple cart appeared thin indeed.

Murder was murder and being expressly forbidden, also by Jack, to keep out of it, did not lessen my determination to solve it. What was the hidden agenda, what were the authorities, namely Inspector Gray, so anxious to conceal? I realised it was becoming an obsession, a permanent itch impossible to ignore. With another week to endure before the Games and our return home, I thought longingly of Solomon's Tower.

What upset me most of all was the change in my long and loving relationship with Vince. We had always been close but since we came to Balmoral and particularly since Lily's death, his attitude towards me had changed completely. To my horror he saw me as a potential troublemaker, meddling in affairs that did not concern me but might have disastrous repercussions on his position as physician to the royal household. I had never seen Vince in a role where he was afraid of anything before but that warning to me held a risk I could not take.

I felt very let down by present events – even Jack had dismissed my suspicions about Lily and I felt wounded, that he should have known and understood me better. However, during those long evenings having drams together while I lay upstairs nursing my wretched cold, I suspected that Vince had persuaded Jack as well of the somewhat vague explanation of Inspector Gray's presence at the castle, all of which added further to my conviction that there was more than a servant girl's murder at its core. I needed to escape for a while from a cottage that had become claustrophobic, my thoughts going round and round like rats trapped in a cage. I needed to lose myself for a few hours in the calm beauty of the landscape, in the hills that had been here long before humans and would still be here when humans with all their griefs and joys were no more.

At least I still had Thane, loyal and faithful, nothing had changed there. At home in Solomon's Tower when I was perplexed by an apparently unsolvable crime, I would climb through Hunter's Bog to the heights of Arthur's Seat and look down on the sprawl of Edinburgh city far below. It always helped to clear my mind and I would return home more often than not with a key to the labyrinth.

It just might work here. I would climb the hill on the Tomintoul road overlooking the castle, with its magnificent view of the undulating hills of Deeside, past Bush Farm, the one-time home of John Brown, who had created such an almighty stir in the late Queen's reign. A troublemaker and worse, King Edward's resolve had been strengthened to remove all traces on the estate of his mother's favourite ghillie.

I would take my sketchbook and Thane, although we had to make our journey across the estate by a circuitous route. This did not seem necessary since Meg's outburst regarding her ownership of Thane unless the King made his own secret arrangements and decided to kidnap him. But in this particular part of the world with royal prerogatives one never really knew what was law and what wasn't, so I decided to err on the side of caution and continue to avoid any contact.

It was a lovely clear day; autumn's changing colours were still to come, with no hint beyond a time of mellowing, of deepening colours and a golden glow over everything. The treetops looked heavily burdened, overleafed and weary somehow. As if having accomplished all that nature intended, blossomed, flourished and provided shelter for little animals and nests for the next generation of songbirds, as well as their more raucous uncouth neighbours, they were ready to sigh and shed their leafy load and go to sleep until spring woke them again.

Our climb was assisted by a slight but welcoming breeze. At last we reached a suitably sheltered place to set up my campstool.

As I began drawing, at my side Thane seemed content after exploring new smells and sounds with canine intensity. He had enjoyed the longer walk and exercise after being restricted to the wood by the cottage.

Suddenly he sat up, alert, a low-pitched growl.

'What is it?'

Turning his head, he stared towards the top of the hill behind us and I saw the glint of sunlight on glass. Twin circles – someone with binoculars was watching us.

I wasn't afraid. Thane would take care of me and he was more than a match for any man. But I felt anger now, all I had wanted was a bit of peace to draw, now it was being invaded and I felt too uneasy to relax. Small chance of that as footsteps were descending, twigs snapping under swift-moving feet. Branches being pushed aside as the watcher was making his way downhill and had to pass us by if he was to continue down the track.

He came into view a few yards away and my heart thudded as my senses recognised that fleeting resemblance, the tumbling locks of dark hair, even the walk. Vince had recognised it. And did anyone who ever knew Danny see it – would Jack too, I wondered?

I stood up, deciding to confront him this time.

'Good day to you, Mr Brown.'

He stopped, a moment's bewilderment as he looked back over his shoulder. And I knew the grim truth, it confirmed my suspicions. That whatever Vince said, Brown was not his real name.

Thane was leaping towards him, seeing him as a threat. I was safe enough. But wait a moment, what was going on? Thane had reached his side and, far from confrontation, there was a lot of tail-wagging, excited barks. Thane had found a friend. And so had Mr Brown, stroking him, ruffling his ears.

'Hello, old chap, how are you?'

I was taken aback. I was not witnessing a polite meeting of strangers but a reunion as Brown crossed the short distance, his hand on Thane's head. He came close, close enough for the echoes of spent tobacco smoke. Even if he didn't smoke cigars, those he associated with did. The smell of old tweed, this male closeness disarmed me. My body yearned to lean into that warmth. It struck a chord long since lost, reminding me of greeting Danny after one of our long absences from each other in Arizona, while he went far afield on business from Pinkerton's Detective Agency. When I never knew if I would ever see him again, always afraid I would lose him. Which I did.

From his tall height, looking down at me, he smiled, an endearing smile. 'You are not lost this time, miss, I'm relieved to see.' And squinting at the drawing. 'That's very good.'

'Thank you, Mr Brown.'

Again that slightly baffled smile, that wavering moment.

'I see you have put your binoculars away. Why were you spying on me?'

That startled him. An uneasy shrug.

'Just walking, were you?' I asked.

Ignoring my question, he said: 'May I?' leaning over so that I could not see his expression clearly, he had taken refuge in turning the pages of my sketchbook.

He pointed to the drawing I had made of Lily, and said: 'This looks familiar.'

I felt embarrassed. There was one of him on the next page, drawn from memory.

'Did you know Lily?'

'Lily?'

'Yes, the girl who drowned.'

He was concentrating on turning the pages. 'No.'

'I saw you talking to her.'

'Did you?' He did not raise his head, the question casual, of no importance.

'Yes,' I said.

He sighed, closing the book. 'I don't remember. Perhaps she was lost,' he smiled. 'Like you, asking me for directions.'

So he was lying. He knew it was Ballater. I felt triumphant.

'I don't think that was the reason.'

'Why not?' He regarded me slowly, a patient smile.

'She wasn't English, Mr Brown.'

He was silent, frowning now, staring down over towards the turrets of the castle still far distant.

I had to know more about him, fill in the gaps. He was no ordinary ghillie, that was for sure. Not one of the visiting sportsmen either. He just didn't belong in either category, or on the Balmoral estate. Alien somehow to these surroundings, as if he had wandered into this place, this time.

'Brown isn't your real name, is it?'

He turned those strange luminous eyes. 'No. The men call me Saemus.'

'You're a Scot?'

He shrugged and I persisted.

'Or Irish. Is it Irish you are?' (Like Danny, my heart fluttered) 'Saemus is the Gaelic for Thomas.'

He looked away frowning, towards the distant hills,

the far horizon as if they might provide the answer.

Then with a shrug: 'I am nothing,' he said coldly.

That seemed odd and I asked: 'Why are you here in Balmoral?'

He had recovered whatever he was in danger of losing by my questions. He smiled. 'Perhaps I am a guest like yourself.'

'I don't think so, you don't dress like the sportsmen, or the ghillies.' I paused. 'No, you are a man here with some purpose. I can recognise that. And you appear unexpectedly in strange surroundings.' I could not say Penby, but I added, 'I saw you with the gipsies when we first arrived, on our way here.'

He gave that a moment's thought. 'A social call. They are my friends, they speak my language.'

'Gaelic?'

Again he shrugged. 'Metaphorically speaking, I understand many languages.'

'So you are a scholar too?'

He looked away. 'Perhaps.'

I took a deep breath. 'I think you knew Lily. And that you killed her,' I said slowly, even knowing it was madness. Looking at Thane, after that show of friendliness I could no longer rely on his protection. In a minute this man's hands would be about my throat, but there was no water here to conveniently dispose of my body and have it dismissed as drowning.

In one swift movement, he dropped down to my side and took hold of both my hands. It was handholding, a warm friendly gesture. He wasn't going to kill me. 'Why all these questions?'

'That is my business.'

Suddenly he was laughing at me. 'You are not a very clever detective, Rose McQuinn.'

That startled me. 'How did you know my name?'

He turned away, his face suddenly sad. 'I know everything,' and letting go my hands, no longer warm, he stared ahead down towards the castle. 'And if I were to kill someone, and I do know how,' he said coldly, 'I would do it differently.' He picked up a twig and snapped it. 'Not dump them in the river, hoping the body might be washed into the sea forty miles away.'

And I knew he spoke the truth. He had killed but then so had Danny and so had I, a necessity of survival against hostile Apaches and bandits in Arizona.

He stood up again, and looking down at me, bowed. It was suddenly an old-world gesture. Whoever he was, he had the manners of a gentleman but without another word, he turned and walked quickly away down the hill.

The weather was changing, a chill wind had taken over, clouds overtaking the blue sky, sweeping in from the west. I was no longer in the mood to draw. I went back to the cottage, going over that odd conversation, remembering those strange eyes, amber in colour. Not in the least like Danny's blue Irish eyes, but tantalisingly familiar.

And I knew where I had seen them before. I looked into similar eyes a dozen times a day, every time Thane leapt up to greet me.

CHAPTER TWENTY-EIGHT

Later the girls, Mabel and I were having lunch in the garden, enjoying the warm sunshine. As I gathered dishes together, I thought I saw Bobby Biggs. He was at the stable door, looking towards the cottage but standing back as if he didn't want to be seen. I held up my hand, gave him a wave of acknowledgement, but he darted back into the shadows.

This familiarity obviously struck Mabel as odd and I said: 'That was the stable boy Bobby who was friendly with Lily. I just wondered if he was waiting to see me. That he might have some news.'

Mabel gave me a bewildered look. 'What kind of news?'

'About Lily.'

'You make very strange friends, Rose.' And her shrug of indifference as we went into the kitchen left no desire to go into the details of our conversation.

The postman was due on his daily round from the castle. I saw him approaching and went to the door.

'A moment, if you please, Andy.' He came in, had a polite word with Mabel, who seemed at a complete loss to understand his accent, but nodded politely.

I picked up the letter I had written to Olivia, searched for a stamp, handed it to him and said to Mabel, 'I'll be back shortly.'

She pointed to Hector, the pony she now regarded as her own whose cart took her on her travels around the estate. He was happily nibbling at the hedgerow awaiting her instructions.

'If you're wanting a lift somewhere, we can take you wherever you want to go.'

She was always generous about that. I was grateful for the occasional offer of transport into Ballater but preferred my bicycle unless we needed emergency provisions.

I smiled and thanked her. 'No need, I'm just going across to the stables.'

There was no sign of Bobby lingering about and Jock said: 'You've just missed him. Left a couple of minutes ago.'

'Did he say where he was going?'

Jock grinned. 'No use asking me, miss. Bobby's never the one to let his right hand know what his left hand is doing. Proper close, he is. He's taken a horse, borrowed the one he used to ride. Said it was urgent, he had someone to see, but he'd be back promptly.'

If I hadn't hesitated to deal with that letter for Olivia, I would have caught him. I had even heard a rider going past the window. It was infuriating.

Jock was looking over his shoulder as if he might be overheard by the rest of the lads. 'Not allowed officially,' but patting his britches pocket, he grinned, 'made it worth my while, if you get my meaning. He'll be back shortly and I'll tell him you were looking for him, miss.'

'Did he say why he'd come back? I thought he'd been fired,' I added, remembering the threat and the ten quid.

Jock stared at me. 'Ye ken more than I do. All he said was that he had to meet someone.'

And I guessed the reason. He had run out of money or just wanted more, a bit of blackmailing which fitted into his character. But it was annoying. Meanwhile it was obvious that Jock found my questions and my interest in Bobby intriguing, especially remembering his reputation with the ladies – bragging about being irresistible to ladies of all ages.

'I'll tell him you're wanting to see him,' Jock repeated and I was conscious of his eyes watching me with a very calculating look as I walked out of the stables.

I could hardly linger outside without more sniggering speculation once Jock told the lads about my visit. Mabel had departed with the pony cart and I decided to sit in the garden with my book, remaining vigilant for Bobby's return. Nearby, Meg and her new friend Rowena were having a game where Thane was involved, his usual dignity suspended, chasing after a stick. He was becoming a very domesticated dog, I thought fondly, wondering how he would react to our return home with Jack and I often out and Meg at school all day.

Rowena was now a constant visitor. I expected all gypsies to look like, well, Egyptians as the name originated, but Rowena was quite different, with red hair and green eyes. A very pretty ten-year-old but her education was no match for Meg who said in tones of awe: 'Rowena has never read a real book, Mam. Never! Just think of that. But she loves fiddle music and knows lots and lots of songs. And she sees things.'

'What sort of things?'

'They call it second sight; all of them – the ladies that is – have it. They can find lost people.'

That was interesting. 'What did she mean by lost, a long time ago or just lately?'

'Oh, both. They can find babies taken from their mothers and bring them together again.'

It all sounded intriguing but very weird, especially looking at Rowena who seemed just a normal happy girl, and if Meg was in awe of her, then she returned the compliment. She seemed slightly in awe of us – the gringos.

It was good to see Meg so happy again, and enjoying the warm sun on my face, I relaxed and put the book aside. I must have dozed off, awakened by the sound of a horse trotting past on its way to the stables.

That would be Bobby returning. I sprang up and hurried across, trying to make it look if he was watching that it wasn't urgent, that I was just passing by.

My excuses weren't needed. Jock was patting the horse which had obviously been galloping, while the other lads gathered round. They looked scared.

Jock saw me and said: 'The beast's returned alone – just look at the state he's in.'

'Has he run away from Bobby?'

Jock shook his head. 'Not likely miss, I think something else has happened. Got thrown off.'

'Never Bobby,' someone else said, 'Great rider, even bareback. Never known him to be thrown.'

'Well, there's always a first time,' Jock replied and as one of the lads took the horse and was rubbing it down, he seemed to realise what I was there for. 'No doubt, he'll be walking back at this moment, cursing the beast. He'll get some teasing, that's for sure.'

I said: 'I hope he's all right.'

'Dinna ye worry, miss, He'll be in a fine old temper after a long walk back, but I won't forget to tell him that you're waiting to see him.'

With that I left them, but I felt a sudden chill of unease. After all they had told me about Bobby and horses, I had a niggling feeling that if the horse returned without him then he must have been thrown and might have been hurt.

I hadn't long to wait for an answer.

I'd hardly set foot in the kitchen when I heard the pony cart return. Mabel rushed in, her face white.

'Oh Rose. I've just seen a young man, lying on the track beyond the wood. We nearly ran over him. I got down, took a look to see if I could help. He murmured something when I asked if he was hurt.' Wringing her hands, she went on, 'I couldn't understand what he was trying to say, and didn't know what to do. I couldn't lift him into the cart, and bring him back here.' She shook her head. 'I know nothing about first aid or what to do with someone badly hurt. So I told him just to lie still and I'd go for help.'

Meg and Rowena had seen her arrive and as she was

237

obviously crying and distressed, they followed her into the kitchen.

I said, 'Go across to the stable and tell Jock there's a man lying injured, beyond the wood. I think it's the lad whose horse came back without him. Tell them to bring a stretcher.'

As I rushed out to get my bicycle, Mabel said: 'Shall I come? I know where he is . . .'

Listening to her directions I said: 'You stay here,' knowing she wouldn't be much use. I had dealt with, nursed and bandaged a lot of badly injured men in my far-off days in Arizona. It was not an experience I expected to encounter on the royal estate.

CHAPTER TWENTY-NINE

It was Bobby Biggs. I was bending over him as minutes later Jock and the lads with cart and stretcher arrived. As I had feared, just one look, and I knew he was dead. His head at a queer angle told a grim tale. He had been thrown and his neck was broken.

As the lads gathered him up, Jock, shaking his head sadly, looked at my face. I was shocked and sad. It seemed such a waste of a young life. Jock said: 'Dinna ye grieve, miss. He didna suffer. Not with that neck. Died immediately.'

Perhaps he was trying to spare my feelings and I didn't contradict him by saying that he had still been alive when the lady who found him gave the alarm.

One of the lads had sent for Vince and he was already at the stables by the time our sad procession with Bobby's body got there.

My presence wasn't needed and in the cottage Mabel was sitting by the window. She had made a pot of tea and asked anxiously, 'Is he all right?'

I shook my head. There was no need for any further explanation. She sighed deeply. 'You were too late to save him. What a pity. Such a young man too.'

I needed that tea and I said: 'Tell me again what happened?'

She repeated word for word how she had almost run over him, and got down to see if he had been injured.

'The horse had thrown him, his neck was broken.'

She gave a shuddering sigh. 'How awful!'

'They said they thought he had died instantly. But he was still alive when you found him. Can you remember what he was trying to tell you?'

She looked at me blankly. 'Just mumbled some words.' And shaking her head, 'I was upset not knowing how to help him, what to do.' She paused, her hand trembling as she put down the cup. 'You know I have problems understanding what people here are saying.' Again she paused and then in a whisper she went on, 'I think it was that someone had attacked him.'

I felt a sudden chill. If that was so and Mabel had heard correctly, then this was a second murder. While Lily's body lay in a temporary grave awaiting further information regarding her parents, her killer had struck again. There was little doubt in my mind now after my visit to the stables and Jock's information that Bobby had come to see someone urgently, that he had returned in the hope of extracting more money to keep his mouth shut and whoever he was blackmailing had killed him.

Vince called in on his way back from telling Bobby's mother. As always these necessary interviews upset him considerably. He had never got used to breaking tragic news. 'Fortunately, her older son and wife were having supper with her at the time. But she was in a terrible state and I got the impression when they tried to comfort her that Bobby, although adopted, mattered most. I got the impression that he and not her real son was the apple of her eye.' He paused. 'It always amazes me how much normally well-concealed family feelings can be revealed by a sudden tragedy in the blink of an eye.'

'What will happen now?'

'Oh, the usual information to the fiscal, that sort of thing. But in the case of accidents on the estate, it's just a matter of course.'

'Is it now?' I asked. 'Are you sure this was an accident?'

He looked at me and groaned. 'Oh, there you are, off again, Rose. If every fatality in a great mass of servants and estate workers and tenants was to be regarded as murder, we'd need a resident police force.'

'Such as Inspector Gray,' I said slowly.

He ignored that. 'The lad's death was the kind that is not unknown, and certainly without any suspicious circumstances. His horse threw him, broke his neck.'

'Mabel said he was still alive when she found him, muttered something about an attacker.'

Vince looked at me. 'Is that so? I would have said that death was instantaneous.'

'He had been fired,' I said patiently and I repeated what Jock had said. 'He was here to see someone urgently. And that sounds to me like suspicious circumstances, namely to blackmail whoever sent him packing into parting with more money to keep his mouth shut.'

'For heaven's sake, Rose. We've been over all this ground before.'

'No, we haven't, Vince. It must have been someone on the estate and that was why he borrowed the horse for half an hour.'

Meg and Rowena came downstairs. They had been playing in Meg's room and Vince said, 'You still here, Rowena? You should have been back ages ago.'

An apologetic shrug from Rowena. 'We were having a fine game, Dr Laurie.'

Vince said: 'Never mind that. It's late and your mother worries about you, so come along with me.'

And as they left I could not help thinking this was the perfect excuse for cutting short our conversation.

Meg and I took Thane for our usual evening stroll. We did a circuitous path as I wanted to avoid the wood where half a mile away Bobby had died.

Meg was asking if Rowena could come and stay overnight and I said yes, if her mother would allow her.

She sighed. 'Her mother isn't like you, Mam. She makes such a fuss about everything. Anyone would think Rowena was made of glass, or just stupid!'

Back at the cottage, I hoped to talk to Mabel but she had retired to her room with her book. My questions would have to wait until tomorrow. I saw Meg off to bed and came downstairs, thinking of poor Mrs Biggs and of Rowena's mother. The devotion parents can bestow like shackles on children who yearn to be free.

I did not sleep well that night. The window had no

shutters, and although the curtains were pretty they were no match for the moonlight which streamed in like a forbidden searcher, lighting every corner and keeping me wide awake, my thoughts going round and round, back and forth, over and over the day's events.

At breakfast next morning, Mabel seemed to have recovered from the shock of her discovery. In fact when I mentioned Bobby Biggs she blinked as if she had never heard of him.

'It just occurred to me last night, Mabel, after you had gone to bed, can you remember if you met anyone when you were out in the pony cart before you, er—found the young man.'

She thought for a moment. 'Well, I did see someone, one of the ghillies, I suppose, about ten minutes earlier. But I thought nothing of that, they are always around the wood. Why do you ask?'

'I just wondered, that's all, if he might have some information.'

'What kind of information, Rose?'

'Oh, just if he saw the horse bolting. That sort of thing,' I lied.

Mabel nodded and I asked: 'What did this man look like?'

She frowned. 'I didn't see him up close. But he was youngish, tall with dark hair.'

She didn't need to say any more, or I to ask any more questions. That cold chill went through me again.

The description matched perfectly: Mr Saemus Brown or whatever was his real name.

CHAPTER THIRTY

If I wasn't satisfied that Bobby's death was an accident, neither was Inspector Gray. He was back again asking questions and suddenly I was a suspect.

'At the stables they said that just after Biggs left with the borrowed horse you came looking for him. Can you tell me why, Mrs Macmerry?'

'I thought he might have information about Lily.'

At her mention, Gray winced. 'Is that so?' And before waiting for my answer, he said. 'The lads thought it was odd that you were so interested in Biggs who had a way with women.'

'What you are hinting, Inspector, is outrageous and ridiculous!'

He shook his head and said: 'It has been known, especially women who look younger than their age.'

That was either flattery, which I did not expect from

him, or more likely a veiled insult. I said: 'Very well, I'll tell you what it was all about.' And I went into the whole story, Bobby threatened, given ten quid to leave.

Gray listened, his face impassive, giving nothing away.

'So when you saw him, you presumed he was here for a bit of blackmail.'

'That is correct. And I think he met up with his intended victim who killed him.'

Gray sighed deeply. 'Mrs Macmerry, the horse threw him. That was how he died. An unfortunate accident that can happen to the most experienced of riders.'

'But there are ways and means of making a horse throw his rider.'

Gray tapped his fingers on the table, a dismissive smile. 'Don't you think your ideas are a little fanciful, Mrs Macmerry? This is all circumstantial evidence that would never stand up in court.' He paused. 'There is another matter. Can you account for the bicycle tyre marks where the body was found?'

'Of course I can. When Miss Penby Worth rushed back to the cottage, she was in a state of shock. She guessed that he might be badly injured but he was still alive and had mumbled something, she thought, about an attacker. I took my bicycle and went immediately.'

A thin smile. 'That could be concluded by a jury as being before as well as after the accident.'

I gasped in amazement. 'Are you accusing me of . . . of—'

'Of murder? No, Mrs Macmerry, but you must admit that knowing your unfortunate propensity to investigate not only imaginary crimes but ones that are none of your business . . .' Pausing, he gave me a hard look and continued: 'The interest you displayed in him might suggest reasons for a *crime passionnel*. A personable young lad, who had rejected your advances.'

'Stop! Stop right there, Inspector,' I interrupted. 'Stop talking nonsense. Have you forgotten that I am a happily married woman, the wife of Inspector Macmerry?'

He shook his head solemnly. 'Indeed no. But does that make a difference?' At that he stood up, leaving me speechless with fury. 'Now I'll bid you good day.'

I was still thinking of a reply, reeling at his accusations and wanting to throw something at him as he made a dignified exit.

That might have been the end of it, except that on the very next day Mabel was attacked.

After breakfast I learnt later she had gone to the stables for the pony cart, to find that there was a problem with one of the wheels and that she would not get it that day. Disappointed, as it was a fine day, she decided to make do with a walk.

Meanwhile I was washing the breakfast dishes with Meg, a willing helper, drying them. Rowena would be arriving later so we prepared to give Thane his morning exercise together.

Suddenly the door opened and Mabel rushed in. Muddied, dishevelled, her face white, she was sobbing, terrified and quite inarticulate.

I made her sit down, tried to calm her.

'What happened, Mabel? Did you fall, did you have an accident?'

She gulped. 'No accident, Rose. I was attacked. A man tried to kill me. In the wood.'

I sat down opposite, she was still hysterical. Meg gave her a glass of water, she gulped it down.

'Have you something stronger?'

Vince's excellent brandy which Olivia had left with us was produced. She made good use of that and it seemed to work. With a sigh, clenching her hands together, her eyes still wide with terror – a frightened horse came to mind – she unreeled the terrifying story. Between sobs, and sips of brandy, I got the gist of it.

Unable to have her pony cart, for her daily excursions for her health, for fresh air and exercise, the latter which I might have questioned as there was little exercise in sitting in a cart for hours, she was making do with a brisk walk following the path she usually took through the wood.

She wasn't concerned that it took her very near the place where Bobby had his fatal accident, but it was just yards from the scene set for a second fatal encounter. This time her own.

Meg was holding my hand. I told her to go to Uncle Vince. He would alert Inspector Gray if he was still somewhere in the confines of the castle.

Mabel was saying: 'I took a path through the trees alongside the river. Thought I heard something. Voices and rustling. Like footsteps. Decided it was just an animal.' She gulped, looking bewildered, remembering. 'Then – then he leapt out at me, threw a sack, a disgusting smelly sack, Rose, put it over my head and tried to push me down the bank to the river.' Wringing her hands she went on: 'I was terrified but I knew I was fighting for my life and thank God I am strong. I struggled, kicked out and the next moment I was on the ground. He had gone.

Those voices I had heard were part of the shooting party with their dogs.

'They got me to my feet, asked what had happened. There was no sign of my attacker and I didn't want to make a fuss. So I said I had slipped and rolled down the bank, and they said I was lucky, another few feet and I would have been in the river.'

She clutched my hand, 'Oh Rose, if those people hadn't been near, they saved my life.'

I asked the obvious question. Could she describe her attacker?

'He felt like a tall man, but I never saw his face. He grabbed me from behind.'

I realised this was something else for Inspector Gray. But it didn't make sense. Why should anyone attack Mabel? Again that missing motive. She had nothing to do with Bobby, although there was a link with Lily.

It was beginning to sound as if we had a madman at large, an unseen maniac now attacking a defenceless woman. Who next? I wondered.

The sound of a motor outside. Meg must have run all the way. Inspector Gray emerged with Vince, who had advised Meg to stay with Rowena.

Satisfied that Mabel had suffered no injuries, Vince departed and Gray took a seat at the table opposite a forlorn-looking Mabel who had not yet attended to her muddied skirt and boots. She would have to do without a personal maid this time.

'Am I to understand that you have been attacked, Miss Penby Worth?'

'Indeed, yes. Just an hour ago.'

And out again, the same story, word for word as she had told me.

Gray listened patiently, an occasional nod, or that habit of tapping his fingers on the table. At the end, he asked for the description of her attacker. Again she had no notion, guessed only that he was a tall man, taller than her and very strong.

A short silence as Gray made some notes and I said from my place by the window: 'As this happened the very next day after Bobby Biggs' accident, do you not think the two incidents might be related?'

Gray swung round to face me. 'In what way, Mrs Macmerry?'

'I've just realised . . . perhaps it was the same man Miss Penby Worth noticed at the time just before she found the body.'

Gray turned swiftly to her. 'So there was someone else on the scene when the accident happened. Can you describe him?'

As she spoke I closed my eyes. I had my own picture of that tall youngish man with dark hair.

'If he had attacked the stable lad, Inspector, then perhaps he believed I had seen him, and as it was well known that I went out in the pony cart every morning, it is possible that he was lying in wait for me.'

I looked at her. We had both reached the same conclusion.

Gray thanked her and made another note. There was a certain finality in his action and Mabel asked: 'May I ask what you intend doing about this, Inspector?'

'This is a serious case of assault but we have no reason

to believe there is any connection with the stable boy's fatal accident yesterday. The fact that you were attacked very near the same spot could well be a coincidence. We will certainly look into it.'

I never had any faith in coincidences. I distrusted them implicitly. Later that day Mabel was eager to unroll the full story to Vince once again. Vince was relieved that, although uninjured, she had suffered no after-effects so far, but appalled by what might have been the result. A third death.

The story of Mabel's attack was verified. One man had been with the shooting party who had found her in hysterics by the river, the sack that had covered her head lying alongside.

'It will certainly help Gray in his investigation,' Vince said.

'Who was the man?' I asked.

Vince frowned, thought for a moment. 'Oh, Brown, I think.'

Again that chill went over me. Brown, or whatever his name was, also fitted the description of the man Mabel had seen on the scene of Bobby's accident – or murder. He also fitted the vague description of the man who had attacked her. And it was no problem for him to apparently be the first on the scene to have found her.

CHAPTER THIRTY-ONE

An independent investigation whatever its consequences was now seriously overdue. I was running out of time. Soon it would be too late, the end of the holiday looming in sight, only days away. Walking with Thane that morning I was certain that he would be glad to be home again and welcome the freedom of roaming about Arthur's Seat. If he could have talked, I was sure he would be sharing my sympathy for an outdoor animal confined for a month to the area around the cottage and woods with scant chance of the exercise he was used to. Or often having to sit for hours on end alone or with Mabel when the girls and I went to the castle gardens and areas forbidden to him.

Mabel still referred to him as That Dog and endlessly complained about him, although once she had mellowed enough to suggest he might like to run alongside the pony cart. Declining her offer with suitable excuses I wondered if this was because she feared another attack.

At that she laughed. 'You need not worry about my safety, Rose.' She smiled. 'I will be armed if there is a next time.' And I remembered that according to her, she was a crack hand with a rifle.

At least she seemed to have overcome her initial hostility to That Dog and conceded that some animals could have quite exceptional, almost human, intelligence. Perhaps this was after Meg had reported our encounter with the King. In Mabel's eyes, if royalty cast an approving glance on him that marked him down as somehow rather special.

I talked to Thane a lot, but I felt the bond we had shared for ten years was slowly diminishing. He often seemed to belong to Meg, and he certainly favoured her presence. When she was in the cottage, he took up a place by her side. Elsewhere, out of doors, there he was at her side, behaving exactly like a domestic pet at heel.

Maybe I was just a little jealous – as I was, I must confess, about Jack too. Thane wasn't the only one I feared I had lost since Meg came into our lives. I remembered that beastly cold and although I told myself that Jack should keep away from me, he seemed almost too ready to do so. I was lucky if he came up to see me for half an hour each day. And the sounds of their merriment, tales of great excursions they had together, did little for my soul.

All these sorry matters I confided to the only one I could ever talk to, and that was Thane. He looked at me with that almost human expression. But did he or could he ever understand? Was I expecting too much? As Jack would say, and Mabel too, he is only a dog.

The question remained, was he? He had certainly been more than that but had this holiday changed him as it seemed to be changing me, and Jack and Meg? And of all the changes, my relationship with Vince was hardest to bear. I realised that he had a busy life and since Olivia and Faith had gone home he spent little time at the cottage, looking in of an evening for a chat. Over the last ten years since my return to Scotland, I had been delighted and grateful for those brief visits when the royal train stopped in Edinburgh en route back and forth to Ballater.

On this holiday I had expected to spend a lot of time with him, but now our conversations were guarded, especially if any reference was made to the mystery I felt surrounded Lily's death.

I soon discovered that Bobby's was to be treated in the same manner. I said I did not believe that he could have been accidentally thrown from his horse, an opinion endorsed by the stableman Jock's assertion that Bobby could ride anything. I regretted that immediately, as Vince's lips tightened.

'There you go again, Rose. You are the absolute end. The slightest accident has you immediately believing that murder was intended.' His laugh was rather mirthless, he was annoyed. 'A good job you don't live here on the estate permanently, or you'd have a succession of crimes waiting to be solved. As a doctor, one gets used to accidents that are quite inexplicable, often domestic accidents where it is wise not to dig too deeply into their cause.'

He paused and said: 'You simply ask for disasters, Rose, and the sooner we get you home in one piece, the happier I will be.'

Wounded that he would be glad to be rid of me, I said sharply: 'It can't be too soon for me either!'

His eyebrows rose at that. 'Well, well. Scant thanks I am getting for negotiating this holiday for you. I have to say that if you haven't enjoyed it, then it is your own fault for interfering in things that don't concern you.'

His words were so like Gray's that I said angrily: 'Such as two quite inexplicable deaths.'

He stood up, shook his head, came over and hugged me. 'You'll be the death of me, my lovely Rose. Now don't cry,' he said softly and holding me at arm's length. 'What I most want for you in all the world is that you go back to your happy life at Solomon's Tower, stay there and resolve to be a good mother to Meg and a good wife to Jack.'

'I'd love to be both, but Jack seems to have deserted me too on this holiday.'

'He's a policeman, Rose, duty calls. You knew the score when you married him,' was his stern response.

'Is that so? Talking of which. I'd very much like to know what the duty is that keeps a senior detective inspector like Gray here in Balmoral.'

Vince gave me a weary glance. 'There you go again. Things that don't concern you, police matters that are none of our business.' He sighed, looked at the clock. 'I'm off. I have my early morning surgery in Crathie tomorrow.'

And he was gone. I went to bed, feeling sore and misunderstood.

After breakfast Mabel was waiting for her pony cart to be restored to her. She said it had developed a creaking wheel which she found both alarming and disturbing.

Considering its daily use over fairly rough ground I was not at all surprised and the sturdy little pony must have been relieved to get a day off.

Rowena arrived; always hungry despite a substantial breakfast with her mother in the royal kitchens, she had a second one with Meg. They went off to play in the tree house they were making with Uncle Vince's occasional help while I took Thane for that walk in the woods. Not many of these left, I told him. Soon be home again.

He turned and looked at me, the equivalent of a grin that said that prospect was joyful to him.

Returning to the cottage, there was another drama afoot. The girls had seen a rat.

'A huge black rat, Mam,' said Meg. 'It was at the base of the tree.'

'How horrible!' said Mabel.

Meg turned to her. 'No, it was quite pretty.' And turning to Rowena for support. 'Wasn't it?'

Rowena nodded eagerly. They weren't scared, just excited.

Mabel sighed deeply. 'So we have rats now.'

'No. Just one,' Meg corrected her.

Ignoring that Mabel continued: 'That Dog is to blame, he is attracting vermin. A good job we are leaving, the place will be quite overrun.'

Defending Thane, I said: 'Quite the contrary, Mabel. Dogs get rid of rats,' and glancing at him I decided that he would be on to it and we need not worry. We would never see that fine black rat again.

He was used to eating meals from the kennels here in Balmoral but he was used to making his own arrangements at home on Arthur's Seat. We fed him while we were at home but I knew when we left him for days he never starved. A matter I did not look into too deeply but guessed the rat that the girls had seen would, like many others before it, be marked down to provide him with an excellent lunch.

Mabel had other ideas. With little faith in That Dog as rat-catcher extraordinaire, and unknown to me, when she was over at the stables she had explained the problem and Jock had said he would tell one of the gardeners to put down poison.

Which was to have dire results.

CHAPTER THIRTY-TWO

Rowena was now spending most of every day with us. That her new friend had apparently taken over Faith's part in Meg's life, I was thankful for indeed. My only fear now was that this would be another parting to dread when we left at the end of this week, with Meg insisting that Rowena come to Edinburgh with us.

To my relief that did not seem likely when I discovered that Rowena was devoted to her Romany mother, Yolande. Since Olivia and Faith's departure, they brought us meals each day and carried off our washing, two domestic duties I was glad to relinquish, particularly the latter. Laundry facilities had been omitted from the cottage, for the obvious reason that the King's important guests were not expected to soil their hands with such menial tasks, and with lesser mortals like ourselves, lines of our undergarments blowing in the wind would definitely lower the tone of the estate and be severely frowned upon.

Yolande had never identified herself as Rowena's mother before her friendship with Meg and I remembered that I had seen her talking to Lily, who she of course recognised as a fellow servant in the higher echelons as lady's maid. But although our children were friends she would never cross the invisible boundary between employer or mistress and servant, one that I hoped to eliminate completely once the success of the suffrage movement was achieved and all women were equal!

I wondered what she and Lily talked about. Then I realised that they observed the same boundaries, perhaps the castle influence made rigid by Queen Victoria (with the exception of presentable ghillies like John Brown), and although those daunting, self-effacing measures such as darting into cupboards at the approach of royalty were still observed, Lily, who was silent with us, evading eye contact, talked freely to the stable boys, and if Bobby was to be believed, did a lot more than talk.

Thoughts of Lily reminded me that she had, according to the stable lads, been good with horses and Rowena too had a way with animals, part of her second sight, this extra sense, according to Meg who, observing in awe, said: 'Animals, even quite wild ones, come to her. I have to be very quiet and she lets me watch her feed the birds, blackbirds and blue tits, they come down and sit on her hand to take crumbs. Those adorable red squirrels, oh I'd love to stroke them, like she does. They aren't afraid of her at all, but they are terrified of me, Mam. It isn't fair,' she said resentfully.

I remembered that maybe it wasn't all animals; I said

she had been wary of Thane at first. Meg agreed. 'She was scared of big dogs, but they're the best of friends now.'

And as Mabel put it, 'What do those children see in That Dog? He's not a little lap dog, he's twice their size – as big as my pony,' she added referring as she did these days to Hector.

I thought I'd seen the last of Alice von Mueller after our brief interview when I had to confess that her domestic problem was out of my sphere of activity as a lady investigator. However, after walking back to the castle with Vince, an evening stroll I enjoyed, I saw Alice approaching.

Although her greeting was polite and casual, I had a distinct feeling that she had been lying in wait for me. It did not take long for her to come to the point.

'I know you were unable to help me, but matters have changed since we spoke together.' She took a deep breath. 'You see, my husband is trying to kill me.' Pausing dramatically, she waited for my response which I could not frame in more than two words:

'Surely not.'

She nodded vigorously. 'Oh yes, yes! I know he wants to get rid of me, and it seems that it would be easier here than taking me back to Munich.'

Kill her at Balmoral Castle, now that seemed a weird solution. Had she no idea of the complications that would ensue?

She indicated the garden seat we were walking past. 'Can you spare me a few moments, please Rose?' The sky was darkening with more than approaching night.

A strong breeze indicated storm clouds brewing over the horizon. 'I will be as quick as I can.'

We sat down together and I noticed that she looked pale and frightened.

'I have known for a long while that Hermann hated me for being English. He could not abide the idea of spending his life with a woman from the country he despised, the country that should be ruled over not by your King Edward but by his beloved cousin the Kaiser.'

She paused and I said: 'That could never be, Alice. Even if we didn't have Edward, there is the next in line—'

She held up a hand. 'Oh yes, I am aware of that. I have tried to tell him, but you see, he is quite deranged. Quite mad.' She shrugged. 'Whoever is your king does not greatly concern me, but my life does. And now that he has taken the children away from me, he wants to be free to marry this other woman, his mistress. And the only way is to kill me first.'

She looked towards the castle. 'He will not do it himself, of course, but he has already made an attempt.' A shuddering sigh. 'Last night on this very spot, on my way back to our lodging, I was attacked.'

'You were attacked – here?' I repeated.

'Yes. A man leapt out from among the shrubs over there and tried to strangle me. I struggled, I was terrified.'

This was very startling news especially when I thought of Mabel's recent attack.

'What was he like, this man?'

'I never saw his face. I knew he was tall and strong and grabbed me from behind, his arm about my throat,' she said with an illustrating gesture, 'like this.'

'But this is terrible, Alice! How did you get away?'

'I was very fortunate. A young couple were approaching. They were laughing and he heard them too. He let me go, and darted away.'

'So they never saw him either. I hope you reported it.'

She shook her head. 'No. What use would it have been? No one had seen. I knew Hermann was behind it; he has plenty of willing servants to do his dirty work. So what was the use, Rose?'

I had to agree with her there.

'What are you going to do now?'

She shrugged. 'There are just a few days left and I will pretend nothing has happened with Hermann. But I have made my mind up. I cannot go on living with him. Now that he has taken my children, I have no reason to go back to Munich. I intend to stay here.'

'Have you family in England?'

She laughed for the first time. 'Yes, Rose, I have, but I am not going back to them. I have met a Scottish gentleman, who has a place in Argyll. He once visited us. We became friends and when he saw how vilely my husband treated me, he realised that I was living with a madman and has offered me sanctuary.'

'What kind of sanctuary? Is he one of the shooting party?'

I could see more ominous clouds than a mere storm gathering at such a prospect.

She smiled, radiant for a moment, and laughed again. 'No, he declined the invitation – for obvious reasons. He said that he would be tempted to shoot Hermann. But I have sent him word to expect me.' She took my hand.

'This is our farewell, Rose. Will you tell Olivia when you see her that I will be in touch? And wish me well in my new life.'

I hoped she was right about her Scottish gentleman and that in due time things would sort themselves out to her satisfaction. At the moment, though, the whole situation filled me with misgivings.

As we parted and I made my way back to the cottage I had a lot to think about. Was her attack, as she thought, instigated by her husband? The alternative was even more terrifying.

I thought of her description. A tall strong man, unidentifiable. But curiously enough the method of his attack also fitted Mabel's assailant, and all pointed steadily in one steady direction.

We had a madman at large. And what if his ultimate target was to kill the King?

Jack's unexpected appearance just two days before the games put things in quite a new perspective.

CHAPTER THIRTY-THREE

I had a disturbed night troubled by anxious dreams about Alice and her England-hating husband. Meg was still abed as usual when I came downstairs and Mabel's breakfast dishes were in the sink. Thane was usually waiting to greet me but not this morning. He lay asleep by the peat fire.

'Are you being lazy too?' There was no response. I went closer. He was lying very still on his side. As I bent over him I noticed he had been sick. I had never known him ever to be sick in Edinburgh. If he was, never in the house.

There was something terribly wrong. My heart raced as I bent over him. I stroked him gently.

'Thane, Thane!' I said. He moved his head as if it took considerable effort and opened one eye, an eye that seemed glazed over.

And I knew what was happening. Thane was dying.

I screamed. The door opened and Mabel appeared.

265

'What on earth is wrong?'

'Thane's been poisoned,' I cried.

'What nonsense, Rose. All animals get sick. Only to be expected. I've told you before, That Dog should be in the kennels with the others. It put me off my breakfast, I can tell you. How can one eat in a kitchen full of dog sick? I wasn't going to clear it – quite revolting.'

At that moment, I knew I hated her. I wanted to strike her and I knew what it felt like to have murder in one's heart, as all the little resentments, all her silly remarks and her snobbery boiled up inside me. I felt my hand rise to strike her as she stood, her back to me by the window which she had thrown open for fresh air.

Thane moaned and that brought me to my senses and saved her from being struck down. Then suddenly Mabel was no longer of any importance. Only my Thane dying on the floor beside me mattered.

I had to find someone and at that moment I heard the motor coming down the road. Vince was on his way past. A miracle, I thought, as I rushed out into the road.

'Something's happened to Thane!' He took one look at my face, switched off and followed me inside, knelt down beside Thane, sniffed and looking up at me said: 'Poison. I'll take him into the vet.'

Meg appeared, alerted by all the noise. She took one look at Thane and cried: 'That rat poison!' She began to sob. 'I tried to keep an eye on him . . . Oh, he's not going to die, Uncle Vince. You can't let him die.'

'I can't do much for him, Meg. I'm only a doctor for humans not animals. I'm taking him to the vet, he'll do what we can for him.'

It seemed as he spoke that Vince hadn't any great hopes, trying to lift him up, a very large deerhound almost as big as me. Between us we managed to get him out and into the back of the car, lying on the floor wrapped in a blanket.

'I'm coming with you.'

'Me too!' sobbed Meg.

'No. There isn't room.' Vince said sternly and I realised that two hysterical females was the last thing he needed. 'Try to stay calm, the pair of you.'

'Where are you taking him?' cried Meg.

'To Ballater.' And I remembered that this was Vince's day for collecting drugs, like laudanum known as 'ladies' medicine', for use at the castle as he went on: 'We have a great vet there, takes care of all the King's dogs.' And he drove off.

I led Meg back into the house, still sobbing, aware that if he died then I would blame myself for bringing him here, away from Edinburgh, from his home. Obviously the secret of his survival – for I had once seen him shot, get up and walk away – that secret lay in the depths of his origins in Arthur's Seat. His magic, if you like, could not be sustained, it didn't work in an alien place.

Trying to calm Meg, I thought of all our years together, how he had saved my life so often and now I was helpless. I could do nothing. And I thought of his loyalty and protection for Meg and me, and how miserable he must have been here in his restricted life.

Meg sat at the table shivering. 'That rat poison, Mam. That's what did it. Why didn't we just keep the rat? He wasn't doing us any harm. And Thane would still be alive.'

'Meg,' I said sternly, 'Thane is—is still alive.'

'But he's going to die. I know it!'

'No, darling, this vet that takes care of the King's dogs, Uncle Vince says—'

She shook her head. 'But Thane's not like them. He's not an ordinary dog. You know he isn't.'

I put my arm around her. 'I know. But he'll be all right. We must have faith.'

She looked up at me as if she'd never heard the word before. The nuns hadn't got very far with her religious education. I said: 'Magic, then. You believe in magic, don't you?'

She nodded and said: 'Will it take long before Uncle Vince brings him back?'

'Maybe an hour or two.' I had no idea but knew we couldn't sit around and wait for news. Vince had said as he drove off that it might take a while for the vet's treatment to work. Neither of us could eat so I offered her one of some forbidden chocolate bars, the very special treat that she loved and craved. She unwrapped it and I said: 'Are you seeing Rowena today?'

She looked at me as if she had forgotten their almost daily meetings and shook her head. 'Her mother gives her a cookery lesson this morning.' I gathered that Yolande was obviously hoping to train her daughter for duties in the royal kitchens.

Which was just as well today. Rowena was fond of Thane and our distress would be infectious. I could not have dealt with two hysterical girls in floods of tears.

I crumbled up some bread. 'Here you are.' Anything to distract her. 'Don't forget the birds. They'll be waiting.' Her after-breakfast task.

I wanted to clean up and just hoped that Mabel would stay upstairs in one of her huffs and not come in to lecture me on That Dog or I would most certainly do her an injury.

And I had an idea of how to fill in those dreaded waiting hours. Meg had always wanted to go across to the little island with the monument Queen Victoria had set there. It wasn't an island at all really, just a raised bit of land in the middle of the river, a kind of peninsula, but it had lots of trees and Meg was sure it was a magic glen. Doubtless shades of Sir Walter Scott's 'Lady of the Lake' that I had been reading to her.

It was a lovely, sunny morning, the earth smiled, oblivious of our anguish. When I told Meg my plan, she brightened. How would we get across?

'Remember that little rowing boat moored on the shore?' I said, wondering if it was still there and more to the point, seaworthy.

Meg clasped her hands. 'Do let's go, then.' She frowned. 'Oh Mam, will we be back in time for Thane?'

I said Vince had hinted at afternoon, and as neither of us had eaten, we could take a picnic.

Ten minutes later, with thankfully no appearance from Mabel, although she watched us leave from her window, Meg said: 'Should we ask her to come along?'

'No,' I said firmly, 'there wouldn't be room in the boat.'

We walked through the wood down to the river path and there was the boat: dilapidated, ancient and unused. I sighed: if needs must.

Meg stepped in and took up one of the oars. 'Rowena would have loved this.'

I was always very careful with Rowena and her overprotective mother. If she got a scratch on her or a tear on her pinafore, Meg would shake her head and say: 'Her mother will be in such a state.' I hated to think of that state if Rowena had returned thoroughly soaked.

With an oar each we set off. There was quite a swirl on the current and the water had looked a lot smoother than it felt. I looked across at the little island and was glad it was a journey of about thirty yards, remembering my tendency to seasickness.

At last we wobbled onto dry shingle and pulled the tiny boat after us, fastening it to an overhanging branch of a tree.

'There has been a castle here once,' Meg said, 'look at all the stones. Do you think people lived here before they built the castle?'

I thought that very unlikely as it had only been an island since the river changed its course. The reason for the monument was that it most probably brought the Queen treasured memories of Prince Albert and the love story of a truly romantic couple.

'That boat might well have been theirs,' said Meg.

True enough. It didn't look as if it had had much use in the present king's reign. And on further thought, if I had always had doubts about bringing Thane over, then for such a large man it would have been somewhat hazardous.

The scene was certainly very pretty but there was this air of desolation, of neglect. No one ever came here any more. Not nearly grand enough or big enough for King Edward and his society. He liked his romance taken in luxury and I couldn't imagine him bringing Queen

Alexandra, even without their six children, for a pleasant outing without a stream of servants carrying the picnic.

I was very glad to see Meg's appetite had returned and every time she frowned and asked the time and mentioned Thane I insisted that we were not to worry, that the King's vet was very clever and doubtless lots of other dogs much smaller and more fragile than Thane had been poisoned and survived.

I hoped that was true.

As always, the sun seemed to be on shift work. After a fleeting appearance, work done, it now retreated. The sky had greyed over and we decided it was time to get back and continue our vigil in the comfort of the cottage.

Except . . . except that there was no boat! At least, there was no boat on the overhanging branch. It was bobbing merrily about in the middle of the river. Far out of reach and completely inaccessible.

We were marooned.

CHAPTER THIRTY-FOUR

'What will we do now?' Meg wailed.

She couldn't swim and neither could I. We could try shouting for help if there was any hope of our cries being heard above the swirling rush of the water, or if anyone happened to be passing by, a fisherman perhaps. We had seen groups of them with their fishing rods on this part of the river.

'He-ll-o!'

A miracle – our shouts had been heard.

A tall man stood on the mainland side. The one my heart recognised before I did. Mr Brown.

We pointed to the boat. He nodded, elaborate gesticulations accompanied his words that we couldn't hear distinctly, indicating that he would push it across to us.

Wasn't it too deep for him? 'You'll drown,' shouted Meg.

He shook his head. 'You'll – get – very – wet.'

He laughed, kicked out a leg and we realised he was wearing thigh-length waders, the usual accoutrements of the eager fishermen.

He disappeared from view, as had the boat, which had drifted out of sight. The silence took over. It seemed like some time as we waited.

'Do you think he's coming back? Did he mean it?' asked Meg. 'Maybe he can't get the boat.'

I only knew that once again he was to be my rescuer. And there he was, wading across, ten yards away, coming closer, treading water. But no boat.

Stepping ashore, he shook his head. 'Boat's leaking, I'm afraid, and sinking fast. Your combined weight must have been too much for it. Fortunate it didn't fill up while you were crossing.'

He smiled at Meg. 'Hello.' And to me. 'You don't have much luck with water, do you?'

Ignoring that I asked sternly: 'What do we do now?'

He seemed very tall as, hands on hips, he looked down on us grinning. 'Well, I shall have to carry you across.'

'Both of us? Isn't that going to be difficult?'

He smiled. 'Only one at a time. I'll take the little lady first.' He knelt down. 'Up you go!' And setting Meg on his shoulders, her arms about his neck he stood up. 'Comfortable, are you? Hang on tight.'

Meg laughed. She was enjoying this adventure.

As they stepped into the water, he looked back at me. 'Don't go away, miss. I'll be back shortly.'

'How—?'

'I'm coming back for you, of course.'

I watched them go, Meg laughing merrily as he waded

steadily through the water. On dry land, she waved to me and then he was coming back. I waited.

Reaching my side, thoroughly drenched, he regarded me solemnly. 'I don't think my shoulders would be quite appropriate. I'll carry you. Here we go.' I gathered my skirts modestly about my legs and he lifted me up. 'You're as light as a feather.'

I was in his arms, close to his beating heart. Smiling, he looked down into my face.

'Rescuing you is getting to be a habit.'

'Thank you. We were lucky you were passing by.'

He laughed. 'I decided to do a little fishing. I was told the trout was good here. I didn't expect the catch to include two damsels in distress.'

I could think of no clever rejoinder. Every step listening to that heartbeat, his warm breath, his closeness, my head under his chin, deprived me of speech. I just wanted it to last. I felt so safe, so comforted.

My feet set on dry land again, I felt chilled without his warmth and looked round for Meg.

'She didn't want to wait. She thought Thane might be back by now. What's this about? Him being poisoned?'

'Meg and Rowena saw a rat in the garden. Aiken had poison put down. He must have got some of it.' I could feel the tears, the agony of it all welling up again.

He put an arm around me. 'Don't worry. Thane will be all right.'

'How do you know that?' I sobbed.

His smile gave his eyes that strange light. He took my chin in his hand, said softly, 'Like I told you, Rose. Remember? I know everything.'

He had never called me Rose before. It seemed so intimate that my heart gave a little leap.

The cottage was in sight. 'Safe home, at last.'

'Thank you.'

He bowed. 'Glad to have been of service. I bid you good day.'

I looked at the cottage. No sign of Vince or Thane. Turning to say thank you again, he was gone. No sign of him, either. He had an extraordinary way of just disappearing that was quite unnerving.

As I opened the door, there were voices. The last one I wanted to hear. Inspector Gray was sitting opposite Mabel, the table between them.

'Ah, Mrs Macmerry.' He didn't get up. Looking across at Mabel, her expression angry, eyes turned stonily towards the window, Gray indicated an envelope: 'Some documents for Miss Penby Worth's attention. We are legally bound to pass on copies of death certificate and so forth for the young woman's next of kin – if they can be found – before the necessary arrangements for her interment can proceed.'

It was an irresistible chance to drag more information out of the inspector. 'The case is closed, then?'

'Of course.'

'Nothing further about the stable boy Biggs, either?'

He sighed deeply. 'You have heard the facts, Mrs Macmerry, and that case too is closed.'

'You never discovered who he was on the way to meet when the horse threw him?'

He shrugged. 'That is irrelevant whether he met someone or not, we are satisfied that this was an unfortunate accident. Perhaps it was yourself, Mrs Macmerry, since your bicycle tyres were on the scene of the accident,' he added smoothly.

'I have told you why, Inspector, you know my reasons and I'm not going over that again.' I paused. 'Have you had any success in discovering Miss Penby Worth's attacker?'

He didn't want that one. He frowned across at Mabel who was now eyeing the tabletop very intently, giving it her full attention as if it held some hidden message for her.

'We are still working on that.' He stood up. 'Now, if you will excuse me.'

'There is something else you might like to work on, Inspector. It is possible that someone tried to poison our deerhound Thane, a very valuable animal.'

'From what your daughter told me' – Meg must have gone to her room – 'it was an accident with rat poison. Unfortunate, but we cannot risk vermin in the cottage.'

'Thane would never have taken poison. He is a very intelligent animal and not greedy.'

Gray held up a hand. 'Intelligent or not, dogs will eat anything if the package appeals to them. I would suggest that a large rat might have been acceptable to a hungry dog.' With a bow to Mabel, who without a word to me, obviously still bearing in mind our exchange of words regarding Thane that morning, was heading in the direction of her room.

As he departed, Meg dashed downstairs. 'He told me I wasn't needed and to make myself scarce. What a rude man!'

I could not but agree as she poured herself a glass of milk. 'I like that Mr Elder a lot. He is nice, isn't he?'

So he had told her that his real name was Elder. She had made some advance on short acquaintance but I wasn't sure that 'nice' was quite the description I had in mind. 'Wasn't it lucky for us that he was there, Mam? We might have still been marooned on the island for hours and hours—'

The sound of a motor approaching cut her short.

We dashed out.

Vince stepped out. Alone.

Meg ran to him, screamed. 'Thane! No! No – he-he-isn't—?'

Vince picked her up, took her in his arms. 'No, Meg. He'll be better soon.'

I could see she didn't believe him. He looked across at me. 'He's going to be fine, Rose, but he'll stay with the vet for a day or two. Bain wants to keep him, that's the usual procedure with poisoning. Wants to be sure it's all out of his system.' And to Meg, 'Now wipe your tears, dear. It's just like being in hospital, being looked after.'

'Are you sure, Uncle Vince?'

'Sure, I'm sure.'

Later he said to me: 'Thane has a charmed life. Bain said there was enough rat poison in him to kill a dozen dogs.'

CHAPTER THIRTY-FIVE

With not much time left before we left for Edinburgh, another problem. Would Thane be fit to travel? But to my delight, even as I worried, Vince brought him back to the cottage the next day.

I regarded him anxiously but he seemed to have taken no lasting ill effects from the poisoning, which was usually fatal. Once again I felt he had missed death by inches. As Vince said, he did indeed have a charmed life, maybe even more than one!

I gathered that the vet had been very impressed. He had been so ill that he had felt there was little hope of survival, that his digestive organs might have been destroyed, and was amazed at such a complete recovery.

Vince stroked his head proudly. A remarkable dog indeed.

'We must watch his food, Rose. It seems that he had

been tempted, as any normal animal would be, by a rat which unfortunately had just consumed the poison. Where's Meg? She'll be so pleased.'

'She's at the castle with Rowena. There's a children's picnic tea.'

The royals were very fond of having their children mingle with those from the household. The Queen was very enlightened in this respect and considered that knowing and understanding the 'common people' would be very useful in days to come, an idea fully appreciated by her husband who enjoyed mingling with his subjects, particularly if they were female, young and pretty.

I was so glad to have Thane back, restored to health, such a sense of relief that I knew would be shared by Meg. Such a pleasant surprise for her at six o'clock, when she came home for supper.

But six came and passed and seven too. She was later than usual. That didn't worry me particularly until at seven-thirty I opened the door to be confronted by a terrified Yolande.

'Where is Rowena? Is she not here with Meg?'

As I explained about the picnic, her eyes were darting round the room as if they might be hiding somewhere, then she cried: 'No. I knew about that and when Rowena didn't come home I decided to go and collect them both.' She put her hand to her mouth. 'And what did I find? Neither of them had been to the picnic party.'

I stared at her, anxiety was catching. I did a quick calculation. In other words, they had been missing since midday. Where were they? My turn for panic, mild compared to Yolande's who screamed: 'Why are they not here? Because they have been kidnapped, that is what has happened!' and she sat down heavily on a chair, looking ready to faint.

I said with a calmness I was far from feeling: 'That is nonsense. Who would want to kidnap two little girls? They aren't royals—'

She gave a shriek: 'But there are strange stories about here just now. Haven't you heard, bad things happening at the castle?'

I was no longer listening; trying desperately to think of a logical reason why Meg and Rowena would miss an event regarded as such a treat. I had a sudden flash of inspiration.

'Could they have gone to the gipsy camp?'

'Why would they miss a picnic for that?'

I thought about Rowena and the gipsy camp again. She never talked of her father, perhaps he was there. At the mention of him, Yolande began to cry again. 'I do not know where he is. He left years ago. I do not even know his real name – he worked on the estate, that was all. He wanted to marry me, so he said, but when he knew I was pregnant, he departed and I was forbidden to return to my family for associating with a gringo. And so was his child.'

Her tears were now accompanied by a wringing of hands. 'My precious little one! What will I do without my Rowena?' I put a hopefully comforting hand on her shoulder. 'Please, don't upset yourself. We will find them.' Adding confidently: 'They can't be far away.'

She stood up, the clock had struck the hour. 'I must

go. I am on duty in the kitchen and if I am late I will be discharged. That is the rule. All my years there will mean nothing. It is a strict regime, be late and be sent off without a reference. Lateness will not be tolerated, even minutes. Unreliable.'

I said, 'You must go. I will get my bicycle—'

'Will you please tell the policeman?' she interrupted.

I presumed she meant Inspector Gray. I didn't know where to find him and he wouldn't thank her or me for raising the alarm for two little girls missing on the estate since midday.

Ignoring her plea, I said: 'I'll take Thane – we'll find them.'

Thane had come to my side as if he understood the conversation and the urgency. She eyed him doubtfully. 'He is only a dog. It is a man, a policeman you need.'

There was a logic in that but the clock was ticking relentlessly. I told her again not to worry, that I would find them both, and pushed her towards the door. As she stood there wavering, torn between losing her job and finding Rowena, I made a promise I was far from certain I could keep. I would find them, while reason told me that with several hours' start, they could be far away indeed.

As I was closing the door, Mabel appeared. 'What was all that dreadful noise about? That servant screaming her head off about children being kidnapped?'

She had overheard the conversation and instead of consolation said grimly: 'After my attack, anything is possible. Dark forces are at work,' she added, echoing Yolande's sentiments. 'Would you like to take the pony cart? Where will you start searching?'

I had no idea but there were hours of daylight left. 'My bicycle is easier to negotiate than the cart over rough ground.'

Thane had been listening. I said to him, 'We'll find them, won't we?' and he gave me that eager look, that almost human response. I decided I would have to rely on his instincts that were more appropriate to a shooting party and retrieving game than finding little girls who had gone astray.

And I was by no means as confident as I had sounded.

CHAPTER THIRTY-SIX

'The gipsy camp, Thane.' I decided that would be the first place to look, but where was it now? Would it still be by the roadside en route to the castle as we had seen it on our journey almost a month ago?

Retracing our steps took some time and I was about to give up in despair when smoke and the distant smell of peat fires indicated the road. The camp was still there.

Our approach had been noticed. I could have wept with relief as Meg and Rowena raced toward us.

They weren't interested in me or in Yolande's anxiety.

'Thane! Oh, Thane!' They shrieked, laughing with delight, Meg tearful with emotion at her precious pet restored to them.

They flung their arms around him, ignoring my stern remonstrations about Rowena's mother being out of her mind with worry.

It got through to them at last. Meg looked up and said: 'It was for Thane we came here, Mam. Rowena knew that her great-grandmother who is the chieftain of the Faws here would have a cure for him. She has wonderful remedies. Rowena says she has cured people who were hurt in battle long ago or poisoned. Isn't that so?'

Rowena nodded and took my hand shyly. 'I am sorry to have upset Mamma, but I knew if we told her she would not allow us to come here. I would like you to meet Great-grandmother Katya.'

She led the way through the camp to an exquisitely painted caravan and sitting on the step enjoying a clay pipe was a very, very old woman, her long white hair in braids. Once, when young, she had been beautiful and the remnants of that lost beauty still lingered in her finely carved features.

The introduction was in Romany, I presumed. I wasn't sure whether a curtsey was indicated. There was no doubt about her regal manner, she was still Queen to her tribe.

After Rowena finished speaking, Katya, who had been observing me closely, nodded and in perfect but halting English, indicated Meg. 'You are not her mother.'

Rowena looked embarrassed. 'But she is—'

Katya held up her hand. 'Be silent, child.' And pointing to Meg she said: 'This child you call your daughter, but you did not carry her and bring her into the world.'

I looked at Rowena, I doubted that Meg had ever told her that I was her stepmother.

Katya had not taken her eyes off me. She shook her

head. 'She is not your child, she is Romany.'

That was absurd. I thought of Jack her father, of how like him she was and then I thought of her mother, a woman he met in a Glasgow bar about whom he knew nothing, about whom he never spoke, just as he never spoke of that brief marriage of necessity.

Katya was saying: 'We keep track of our Faws, those who are the highest in the tribe. This child's mother and sister did not keep to the rules so they were sent away. Margaret, the child's mother, and her sister Pam were wilful and disobedient. They wanted a different life but neither had any knowledge of what it was like to be a Faw living in a great city like Glasgow.'

She paused, sighed. 'It was soon apparent that there was only one means of staying alive. In the age-old tradition of starving women, by selling their bodies. They had good looks to offer. Pam was fortunate, she met a working man who offered her marriage. Margaret met a gringo who set her to work in his public house.'

Pausing, she glanced at Meg who was sitting a few yards away from us laughing happily with Rowena. Thankfully they were not interested in Katya and me as all their attention was on making a great fuss of Thane.

'Margaret met a policeman.' Katya pointed to Meg. 'She became pregnant and he married her but she died shortly after the child was born. Her sister Pam took the little girl, and all was well until she died.'

'Wait a moment,' I interrupted, 'how do you know all this?'

She smiled, a gap-toothed smile which did not mask the ghost of a once lovely face. 'Because they were inheritors of our dynasty, of the Faws – and we have means of keeping track of important members.'

I shook my head. All she said I knew was true but quite unbelievable. She saw my expression and said: 'We do more than sell clothes pegs and tell fortunes, dear lady. We have still extra senses which we inherited from the nomadic races centuries ago, like the ability to see into the future, what the gringos call telling fortunes. We believed that everyone on earth was born carrying a map of their future in the palm of their hand.'

I looked at Meg. Was she some sort of a gipsy princess? Jack would never believe that and suddenly I wondered what this queenly old woman intended.

I said: 'She is our daughter now. We love her, her father, who is a policeman of high rank, absolutely adores her. We had some difficulty tracking her down after her aunt died.'

Katya nodded. 'Your activities on her behalf were noted, dear lady. We were glad to see her restored to her rightful father. Had the situation been different, then we would have moved in and brought her back to her rightful place in the tribe, where one day she would sit where I do this day.'

I wondered if that was where being kidnapped by gipsies originated, and watching Meg with new eyes, I could not imagine her being happy – and yet, she was fascinated by gipsies. Perhaps something in her being, a strand of recognition she had inherited. Suddenly I was afraid.

As if Katya read my mind, she stretched out a hand and touched me. 'Do not fear, dear lady, the Faws are happy that she has a good home, we have no intentions of taking her from her father.' Pausing, she looked towards Meg and said: 'She has a great inheritance and will go far in your world.'

'She is very clever, so her teachers tell me.'

Katya smiled. 'Ah yes, the good nuns. They mean well, but there are other spiritual forces at work as well as the ones they teach.'

I think I knew now how Meg was just a little different from her schoolmates, and had always been so. And seeing her with Rowena, why the two girls had an instant friendship.

Katya followed my gaze. 'They are not related, except by their tribal origins.' She pointed to Rowena. 'Her mother Yolande was also sent away. She also brought disgrace upon the Faws by bearing a child to a gringo man who was already married. But Rowena has made her way back to us, and has been welcomed—'

She was interrupted by a commotion, laughter and shouts of greetings which erupted as a tall man strode across and my heart made its usual giddy jump.

Mr Brown or Elder again. Thane left the girls and raced over to him. A scene repeated of recognition between the man and the deerhound.

Then still stroking Thane's head, talking to him, he saw Katya. She had stood up and held out her thin arms.

'Tam, Tam, it is good to see you, son.'

So he had a first name that wasn't Saemus, the Gaelic for Thomas.

She hugged him and they spoke in Romany, about me and the girls, judging by their glances in our direction.

He smiled at me, shook his head and sighed. 'So we meet again.'

My thoughts were racing. 'How did you get here?'

'I met Yolande in hysterics. Rowena had been kidnapped, Meg with her, and that you had gone in search of them.'

'And you just guessed that I had come to the gipsy camp.'

Again he smiled. 'Just as I told you, I know everything.' Then he added, 'These people are old friends of mine, miss. And I guessed if the two lasses weren't with them, they would certainly be the people to find them. Now, shall we go, get Rowena back to her mother as fast as we can?'

Katya had been listening, so he didn't need to translate, she was nodding approvingly. Meg and Rowena came over, explaining about the cure they thought Katya would have for Thane, but it had taken longer than they thought. They had lost track of time but fortunately Thane didn't need a cure.

Katya took my hands in parting. 'It has been good to meet you, dear lady, and to know that you will be a good mother to our lost child. She will be happy and content with you and her father, a good man for a gringo policeman.' And nodding vigorously, 'We are very pleased with him. It seems that all worked out well in the end. Sadly, not at all well for poor Pam, whose husband is one of your people and a ne'er-do-well.'

And so we left them, the girls holding a hand each of the man whose first name I now knew.

This was the twilight hour known romantically in

Scotland as the gloaming where the world takes on a special glow and the tall trees settle down to sleep. It was a romantic night, for there was a full moon, and I felt a little isolated, listening to the gentle laughter of the trio in front, Thane and I walking behind as I pushed my bicycle through the narrow tracks in the wood.

Suddenly I realised we had missed the track back to the cottage. A moment's panic. Where were we heading?

CHAPTER THIRTY-SEVEN

Ahead of us, the girls stopped and waited.

'What is wrong?'

'Nothing wrong.' He pointed. 'This is the quick way back to the castle. Yolande will be waiting anxiously for Rowena.'

It was considerably shorter. He certainly knew his directions and a few minutes later, Rowena was restored to her tearful mother who couldn't decide whether to slap her for disobedience or cuddle and kiss her in relief.

Her rescuer was thanked profusely and turning about we were heading back down the road to the cottage. With Meg and Thane leading the way, I cursed the bicycle that kept me apart from the man who kept appearing in my life, so full of surprises.

'Let me,' he said and took over the bicycle, pushing it with one hand, he offered an arm.

I decided thanks were in order. 'You were very clever to guess about Katya's camp. You headed in the right direction.'

'Thane pretty much led the way.' He smiled.

I said: 'I remembered seeing you with the gipsies on the day we arrived to take up our holiday cottage at Balmoral.'

'As I told you, they are my friends. I am always welcome with them. Katya is an old friend.'

All too soon for me, the cottage was in sight. Meg turned, ran back and threw her arms around him. 'Thank you, sir.' And with a reproachful look in my direction. 'We were never in any danger, Mam. It seemed a good idea of Rowena's that her great-grandma could make Thane better.'

'And someone succeeded, didn't they, old chap?' Thane was having his head stroked and added his thanks by wagging his tail energetically. With Meg he ran down the path and vanished indoors, leaving me alone with the man who I had reason to believe, however reluctantly, had attacked Mabel and killed Lily and Bobby.

I thought of the clues, the evidence I had lined up against him. My prime suspect. If he hadn't killed them, then who had? It was a sickening thought but I had to know.

'The girl who drowned,' I said slowly. 'She was Miss Penby Worth's maid.'

He seemed to know that. He nodded. 'The lady with the pony-cart. Ah, yes I often see her watching the shooting party.'

'As you know, she was attacked in the wood. Did you see the man?'

He shook his head. 'All I saw was this lady in hysterics, saying a sack had been thrown over her head and someone had tried to kill her.'

He sounded faintly amused. I gave him a hard look and said. 'Apparently your arrival saved her. He ran off.'

'Was she hurt?' He didn't sound very concerned.

'Fortunately, no. Just shocked, terribly scared.'

He nodded. 'Are you sure she didn't imagine it?'

'Of course not. Why should she?'

He was smiling again. 'Ladies can sometimes let their imagination run away with them where men are concerned.'

I couldn't think of a reply and didn't feel like defending Mabel, but the time had come to thank him and not knowing quite where to begin, wanting to extend the moment, I said: 'You must have thought us very foolish, Yolande and I getting into such a state about our little girls.'

'Children are very precious, the greatest of gifts,' he said. There was a sadness in his voice.

Was he married then? 'Have you any family?'

He looked away, his expression unreadable, blotted out by the moonlight behind us. 'I had once, a very long time ago, I think.'

It was an odd statement and the silence indicated that I was not to hear any more about that. The moment was almost over. I could think of nothing to say to extend it, to detain him.

As he took my outstretched hand, the moonlight touched a curiously shaped scar on his bare wrist.

'Have you been hurt?' I asked.

He put his hand over it. 'No, that is my passport.'

'Passport to what?'

He didn't answer, perhaps there was no answer.

I said, 'Thank you, Mr Elder – or is it Tam?'

He shook his head. 'It's not Elder, it's Eildor. Tam Eildor.' And leaning forward, his face blotted out the light as he kissed my cheek. So gently, a butterfly touch, so swift that later I would wonder if I had dreamt it. 'Fare you well, Rose McQuinn.'

I wanted to say something about our paths crossing again. But the words stuck in my throat for those five words of his held finality and I knew that this was farewell, that we were never to meet again.

Thane had returned. He was watching us both intently. 'And you too, old chap, watch over her.'

Inside the cottage everything was normal again. Mabel had retired long ago and Meg had her supper, full of chatter about the gipsies and how she would love to live in a caravan. I thought of what Katya had told me and decided that maybe one day when she was grown up I would tell her the story of her Romany mother. But not now and certainly not before I told Jack. And I wondered about that too. Would it stir the old unhappy memories? Was this a secret best kept to myself?

I didn't sleep well that night. The evening's events had given me so much to think about.

I also came to my senses that night and realised that he was not really like Danny at all, after that first impression. As I now knew him I saw that the illusion was mine alone. Clever Vince who knew me well had spotted the superficial likeness, the dark hair falling over his brow, his height, the way he walked.

But those eyes, strange, luminous, amber-coloured, by no stretch of imagination could they be described as Irish blue eyes, and I knew now that I had been writing him into the role of Danny.

Tam wasn't a gipsy, but having seen him with Katya I knew there was something beyond the powers of explanation. A common bond, like the one Thane recognised, man and deerhound sharing that strange extra sense most humans had lost long ago, existing in only a few of us still as rare flashes of intuition. The precious link between the present and an ancient forgotten code that rules still in secret places on our earth, like Arthur's Seat that had carried Thane into the present day and into our lives.

And even with all my ingenuity for interpreting clues, real or false, and for once losing my prime suspect, here was one mystery I could never hope to solve.

CHAPTER THIRTY-EIGHT

With only a couple of days before the Games and our departure, it was time to think about repacking, leaving the cottage in the same immaculate condition as it was when we moved in. Vince said not to bother, that the two servants would do it. But my pride would not allow that, especially for Rowena's mother. I felt I must leave Yolande with a good impression.

I approached the task thankful to be returning home in normal circumstances, but I would never cease to regret that having lost my prime suspect I had not been able to solve what I would continue to regard as the murder of Lily, and of Bobby who had known her and had met with an unfortunate fatal accident, with all the evidence pointing to the fact that he had been killed by whoever he was blackmailing for more money.

Then there was Mabel's attacker. Inspector Gray had

got no further with finding him. Finally the attack on Alice von Mueller. Although her assailant's description could also have fitted that of Mabel's, I was not convinced that there was any connection. It sounded much more like a hit man at the sinister instigation of her husband.

If all of these incidents were connected and no killer had been apprehended, then we had to conclude that there was a potential assassin in Balmoral, who bore all the marks of an insane creature who would kill again when I, along with Inspector Gray, had walked away leaving two murders and two attempted ones unsolved.

And always, there was no escaping that one vital element.

The motive. In Lily's case, her death seemed motiveless. When I talked to Bobby at Crathie, he was terrified. He said he had been threatened by someone in authority, a man with a posh voice, who had given him ten quid to clear out. And although that fitted Vince's interpretation of Biggs having given offence to someone at the Castle, I was sure that there was a deeper, more sinister reason. His association with Lily. Was he killed because believing he loved her, Lily had confided in him or asked for his help?

I had cases in my logbooks solved successfully on far less evidence. A picture was beginning to emerge where I had all the pieces, if only I knew how to put them together in the right order.

Then Vince provided that possibly vital missing piece when he said that before the Games, extra precautions had to be taken for the royal family's safety. When questioned, he turned evasive and looked remarkably like a man who, having said too much, regretted it instantly.

'There have always been these insane attempts, you know that from Stepfather, surely. He was the Queen's personal detective here in Balmoral, after all. Saved her life once or twice.'

He tried to shrug off my interest, change the subject, but I was on to it. 'You mean that the King's life is in danger?'

That accounted for many things which now slid into place, like Inspector Gray's continued presence and the number of ghillies I'd seen wandering about during my walks in the wood with Thane, far enough away from the castle. I recognised at once that these were ghillies in name only. There was no disguising their discomfort or embarrassment in that particular Balmoral uniform of kilts and glengarry bonnets, they still looked and walked like policemen.

I now knew what the venue would be. It didn't take a great deal of imagination to guess that the Games at Invercauld would be the perfect camouflage, the crowds providing perfect cover for assassins to strike and make good their escape. The police would have to be very vigilant indeed and extra pairs of eyes in the backs of their heads would have been a considerable advantage.

At last I seemed to have all the ingredients if only I could sort them out. The victims so far, Lily and Bobby. Was there a vital link I had overlooked? Was Lily, in fact, a spy? From the vague background Mabel had provided I had concluded that she was foreign, didn't speak English but spoke and understood it perfectly. Perfect camouflage for a spy to be able to overhear conversations.

Even being so colourless was an excellent disguise for

Lily, who according to the stable lads loved horses. White horses like the Lipizzaners suggested Austria or Germany, and hinted to a possible link with Alice's husband, who hated the English, obsessed by the belief that his distant cousin Kaiser Wilhelm, who blamed his mother, Queen Victoria's daughter, for his withered arm, was the rightful king of England. Accepting the invitation to Balmoral gave Hermann von Mueller a sinister reason for his presence, the perfect opportunity of serving his beloved Kaiser.

Who was the man who had threatened Bobby? Was the reason for his murder because believing he loved her, Lily had confided in him or asked for his help? Who was the man who had threatened Bobby and given him a ten-pound bribe to clear off? That wasn't enough for the wide boy and greedy for more had cost him his life. Was this unseen tall man 'with the posh voice' Bobby had described also Mabel's attacker? If so, then she would never know what a narrow escape she had that day.

This discovery was so vital, so urgent, that I had to tell someone. Even Mabel would do, except that she was away with the pony cart, probably to Ballater for some last shopping.

Vince's daily visit to the cottage was still hours away. If he wasn't in his surgery at the castle then I could leave an urgent message. I was just about to leave when I heard a lot of strange noises upstairs. From Mabel's bedroom. I ran upstairs and poked my head around the door.

And what a scene. A large bird, a young jackdaw by the size of it, had fallen down the chimney, carrying with it a vast quantity of soot, and trapped, its frantic rushes at the window had made a terrible mess of the room.

I opened the window and after considerable effort with a towel from the bathroom managed to steer it to the windowsill, where with an indignant squawk it flew out and disappeared.

I looked around in dismay. Soot marks and droppings everywhere. I hadn't the heart to let Mabel come back to this, she was useless as a housewife, nor did I feel I could call on Yolande and Jessie who would be busy in the kitchen at this hour. I would have to tackle it myself so I went downstairs, returned with bucket and brush and began cleaning the room.

I had almost finished when in one corner of that overcrowded little room there was damage I hadn't noticed. The jackdaw's descent from the chimney had knocked down a large jar. Praying that it wasn't a priceless antique from Abergeldie Castle for the lid was chipped, I lifted it carefully.

There was something inside wrapped in newspaper. I knew as soon as I held it in my hand what it was. A gun, a derringer. I had one exactly like it at home. In the barrel, ready for firing, two bullets. Had it been forgotten by some previous occupant? Was Mabel aware of its presence?

Then I looked at the newspaper – *The Times*, which Mabel conscientiously bought each time she went to Ballater. And dated two weeks ago.

There was my answer. The gun was Mabel's and she had hidden it in the vase. Then I remembered how after our concern for her attack she said if it happened again she would be armed. And that triggered another memory. How when she first went out in the pony cart to follow the shooting parties, she had said wistfully that she was a lot better than most of those men.

I was still wondering whether I should mention the gun to her when there was another crisis. Cries from the garden where the two girls had been playing. Rowena rushed in followed by Thane. 'Mrs Macmerry, come quickly. Meg has fallen out of the tree.'

I rushed out. Meg was lying at the base of the ancient tree; its potential as a possible tree house abandoned, one of its large branches had been a delight to swing on. Now it lay on the ground beside Meg, who was crying and clutching her leg.

'My ankle, Mam. It's broken,' she sobbed.

I knelt down beside her. Thankfully it didn't feel like a broken ankle, but it was badly sprained. Trying to calm her, I carried her into the cottage. In a lot of pain, I must get her to Vince.

At that moment I heard the pony cart. Mabel had returned from Ballater, and coming in with her parcels, she took one look at the scene and demanded: 'What on earth has happened now? You girls, always in trouble.'

'Meg fell off the tree,' Rowena said. 'We were swinging and suddenly it just snapped.'

'Didn't I warn them? Every day I said—'

I cut her short. 'Can I take the pony cart? I must get her to Vince.'

She shrugged. 'Of course, I'm finished with it for today.'

I wrung out a towel in cold water, wrapped it round the injured ankle, and with Rowena helped her into the cart.

Mabel stood at the door with Thane. My questions to her would have to wait.

Vince was not at the surgery. The nurse who assisted him said he should be back shortly and that he had gone to the railway station to collect someone in the motor. A kindly, middle-aged, cheerful lady, she immediately took over Meg who had given up attempts at being brave as the nurse examined her ankle. After some soothing drops to kill the pain and some expert bandaging, she took me aside.

'No, it isn't broken, Mrs Macmerry, but it's a very bad sprain, I'm afraid. Dr Laurie will confirm that.' She sighed. 'I doubt this little lass will be able to go to the Games.'

Relieved with her verdict, I knew that Meg would be only slightly disappointed, as neither she nor Rowena liked sitting still for hours. And then there was Thane. What to do with him while we were all absent for several hours?

The answer was simple. Rowena and Meg would stay with him. I thought of the old adage about ill winds. I heard a motor outside.

At the window, Meg said: 'It's Uncle Vince!' She waved to him. The door opened and he came in. Followed by Jack.

What a surprise! A brief kiss and he rushed to Meg's side. There was a lot of hugging, consoling, soothing words, before Vince separated them and got to work examining Meg.

'No need to wait, you two. I'll bring her back in the motor. Yes, Rowena, you can stay.'

It was my turn to be in line for hugs. As we walked back to the cottage, my first question was: 'What are you doing here?'

'Have to be in Aberdeen tomorrow, a special enquiry. Hoped to be given time off to come to the Games, so that we could all go home together. But duty calls, as always.'

'I'm so glad to see you again.'

He put an arm around me and sighed. 'Me too, Rose, never get used to being away from you both.'

We kissed and I said: 'It doesn't look like Meg will manage the Games.'

'Too bad.' I explained about Thane and he smiled. 'Good thinking. She would soon be bored with all the ceremonials and the competitions. Not my thing, either. But I got quite a shock, I can tell you, when Vince was about to drop me off at the cottage and there was Mabel waving frantically. I guessed there was something wrong.'

So I told him about Mabel's hidden weapon. He merely shook his head and seemed to find it amusing, eccentric, and somehow typical of her. It was a very short visit. The next time we were to meet would be home again, in Edinburgh.

Dave collected him in the motor for the train from Ballater. Meg arrived back with Vince, leaning on a crutch. But it was not until after supper, when Mabel retired and we got Meg upstairs to bed, that I was able to tell him everything.

CHAPTER THIRTY-NINE

At last, the day of the long-awaited Games, and for me an even greater excitement. Tomorrow Meg and I and Thane would be home in Solomon's Tower, picking up the threads of my life, writing up my logbook and seeing what clients (if any) I had awaiting my services as a lady investigator. I wished Alice well but hoped the world of political intrigue, which wasn't at all my kind of world, would be closed for ever. And I certainly wouldn't be sorry to see the back of Mabel as we put her on the London train.

Dave came with the motor. Mabel and I climbed aboard, watched by the two girls with Yolande (who had been allowed a day off but didn't like the Games, declaring them too noisy!). Promised sweeties from the stalls, they waved us off with Thane at their side.

The noises grew louder over the short journey to the

venue and the smells I always associated with fairs and circuses in Edinburgh's Queen's Park grew stronger. As the car was parked and we walked the short distance to our seating area opposite the royal box, a small platform covered by an awning, I noticed there were gipsies among the crowd, obviously permitted to sell their wares and tell fortunes.

There was a great air of expectancy as the royal family arrived in their car. We couldn't see them but we heard the pipers and then everyone stood for 'God Save the King' and across from our front seats, which Vince had acquired for us, just yards away, the king and the princes in kilts, the Queen suitably robed in tartan, took their places.

Nearby I was aware of those policemen pretending to be ghillies and I had a glimpse of Inspector Gray and 'Mr Elder' in the group of seats occupied by the ambassadors, and foreign guests. The rain that threatened had given way to sunshine but there was a slight breeze, welcomed by the performers, especially the Highland dancers, the tug o' war teams from Braemar and Ballater, the weightlifters and the local hero tossing the caber.

Mabel was at my side, silent and I thought watchful. Suddenly I saw out of the corner of my eye a scuffle among the foreign guests. Hermann van Mueller was on his feet, saluting, shouting and raising a rifle, directed at the royal box, at the King.

As he was seized by the inspector and the man they knew as Mr Elder, at my side Mabel sprang to her feet, withdrew that derringer concealed in her pocket, raised it and screamed: 'No, no! He is mine. He is mine!'

As she levelled the gun, I threw my shawl over her

hand and seized her wrist. She struggled and the gun was towards me, in the region of my stomach. As I heard the click, I closed my eyes. What if there had been other bullets than the two I had seen? Then Vince and one large ghillie-policeman were separating us and seized her bodily.

Amid murmurs of astonishment among the people beside us Vince said, 'Please make way. The lady is ill. She has taken a bad turn. Excuse us.'

Many recognised Vince as Dr Laurie as the lady in question was shouting, 'The King – he is mine – he is mine!' Luckily I hoped no one heard her scream and sob: 'I am to kill him.'

Then we were in the motor with Dave driving, Mabel now reduced to angry tears of frustration, no longer a threat to anyone, held firmly between the policeman and Vince.

He looked at me, grinned and said: 'Good job you removed the two bullets, Rose.'

'Good job she didn't check.' I had searched the room but found no hidden cache, but one could never be sure.

He shook his head. 'An accomplished assassin would never make that mistake.' As we reached the cottage he said, 'I'll have to go back, but I'll leave Craig here to stand guard in case she makes any trouble.'

I thought that was a splendid idea, seeing that I was only half her size and if she attacked me, I would be another victim. Somehow I didn't feel that I was in any danger or that she was capable of violence any more. She had been defeated, but we still didn't know why she wanted to kill King Edward. That I had to find out. She made no resistance as we entered the cottage, just made for the stairs and her room. Meg and Rowena were playing cards, surprised at our return.

I said Mabel had taken poorly. They nodded sympathy and went on with the game, their hands watched over by Thane with an almost human expression as if he knew which card to play.

I seized the bottle of brandy kept for medicinal purposes in the sideboard and carried it up to Mabel who was sitting, her shoulders bent, by the window.

I poured a liberal glassful and said: 'Drink this.' She took it from me without a word and continued to gaze into the garden. I drew up a chair and sat beside her. 'You do realise the serious nature of what you – almost – did, don't you?'

She looked at me. 'I wanted to kill him for what he did to us. He ruined our lives, turned my mother into an invalid for life. A botched suicide.'

'That was hardly his fault.'

'It was, it was. He seduced her. They were lovers. And when he used to visit Penby, she believed he loved her. I used to watch them together, spy on them.'

Such sexual antics were hardly suitable viewing for young eyes, I thought. Was that why she had never married and despised men? 'He loved a lot of women, Mabel, but they took it in their stride, they accepted the generous pay-off in the form of some gift. They didn't try to commit suicide.'

'She was a beauty. She believed she was different to the others.'

'How could she? Married with a young daughter – how old were you?'

I remembered the photograph in the hall at Penby when she said: 'I was eight, I saw it all.'

Just a year older than Meg, I thought sadly, as she went on. 'Mama said he would give us an even grander house, make us a substantial allowance and introduce her into society. We would live in the lap of luxury,' she paused. 'Well, you saw for yourself what it was like with the broken old woman, the invalid I pretended was my aunt. Don't you think he deserved to die?' Without waiting for my response she went on, 'I have hated him all my life, I made a resolve long ago to kill him. I always intended that and you – you stopped me. Bitch! How did you manage to do that?' she exploded.

'All I did was remove the bullets.'

'You had no right in my room. How dare you?'

'I went in to release a trapped bird. And I saved you from hanging.'

'You have destroyed my mission in my life, and I hate you. Hate you, Rose Macmerry!'

But she was crying now. Ambition thwarted, her lifetime dream, terrible as it was, turned to ashes. I thought of that scene back at the Games, which now seemed almost farcical.

Not one, but two assassins there planning to kill the King, neither with any notion of the other's existence. Had they had such information and joined forces, the ending could have been much much worse and the young Prince of Wales would now be king.

Refilling the glass which I thrust into her not unwilling hand I said: 'No, you don't hate me, Mabel, someday when you are calmer you'll realise that I saved your life.

311

You would undoubtedly have died, by hanging, sentenced to death for treason, for attempted murder if anyone had seen you raising that gun.'

I paused. 'And you already have two murders to account for.'

She looked at me and began to cry again. 'I didn't mean to kill her. She was a devil. Always listening at doors. She overheard me talking to Mama in Penby, knew what I intended and she decided that she could blackmail me once we got to Balmoral. She threatened to tell all. I knew I had to get rid of her. But I only intended to hurt her, scare her, then I lost my temper in the pony cart. She was so rude, laughing at me, and I hit her, I wanted to push her out of the cart, make her walk back. But I must have been too strong. She fell and rolled down into the river.'

I listened patiently, wondering if that explanation would stand up in a murder trial. I thought not.

'What about the stable boy Bobby? Did you intend to kill him too?'

'He was just as bad as her, thick as thieves they were. I guessed that she had probably told him and they were going to share the profits. I could not take chances, so I sent him that note, got him to meet me – I make a credible disguise as a man – gave him the money and thought that would get rid of him from Balmoral. But like all blackmailers, he wanted more. I had got rid of Lily and I couldn't let him stay around. He was now the greatest threat to my plan.'

She paused, her face grim, remembering. 'I drove the pony cart at him. The horse threw him. It was easy, really. No blame would be attached to me – I thought.

'It had all gone so well. I had been so lucky, it was like God's will, if one was a believer, the steps laid for me to follow. I had no idea over the years how or when, until Olivia wrote that she was going to Balmoral. I knew Vince was a royal physician. What an opportunity. Although I was involved with women's suffrage, that was originally only a desperate measure to join some organisation that might also present an opportunity to accomplish my mission, which had never been out of my thoughts for a single day since Mama's terrible injuries.'

'What about your own attack in the wood?'

She smiled. 'I engineered that very well, I thought. I realised the boy's death would look more plausible if whoever had made the horse bolt had also attacked me.'

That was true. It certainly wasn't an accident that he had been thrown, as Gray had maintained, as she said: 'It was quite simple. He was waiting to meet me, to get more money, and I simply drove the pony cart at him.'

Her face darkened. 'But you didn't believe it, did you? You were smarter than the rest.' And I realised I had made another enemy. 'Just being true to your role as a lady investigator, poking your nose into things that didn't concern you.'

Maybe the brandy was having an effect, she was getting bolder, a glint of the old Mabel again. 'What is going to happen now? Are you going to tell them? They won't believe you.'

I didn't believe in those tales of accidental murders but knew there was only circumstantial evidence if this confession was not signed and sealed and made legal.

Aware of what a dire effect this revelation would have

on Vince's career – the end of his life as a trusted royal servant – rather than having any feelings of sparing Mabel the consequences of her plan to kill the King, I said: 'I think you should leave now, while you can, before the inspector gets wind of what happened at the Games and suspects the truth about those two "accidental" deaths you engineered so carefully.'

'It is the truth. I shall always insist that I never intended to kill either of them.'

I left her then. She wouldn't run away. She was a prisoner. PC Craig was downstairs, on guard. He had been given a hand at cards with the two girls and, with an eloquent shrug, indicated that he was losing. 'Feel at home, I've got a couple just like them. Good job it's only sweeties and not money.'

I decided to go on with our packing and leave them to it. Meg said wistfully: 'Can Rowena come and see us in Edinburgh – just for a holiday?'

I said, of course, if her mother approved.

Rowena said, 'I would love to come, Mrs Macmerry. I've been before, my Ma has friends who are servants at Holyrood.'

And that was one problem less among many that had been solved.

CHAPTER FORTY

The Games over, the royal family safely back in the castle, PC Craig remained at the cottage with Mabel in custody, although that seemed unnecessary since she was not a danger to us or anyone else.

I told Vince about my long talk with her, going over it all, her version of the two 'accidental' deaths, for his benefit. If I expected him to be shocked and demand that she be put on trial when she reached London I was in for a surprise.

'She won't be going back with us. Craig will take her into Ballater and I've made independent arrangements for her to go straight to London under guard, on account of her health.'

'You approve of her getting away with intending to kill the King?'

'No, Rose, I would gladly see her stand trial, although

from what you have just told me, the woman is quite mad and if the truth came out she would spend the rest of her days in a lunatic asylum rather than be hanged.'

He sighed. 'However, I have another stronger and more personal reason for keeping silent.'

'I know, Vince. If this reached the King's ears or became public news.' As he had once warned me off getting involved in two deaths that I believed were murders, I could now fully understand the consequences if word got around that he had entertained an assassin as a guest in one of the estate cottages.

He nodded, his expression grave. 'HM is the most genial and understanding of men to a point, but he would certainly be persuaded by those who have his interests, rather than mine, at heart, that I was no longer a suitable person, since I had such criminal friends, to occupy a position of trust in the royal household. Just think what would happen if Inspector Gray got hold of this. Fortunately he never saw the incident at all. He and one of the ghillies were busy disarming that mad German, who regrettably is the King's distant relative.'

'The ghillie, was that Mr Brown?'

'Yes.'

'Do you know anything about him?'

Vince seemed surprised at the question. He shrugged. 'Only that the King had met him in London, took a liking to him. He's like that, quite unaccountable in taking a shine to people. Why are you so interested?'

He smiled slyly then sighed. 'Poor Olivia. She'll be absolutely shocked when I tell her about Mabel.'

I was wondering about Alice and how the scandal regarding her husband would affect her future and that of her estranged children. I hoped it would all work out and that she would be happy with her Scottish gentleman.

And so we returned to Edinburgh. Jack returned a couple of days later.

'Had a good holiday?'

I waited for him to mention the incident, but all he said was: 'You look well.'

I wasn't sure about that, my nerves still felt shattered, but he was more concerned about Meg's ankle which was healing nicely thanks to Uncle Vince's attention. She was still limping and would do so for a while yet.

'Anything exciting to report?'

Was that an invitation to confess all, I wondered? I said, 'Not really.'

'I gather Mabel had a bad turn and was sent back by special train.'

Very special, I thought, probably under lock and key. As for that bad turn, it could have been worse.

'Has Inspector Gray reported anything about his presence at the castle?'

'Nothing, just the usual precautions that accompany the shooting party each year, illustrious guests and that sort of thing, grumbles about getting loads of extra policemen, calling it a waste of time and money.'

In other words, a great cover-up. I was fairly sure that Jack knew, but only Vince and I were aware of Mabel's abortive flourish with that empty gun. As for von

Mueller's insane attempt to get the justice he imagined was his cousin the Kaiser's due, it would be safely shelved away from public scrutiny.

Under the label of 'personal – most secret' information it would take its place and gather dust alongside numerous other assassination attempts, going down in unwritten history, filed as 'The Balmoral Incident 1905'.